# The Titanic Girls

# The Titanic Girls

JULIE COOK

Copyright © 2022 Julie Cook.

A catalogue record for this book is available from the British Library.

No part of this publication may be reproduced, stored in a retrieval system, or transmitted in any form or by any means, electronic, mechanical, photocopying, recording, or otherwise, without written permission of the publisher.

This is a work of fiction. Names, characters, businesses, places, events, locales, and incidents are either the products of the author's imagination or used in a fictitious manner. Any resemblance to actual persons, living or dead, or actual events is purely coincidental.

All rights reserved including the right of reproduction in whole or in part in any form. The moral right of the author has been asserted.

www.blkdogpublishing.com

I dedicate this book to my great-grandparents Emily and William Bessant and to all those who perished on the Titanic and to all those whose lives were changed forever after the tragedy.

# Chapter One

**Catherine**

From her spot on the front doorstep on her knees, feeling the cold stone radiating through her bones, Catherine Gregory looked up as three pairs of perfectly white-stockinged legs jumped past her.

'Oopsie,' one of the little girls giggled, as she hit Catherine's full bucket with her shiny ankle boot, knocking a slop of filthy soapy water over Catherine's pinafore.

Their mother followed, not even bothering to chastise her daughter but stepping over Catherine as if she wasn't even there, or was, at best, an insect that she'd rather not trample on.

'Girls,' the matriarch called out. 'Do not shout or laugh in front of this house! Come back at once.' She gathered her girls to her like a duck with its young, deftly extended her parasol up above her head and off they walked down the street, clean, fresh, smelling of soap, boned corsets shaping impossibly tiny waists into a V-shape.

Catherine watched them walk away. Despite her jet-black hair, her dark eyes and thick eyelashes, to the rich she was invisible. She was only 19 but felt fifty years older some days, mopping and cleaning, charring and scrubbing.

She felt her sopping wet pinafore skirt that had now permeated through to her stockings. Gripping her rag and brush harder, she scrubbed the stone step with even more vigour. *One day ...* she thought. *One day I'll be doing the stepping over people like me ... One day I'll be knocking buckets over with a new pair of boots ... One day ...*

But would that one day ever really come? She gritted her teeth as she scrubbed. Life at home was no better than her days spent cleaning and charring. Her father was a stoker on the big ships, or the 'killer ships' as everyone local called them. A stoker – or fireman – was there to stoke the huge boilers that fuelled the gigantic coal ships. The stokers stood there at the furnace in fifty-degree heat, loading their shovels with coal and throwing it into the boilers. While the first-class passengers took their tea in the luxurious lounges on the top deck, people like Catherine's father were toiling in four-hour, non-stop shifts in the bowels of the ships, sailing the rich across the Atlantic to New York on working-class muscle power.

Catherine shook her head, thinking of her father. He'd worked on all the big liners that came and went from Southampton – his most recent being the *Oceanic*, one of the White Star Line ships. When the liners steamed into the port of Southampton, they dwarfed the grey-brick buildings on the shore. They were ungodly, like something from outer space landing on earth. Her mother always said you could get lost on one of those ships, they were so big.

Her father worked hard. Too hard. All of them did. They'd get confirmation they had work, sign on and then you'd see a queue of them outside the pawn shop before leaving on another voyage. Each of them carried a bundle in his hands. They had no gold or rings to pawn. No, her father and these men would pawn their 'best' shoes while they were at sea. They'd get the meagre coins the pawnbroker would hand them and give it straight to their wives to run the household while they were away.

Catherine's father Alfred did the same. That wasn't all. As a girl, she'd even had her school pinafore or school boots pawned on a Friday for some money for Saturday and Sunday, before her mother would get them back on the Monday.

Her mother's various phrases suddenly popped into Catherine's head as she wrung out her sodden rag in over the bucket. *Hand to mouth ... worked to the bone ... tooth and claw ... do your work heartily as for the Lord ...*

Her phrases had always seemed so hard, so cold and yet with an undertone of the Bible about them. Her mother Alice was a hard woman. She was only 42 but she could pass for a woman twenty years older. Years of hunger, running back and forth to the pawn shop, washing her father's White Star Line stoker uniform in a steaming vat of hot water before the fire, choking on the fumes from the nearby margarine factory – all had taken their toll.

Some days, her father would have to wait in line at the docks to get work; sometimes, when he'd come in and shake his head, Catherine would run to the other side of the room and duck, covering her eyes. Her mother would then launch whatever she had in her hand – rolling pin, ladle, iron – at her father's head when he confirmed he had not got work, not this time. The stokers were hard. They had to be. But that was nothing compared to their wives.

As her mother had put her to bed each night, she had not sung lullabies to Catherine. Instead, she'd stood there with arms folded and her lips pursed and she'd repeated the same refrain, more so as Catherine had grown into a young woman. 'Get out of this life, my girl,' she'd say, standing at the foot of her tiny bed. 'Get out of this life and get yourself a good 'un. A stoker's wife's life is a hard one. Get yourself a steward or a waiter.'

Then she'd turn and trudge from the room looking bent and haggard and tired of her life.

*One day ...* Catherine thought again, finishing the step and standing up. She placed her palm in the small of her back and leaned back until she heard the 'click' that she needed to hear in her spine.

That 'one day', in Catherine's mind, was getting nearer each day. Catherine's ticket to this new life came in the form of Percy Jones. With her jet-black hair and dark eyes, Catherine had easily caught Percy's eye across the street when she'd stood by Percy's father's shoemaker's shop.

Each day she'd made sure she was there, across the road, as he came out to open the shop with his leather apron on. He was nothing to look at. He was thin, not particularly tall and coughed a lot. But Catherine had enough of being courted by the handsome ones. She didn't care about looks now. She wanted someone who had ambition and who was going up in the world. Someone who wouldn't come in stinking of coal and soot and disappointment.

Percy had that ambition.

'I won't be working for my father forever,' he told her one day as she dropped off her mistress's boots for mending. 'I've got plans. There will be more ships coming in to the docks. I'm going to sign to one of the big liners as a steward.'

'A steward?' she'd said.

'Yes, and stewards get a nice uniform and a lot of tips from the first class folk,' Percy had explained excitedly. He looked around to make sure customers weren't listening. 'Some stewards have even come home with enough tips to rent a house!'

She'd seen the excitement in his eyes and believed him. In fact, it had to be true. Southampton was now 'gateway to the world'. She'd seen it on the front page of a newspaper. Steam ship travel was *the* fashionable mode of transport for the rich and famous. And they all travelled from Southampton. The *Oceanic* had come and gone, and the *Olympic*. Beautiful mega-ships with every modern convenience you could imagine; heating in the cabins for first class when they were cold, and cooling fans when they were hot. Famous people – aristocrats, actresses, singers – they all travelled on the huge White Star Line ships from Southampton. Now, though, there was talk of an even greater ship. The biggest ever made. It was called *Titanic* and Percy swore to Catherine he'd get a job as a steward on the ship and he'd make a fortune in tips.

'Then we can wed,' he'd told her, shyly reaching for her hand and stifling another cough.

And now, as she gazed at the pristine doorstep, the sweat coursing down her back, she let herself form a faint smile. With Percy's tips, who knows what they could do? Get a small house to rent? Get married? Start a business or run a shop? All she knew was she would not be scrubbing steps forever.

Not other people's, anyway.

# Chapter Two

**Lucy**

The baby's face was so red she looked like a giant tomato – if tomatoes had the ability to scream of course. Lucy held the child closer to her chest and offered soothing words. 'There, there,' she cooed, trying to rub her cheek against the baby over the ear-splitting screams. 'There, there, Mother's here …'

Nothing worked. It never did. She jogged the baby on one hip, walking around the nine foot square kitchen. She felt her baby daughter stiffen and take a breath before pausing. Silence. Lucy dared to breathe. But Lucy knew this was not a reprieve. This was the child inhaling before another round of screaming blue murder.

'Oh, Florence!' Lucy wailed as the baby let out an enormous scream again. Lucy wandered from wall to wall, jigging the baby up and down. 'Father will be back soon,' she shouted over the din. 'You'll see.'

A pot was boiling over on the stove. Black mould was spreading its way across the cracked ceiling. Lucy padded towards the front door and stopped in front of the small mirror she'd hung next to it. It was ancient, covered in spots and peeling in places. She stared at the woman staring back at her – fair haired, green eyed, but an expression that said, *I'm so exhausted …*

Lucy feigned a smile at baby Florence, but she knew it was hopeless. Florence would only stop wailing when her husband Joseph came through the door. The baby didn't respond to maternal cooing and warm cuddles against the breast. Instead, she seemed to love the stench of coal and smoke and soot that accompanied Joseph. Rather than being repulsed by it, the child seemed to relish it, finding it comforting.

As Joseph threw his kit bag down and scooped the baby up in his strong hands, she would stop crying instantly.

'Father's here now,' he'd say, rubbing her nose with his and leaving a trace of soot on the baby's face that Lucy would have to clean off with a hankie and a bit of spit.

Lucy smiled. Joseph was one of the few stokers who would forego the post killer ship drinking session at the King's Arms on the corner to hurry home to see Florence. As the baby wailed, Lucy looked at her simple, thin wedding band. She was 22 but her hands told another story. Her face was plump with a youthfulness that had not yet left her, and her green eyes were bright, but her hands were red raw and chapped from constantly washing the baby's nappy rags, plunging her husband's soot and coal-covered clothes in a tin tub in front of the fire between trips.

She and Joseph met in the country, five miles away, working as farmhands. Lucy had never lived in a city before and it had never been her plan to move to the hub that was Southampton, with its huge ships coming and going.

But then she had met Joseph one harvest season in a field. They'd caught each other's eyes and started talking as they gathered hay bales. What had followed was a whirlwind that even she could not explain but they had married just four months later, on Christmas Day – the only day agricultural workers could get a day off.

Joseph was different from other men, or at least so Lucy believed. He hadn't wanted to stay in the countryside. He'd seen – and sensed – the changes coming; the tractors that were replacing people, the machinery that threshed corn and wheat, replacing human strength.

'We need to get out, Luce,' he'd told her. 'There'll be

no work here soon.'

She'd stared into his brown eyes and nodded. The truth was, she'd have followed him to Timbuctoo if he'd asked her.

And so, they had moved to the city of Southampton. After years of physical labour in the fields, Joseph was strong and muscular and was soon taken on by the foreman at the docks as a fireman on the big ships.

'Can't be much difference scooping coal from scooping haybales,' Joseph had said at the time.

But then the reality had set in. He'd travelled the world and would be gone for days, sometimes weeks at a time. When he came home, he was covered in soot, trembling from the hours at the furnace, thinner from dehydration.

People where they lived called the liners the 'killer ships' because they'd see the stokers staggering home after another trip, pounds thinner from when they'd set off, exhausted, their eyes hollow.

Usually, they'd head straight for the local hostelry to spend the first of their pay on ale. Joseph didn't. He always came home. He didn't get drunk like them. He didn't hit his wife, as so many of them did. But at work, he'd had to become hard, to play a role. He was now part of the group known as the Black Gang, so called because they were stokers always covered in soot and coal and grime from their hours at the ships' furnaces. They were also called that because of the negative connotations of being a stoker, of heavy drinking, of fighting, of violence.

Joseph fitted in at work, swearing when he needed to, fighting with his fists for work if needs be. But back at their two-up, two-down in the streets of Northam, Southampton, he was her Joseph again. Kind. Caring. Protective.

'One more voyage,' he'd tell Lucy each time he signed on to another killer ship. 'Just one more.'

The pay was bad. Not as bad as the stewards, who relied on tips, but at six pounds a month for the back breaking four-hours-on, four-hours-off they did at the furnaces in 50 degree heat, Lucy's heart broke at how hard he worked for the money. But he brought it all home to their family. Their baby never wanted for blankets or warmth. They always had coal. They had bread and enough to eat.

And, instead of staggering to the pub with his crew mates, Joseph was often mocked for coming home to his wife.

'She wears the trousers, that one!' they'd call after him as he walked home alone.

Then he'd push the door open, throw his kit bag aside, scoop his daughter into his arms, before collapsing, exhausted and soot-covered, into the arms of Lucy.

She'd feel her hands tracing his back, his neck, his aching muscles that had grown so taut and firm since working as a ship's stoker. She didn't mind the smell of the soot and coal. She'd save water and fill him a bath by the fire and sit beside him as he washed the soot and coal away. As the water turned black around him, Joseph would slowly re-emerge. From behind the jet-black face, his brown eyes would twinkle. He'd kiss her from his tin bath and say, 'One more trip and we'll move on. We'll go somewhere new … we'll do something else.'

His one last trip would be soon – on *Titanic*. She remembered an article she'd seen on the front page of the local paper the *Daily Echo* about it. The ship was hailed as the biggest ship of all time. It would be the most beautiful, the most opulent, the fastest, the best.

'What a way to end all this,' Joseph had said, folding the newspaper and slapping her playfully on the behind with it. 'My swansong will be on the *Titanic*. I might even get myself a glass of port in first class and toast them all!'

She felt her thoughts interrupted as there was a knock on the door. She grabbed Florence. 'It's Father!' she said, rushing to the door.

But when she opened it, Joseph wasn't there.

Instead a girl with a flushed face and brown hair stood on her doorstep.

# Chapter Three

**Susan**

Susan rolled her eyes as she registered the disappointment in Lucy's eyes when she saw her at the door.

'Expecting someone else, were you?' Susan said, walking into the house without an invitation.

Lucy closed the door behind her and led her to the kitchen table. Susan was Lucy's closest friend. Along with Catherine, the girls had formed a threesome. Catherine and Susan had played together in the same road in Northam as girls. When Lucy had moved to the city, Susan had seen her in the road, and they'd got talking. Susan had recognised Lucy instantly as a fireman's wife. It was in her blood. Her father was a greaser on the liners and her three brothers were firemen. Susan had seen Lucy outside the butcher's shop looking lost, hungry and worried. A simple conversation had explained why. Joseph had gone to sea for the first time and Lucy was alone. The two had got talking and Susan helped her find the cheapest places to get a cut of meat, the best places for yarn for darning, even the pubs that didn't turn women away where you could get a quick nip of gin on a hard day.

Susan, now twenty. was a city girl through and through. Her childhood memories were a blur of coal, smog and fumes. She and the other children had grown up in the shadow of the nearby margarine factory. Everyone who was anyone worked at the factory, or on the ships. She'd while away the evenings playing hopscotch in the street or rolling hoops with the other children. The only punctuation to their play was when the horse and cart came down with the man selling manure. Then the mothers would emerge quick as lightning from their houses, aprons on, elbows sharpened, jostling with each other to buy some manure in the hope they might get a better yield of vegetables in the back garden.

The only other visitors were the police or the Muffin Man. But Susan's parents had never had enough money to buy anything from him. Instead, Susan recalled stopping play as girls and standing open-mouthed as some lucky person might buy a single muffin from the Muffin Man's cart. Susan recalled watching the steam shoot out of someone's mouth as they bit into the hot muffin wrapped in its paper bag. Her own stomach had rumbled as she'd shrugged and carried on playing hopscotch, laughing and giggling once again but her insides burning with want and hunger.

Susan's father was a fireman on the ships too. Her mother had worked in the margarine factory. Susan had broken the mould, though, and now worked as a schoolteacher. She was sharp as a flint and with a tongue to match.

'Can you believe the pay they're going to get on *Titanic*?' she asked Lucy now, her blue eyes flashing with anger.

She sat down at Lucy's table and without saying anything, took the now-screaming baby from Lucy's exhausted arms. Florence stopped crying instantly and Susan flashed a smile of victory at Lucy who sat down, aching with tiredness, and put her feet up for the first time that day.

'The *Titanic* will be the greatest, biggest ship ever built and do you know what they're paying the stokers and greasers? Six pounds a month. Six! Stewards will get three! Can you believe it?'

Lucy smiled a sad smile and nodded. She wiped her face with her apron and traced a crack in the wooden table's surface. 'Yes, I can, because they can get away with it,' she said, rubbing her aching neck. 'Did you not notice there's a coal strike on?'

Susan went quiet and nodded. 'True,' she said. 'Father's only just got some work after three months. How could I not know?'

'Well, men are desperate,' Lucy said. 'Even Joseph who said …'

'… one more trip,' Susan interrupted.

'Yes,' Lucy smiled. Everyone knew of Joseph's mantra of 'one more trip'. 'Even he will sign on to *Titanic* if he can. We need the money,' she added, looking at her now cooing angel of a baby who was playing with Susan's stiff collar.

'I just think it's a disgrace,' Susan went on. 'The White Star Line has enough to pay proper wages. The Union is trying for more, but I doubt it will get anywhere.'

Lucy recalled the black eye Joseph had that was now healing from three weeks ago. He hadn't got it in a drunken brawl but fighting for work. Men would gather at the dock gates and thrust themselves forward to be taken on for a day, or even a half day, by the foreman. Fights would often break out as men shoved others out of the way to be seen. Lucy didn't know whether to feel proud or sad. 'Susan, Joseph had to fight for a half day's work,' Lucy said. 'He fought with his fists for half a day just to earn a bit for bread for us. There are hundreds of men and not enough jobs. These men will go to sea for *anything*.'

She hung her head sadly, then looked at the door, hoping he'd come in. Why was he late? Had he had to fight for work again? Silly, but she still got a flicker of excitement when she saw him, still felt herself blush a little, still had to push the hair off her face and pinch her cheeks to show him a pretty face. She turned back to Susan. 'And what about you?' Lucy asked.

'What of me?' Susan said.

'Been in trouble lately?' Lucy asked.

Susan looked at the mould-covered ceiling. 'It would endanger you to tell you,' she grinned.

Lucy laughed. Her best friend had always been the

clever one, always been the one fighting for the underdog. Now she'd got involved with Mrs Pankhurst's lot and was often scuttling off to a meeting somewhere , declaring she was unable to say who she was meeting or why.'Broken any windows lately?' Lucy asked. 'Chained yourself to a railing?'

Susan smiled an angelic smile. 'Me? Never,' she replied. 'Everything we do is within the law, I'll have you know. All I want is rights for women and a vote. So should you. It's not a crime to want to be equal you know …'

Susan was a secret member of a club. She went to meetings once a week and would listen as speakers filled the room with talk of hope, with words like 'emancipation' and 'end to drudgery' and 'votes' and 'hope.' She'd hang on every word before leaving the hall and almost dancing down the street with the sense of new dawns and beginnings. She felt anything was possible after these meetings. Women were more than wives and mothers, destined to bear children into a life of poverty, grime and early death. She had a brain. She longed to use it. She followed politics when her parents weren't looking. She wanted Mrs Pankhurst's words to be heard by every woman. She looked at Lucy and was about to reel off her latest teachings from the most recent suffragette meeting when there was a sound at the door.

Lucy started and jumped up and Susan rolled her eyes. She knew once Joseph walked in, Lucy would go googly-eyed and it would only be the two love birds in the room. Susan had no sweetheart. But she didn't envy women who did. Marriage was an outdated institution, a way of shackling women to a patriarchal society where the rules were made by misogynists.

'I'll take my leave, then,' Susan said, handing Florence back to Lucy; the baby began to scream again the moment she was back in her mother's arms.

Susan passed Joseph on her way out, met with a stench of old coal and sweat. 'Good evening, Joseph,' she said. 'My father and brothers are in the King's Arms, I take it?'

Joseph threw his kit bag to one side and grinned, nodding. 'Where else?' he said.

'Good night,' Susan said. She cast a glance over her

shoulder into Lucy's house. She saw Lucy thrust their daughter into Joseph's black, sooty arms. 'Come here, my little one,' he said, rubbing the baby's button nose with his. 'And you,' he added, reaching an arm out and snaking it around Lucy's waist.

He rubbed her nose too and she cried out, giggling. 'Joe!' she screamed, wiping her nose on a corner of her apron.

He sniffed the air. 'Mmm, liver?' he said.

Lucy kissed him. 'And onions!' she added.

Joseph shut the door behind him and Susan smiled to herself. She stepped out into the night. She had to find her brothers and father before her mother started yelling from her doorstep for them to come home. They might have been burly stokers but when her mother yelled at them, they became terrified lambs.

As Susan stepped across the street and followed the din of voices and the soft glow of the lamps from inside the King's Arms, she stopped for a moment. She breathed in the stale smell of old fumes from another day's churning at the factory. Over the roofs of the houses, she could just make out the funnels of another killer ship. She braced herself, ready to shout from outside the pub to get her brothers and father out before her mother heard they were home.

Suddenly all that hope, all that sense of being on the verge of a new era vanished and she felt an oppressive weight once again. She didn't want to marry a ship's stoker and have to drag him from the pub every night as her mother had done. She didn't want to live hand to mouth, living off pawned shoes and erratic work for a seafaring husband.

And as she stood in the cold, blinking in the streetlamp light, she wondered; could life ever change?

# Chapter Four

**Catherine**

The man collapsed at the kitchen table stank of stale drink, sweat and smoke. 'Father's home, I see,' Catherine said, taking off her sopping stockings at the door and throwing them into the tin bath set in front of the fire.

'Oi!' came the retort. 'Your father's things are in there! Those stockings'll turn jet black!'

Catherine shrugged. What did it matter? Did it matter if her stockings turned black or even bright cerise pink? She was an invisible nobody. A charwoman.

'What's this face about?' her mother said, one hand on her scrawny hip, taking in Catherine's miserable expression.

'Those blasted girls, that's what, kicking my bucket over me and leaving me sopping wet all the livelong day, that's what!' Catherine muttered.

Her mother said nothing, just carried on rolling a meagre sliver of pastry into a pie lid.

'We having pie?' Catherine asked, seeing pastry for the first time in weeks.

'Your father came home with his pay. He passed out drunk, so I went through his pockets and bought some mutton,' her mother replied. 'He won't even remember when he wakes up.'

Catherine wiggled her wet toes in front of the fire. She was the last to fly the nest. Her other two sisters were both married to factory workers. They'd escaped. She, on the other hand, still had to char for a living. She ached with a day's toil at the big house and just longed to sleep. But her hunger was burning. She knew on days her father came home from sea there would be food, so she got up and took advantage of her mother's turned back as she pummelled the tiny slip of pastry and found a loaf of fresh bread. She tore the end off it and stuffed it into her pinafore pocket.

'I saw that out the back of my head,' her mother said, without turning.

Catherine burst out laughing. Her mother was hard as nails but as she looked at her diminishing frame as she hunched over the pastry, Catherine found it impossible not to feel love and pity for her. She went over and rubbed herself against her mother's shoulder, rather like a cat marking its owner.

Her mother looked at her beautiful daughter, grabbed her round cheek with a flour coated finger and thumb and said, 'You'll get out of this, all right.'

Catherine smiled smugly. 'That's right I will,' she said.

Her mother saw her expression, slapped the lid on the pie, deftly crimped the edges, before saying, 'Percy?'

Catherine pulled the chunk of bread from her pocket and tore at it with white, even teeth.

'He told me he wants to wed. Said as much,' Catherine said.

Her mother nodded and pursed her lips. 'When?'

'When he's signed on as a steward,' she said. 'He wants to get on *Titanic*.'

Her mother threw her head back and laughed. 'Him on *Titanic*?' she cried.

Catherine's face fell. 'What's so funny?'

'Every man and his dog wants to be a steward on *Titanic*!' she cried. 'What makes you think the White Star Line will take on that little shrimp of a cobbler's worker?'

Catherine baulked. 'Well ... he's soft spoken and sounds genteel,' she said. 'And he can look the part. I don't see why not.'

Her mother pushed the black tendrils of hair off Catherine's face. 'For your sake, I hope he gets on,' she said. 'But everyone wants to get on *Titanic*.'

Catherine's dark eyes flashed with anger. 'Well, he will, he has to, or else I'm not gonna marry him!'

Her mother's sardonic smile vanished. 'Oh, yes you will, my girl,' she said. '*Titanic* or not, if he's made you an offer, you take it.'

'But I don't even love him!' Catherine said. 'I only want to marry if he can be a steward and get some tips.'

Her mother shook her head. 'When are you gonna learn, missy, that the boats are no life? It's unpredictable. One month you have money, the next you don't. If Percy has a cobbler's, take it with both hands! This is your chance!'

Catherine rolled her eyes. 'I read in a paper a steward got a £10 tip off of a passenger in first class on the *Olympic*!' she said. 'Percy could get that for us.'

Her mother slid the pie into the range and took Catherine's chapped hand. 'Look at me,' she said. 'If someone – anyone – other than a stoker wants your hand, you give it. You hear me?'

Catherine looked at her mother's fingers, red raw from washing her father's coal-streaked clothes.

'You promise me – *Titanic* or not – you marry him,' she said.

Catherine nodded sadly. 'I will, Mother,' she said. 'But know this – I don't love him and I won't ever!'

Her mother laughed, cruelly now. 'See where love gets you?' she said, pointing to the collapsed heap of a man at the table. The two women wandered closer without speaking. Catherine's mother reached forward and gently moved a matted lock of her father's hair off his forehead. Catherine looked at the black, soot-covered face, the wrinkles so deeply etched in her father's forty-two-year-old forehead. His hands were splayed on the table, a mess of blisters from picking up a shovel thousands of times in 50 degree heat.

'You want this life? You want a man coming home from the killer ships with a bit of money, and then nothing for weeks? Who cares if he's a stoker or a steward – don't you see? He may wear a smart uniform and get tips, but it's the same life. If you want my advice, don't tell him to get on the *Titanic* when it comes. Encourage him to work in his father's shop. Tell him so. Then you'll have something for your whole lifetime.'

Catherine nodded as her mother let her father's hair fall back onto his face. He snored drunkenly and shifted in his seat, before sleeping on again. As he moved a waft of stale sweat billowed up towards them and Catherine had to fight the natural urge to gag.

But even as she nodded at her mother's words and knew they were right, she could never dissuade Percy from trying to get on *Titanic*. She knew the stewards earned next to nothing – half of that of a stoker – but the tips could be life-changing. Surely it was worth the gamble of one trip on *Titanic* to see if Percy could get tips that could set them up as a married couple?

The following day, Catherine set off down the High Street as usual. She stood on the other side of the road from Percy's father's cobbler's. She watched as a young apprentice lowered the canopy over the shop to keep the non-existent sun off the windows and then waited. Not long after, a man emerged wearing a leather apron. He placed some boxes of shoes outside the shop and then stopped, seeing her across the street.

He looked over his shoulder, then hurried across the road to Catherine. 'My beloved,' he said, breathlessly, before coughing three times.

Catherine lowered her lashes and smiled coyly.

'Is it true your father is back off the *Oceanic*?' he asked, eyes widening.

Catherine looked at him and nodded. She thought of the heap of man still passed out at the table that very morning and tried not to laugh as she recalled her mother's attempts to move him from the table with a poker from the fire.

'May I ...' his voice trailed off and he coughed again. 'May I come over to speak to your father when I shut the shop?'

'You'd better be quick, or he'll be in the King's Arms,' Catherine replied. 'Why? What do you want to see him about?'

Percy lowered his own eyes now before meeting Catherine's gaze again. 'I just want to talk to him, that's all,' he said. He quickly added, 'Will he mind?'

She thought of her father's reaction when anyone came to the door. The cursing, the staggering gait to get to the door, the yelling. 'I am sure he will be happy to have a visitor,' she smiled.

'Right, right,' Percy said, smoothing down his apron. 'And he'll be in a good mood?' Percy asked, thinking in horror of the stokers he'd seen in his lifetime, brawling outside of pubs, trying to kill each other for work.

'If you catch him at the right time,' she replied.

He nodded.

Catherine walked away, to set off to her day's work at the big house. As she walked, she felt Percy's ardour burning a hole in her back. She turned and saw him standing there, still gazing at her.

'Percy?' she called.

'Yes, my love?' he replied.

'Maybe bring some ale or stout for my father.'

Percy nodded gratefully. 'Yes, yes, I will do!' he called.

Catherine walked away, allowing herself a tiny smile. She had him wrapped around her finger. Her father would accept his request to marry her – he'd be happy to just get rid of another daughter. Now all she had to do was ensure Percy got that job as a steward on the greatest, most opulent ship ever created. If he played his cards right, he could make a year's salary in tips from the rich in first class.

Then maybe, just maybe, her fortune might change.

# Chapter Five

**Lucy**

Lucy was trying to find a word for it. Brown was too generic. Almond was too pale. Hazel was too rich. She stared again into her husband's eyes, kissed him and said, 'I'm trying to work out what colour your eyes are.'

In bed, he kissed her and wrapped his arm around her, pulling her onto his chest. He smelt of soap and water. Clean as a whistle. The baby gurgled in her cot at the foot of the bed. She could tell her father was home and was a dream child once again.

'How about … chocolate?' Joseph said, kissing Lucy on her shoulder.

She giggled. 'And just as sweet?' she ventured.

He pulled her on top of him and began to stroke her leg under her nightdress. But then Florence, like clockwork, began to grizzle.

Lucy climbed off her husband and gave a look that said *Sorry*. 'She's hungry,' she said. She fetched the baby from the cot, got back in bed, propped herself up and began to breastfeed. Joseph stared at the ceiling, one arm under his head.

'They're saying they'll take on hundreds from Southampton,' he said.

Lucy gazed at her daughter. When she was

breastfeeding, it was the only time she could enjoy Florence's beautiful face. The rest of the time the child's features were contorted into angry expressions and she seemed to spit venom at her mother. Now, she was beautiful.

'Hundreds for what?' Lucy murmured.

'For the *Titanic*,' Joseph said. He propped himself up on one side and stared at Lucy. He looked excited. 'Just think. If I did one more trip on *Titanic* that would be six pound a month. Some of that would clear this rent, then we can move on somewhere else.'

Lucy rolled her eyes. 'And where would we go?' she said. 'Besides, we have friends here now.'

'All right, not far then. Just somewhere a bit better,' he said, looking up at the black mould on the ceiling. 'Somewhere with fresher air,' he added, looking at the soot from the factory on the window pane. 'Don't laugh ...' he said.

'At what?' she said.

'I'd like us to start our own business.'

'A business? Doing what?' Lucy cried.

'I know someone who's selling a charabanc,' he said. 'It's decent enough. Needs some work doing. We could run outings, trips to the seaside, paying customers.'

'Driving a charabanc?' Lucy said.

'Yes, there's good money in it,' he said. 'It could be called Joe's Seaside Tours.'

Lucy threw her head back and laughed. Then she saw the hurt in his eyes and stopped. He was serious. 'But Joe, where would we get the money for a charabanc?' she said.

'Just this last trip, that's all I need to get the first payment on it,' he said. 'I've worked it all out. Then, whatever I owe, we can pay back from the trips.'

Lucy gazed at him. He was deadly serious. His eyes shone with something she didn't see in any other man around their way. Hope. 'I ... I don't know. Isn't it a risk?' she said.

She watched as Joseph traced a finger gently over Florence's cheek as she fed. 'I don't know about you but I want more for her than this life,' he said. 'I can handle it. I can do the shifts. I can work. But I don't want to come home exhausted and die young. I don't want to pawn my shoes so you can survive while I'm away. I don't want to see Florence get ill from this place, this smog, this mould, this damp. I want better for us. One last trip ... that's all I need.'

He flung himself on his back again and stared at the ceiling. He was full of energy and youth and ideas. She thought of the other stokers she saw staggering back through the streets after another trip. Some were only in their forties but looked aged and decrepit. Joseph was in his prime now but how long before the killer ships sucked the life out of him, too?

'Don't get me wrong. I don't regret leaving the country for here, it was the right thing to do,' Joseph said. 'And coming here gave me ideas. But now I want to do something else. I can make this a success; I really know I can.'

She kissed his cheek and rubbed it with her own. 'I know you can, too,' she said. She leaned in for a kiss and the baby came off the breast and started gurgling and smiling. Florence shot her mother a look that usually pre-empted a crying fit, so Lucy handed her to Joseph, and he held the child on his chest.

'Well, I think we need a celebration,' Lucy said. She went over to Joseph's side of the bed and saw a paper packet folded over containing his pay.

'May I?' she asked, fluttering her eyelashes.

He laughed.

She took some coins and began to dress.

'Where are you going?' he asked.

'To get us something special for our breakfast,' she said.

He watched as she pulled her corset on, doing up the hooks and eyes with a delicate deftness he could never understand. She pulled on her dress and a pinafore, then her boots and an overcoat.

'I'll be back soon,' she said.

In the street, Lucy hummed to herself. She always felt like this when Joseph was home. When he was away the days were empty, spent soothing a screaming child and eating alone, sleeping alone. When he was here, she felt she could do anything. She jumped to avoid a flooded area in the road and hopped to where it was drier. Then she heard a voice.

'What are you doing jumping about like an elf?'

She turned and saw Catherine. 'Ah there you are,' Lucy said.

'Here I am?' Catherine said.

'I heard you were getting wed. I thought you'd run away to Gretna Green!'

Catherine laughed. 'Not yet. Although I might if Percy doesn't hurry up,' she said.

Lucy clapped a hand to her mouth. 'So he will propose?' she said.

Catherine leaned in. 'He is coming over to see Father later today,' she said.

'How wonderful!' Lucy said.

But she could see from Catherine's expression this was not the sort of love she shared with Joseph. When Lucy had planned her wedding day – a simple exchange of vows on Christmas Day – she had been unable to eat or sleep. Love took over her like an illness. Her uncle even thought she had consumption before the wedding because she was so thin from not eating.

But it hadn't been an illness. It had been nerves. The nerves of loving someone so much. The fear of loving them and losing them. She loved Joseph with all her heart. Now, as she looked at Catherine's cold, empty expression, she felt sorry for her. Why did she not feel the same?

'He will ask my father later on and when he says yes, as he will, he will propose,' she said.

'Well, if it's what you hope for then I'm pleased for you,' Lucy said.

Catherine smiled. But the smile was sardonic. Even with her beauty, when she smiled she had the harshness of her mother, inherited from years of bitterness, hunger and disappointment. Catherine caught the glint of sunlight on Lucy's wedding band. 'I know what you're thinking,' she said.

'Oh?' Lucy smiled.

'Yes, you're wondering why I am not love's young

dream like you,' Catherine said. There was bitterness in her tone.

Lucy stepped backwards a little.

'Well not everyone can fall in love and have a wonderful life,' Catherine said. 'Not everyone can get looks, brains, kindness and the pay to match.' She sneered as she looked at Lucy. She could not help it.

'Catherine. I am not judging you or why you're marrying,' Lucy said.

Catherine kicked at the kerb with her boot. 'You see,' she said, her teeth gritted, 'I don't have the luxury of waiting for my husband to come home and holding a baby all day. I work, you see. I graft. I am on my knees every single day morning 'til night, scrubbing a rich woman's step, doing her laundry, making her cutlery shine.'

Lucy looked at Catherine's beautiful face. She was so pretty. But when she spoke this way she was ugly.

'I want more. I want more than a decent man to "get by". I want more than scrubbing steps. Percy's going to be a steward and he will get tips and work in first class.'

'I don't doubt it,' Lucy said kindly.

Catherine, shaking, backed away and smiled. 'Wish you a good day,' she said. Then she walked off in the direction of the big house to start her day's work.

Lucy cast her mind back to when she'd first arrived in the city three years earlier. Catherine had been so welcoming and kind. True, she always had a streak in her from her mother but that had made her funny and cutting and true. When had her friend become so bitter?

And why, just as she and Joseph were trying to flee the world of the killer ships, was Catherine so desperate to join it?

# CHAPTER SIX

**Susan**

From her desk at the front of the class, Susan could see seventeen children at their tables. She pretended to drop her pencil and bent under her desk. There, gazing across the dusty wooden floor, she counted. *Two, four, six…*

She came up again, smiled, and placed the pencil on the desk. But behind her smile she felt sadness gnaw at her insides. Six pairs of feet without boots today. Three wore some moccasin affairs you'd wear in the house, one wore summer shoes with holes in and two … two wore no shoes at all.

This was a regular occurrence at her school. The coal strike meant that most men were not working. And in a town like Southampton, where virtually every man depended on coal for his job on a steam ship, that meant huge unemployment.

Some children didn't bother to come to school at all. Some didn't have the clothes to come, their parents having pawned their school clothes for enough money for rent. Others tried – like these – despite the cold, the wet and owning no shoes or boots. It broke her heart.

She cleared her throat. 'Today, class, we will learn the countries of the world. Who knows another country other than Great Britain?'

Several hands shot up.

'Jack?' Susan said, gesturing to a boy.

'America,' he replied.

'That's right,' Susan said.

'Josephine?'

'Miss … America as well,' a voice said.

Susan smiled. These children were all sons and daughters of men who worked on the ships. The lion's share of their work took them to America – New York specifically. It was the only 'other' country they heard about.

As Susan pointed to a globe and talked of continents such as Africa and Asia, she couldn't take her mind of the poverty of her pupils. She saw them try to concentrate and fail. She knew why. Their stomachs were rumbling. How could any child learn when they were starving?

At the end of the school day, Susan watched as the children filed out of her class. As they did, she stopped the two children who were shoeless. 'George, Eustace,' she said. 'Would you come here please?'

The two boys came towards her in their bare feet. They were 13 but their weary faces looked older. 'Yes, Miss,' the chorused.

'Where are your boots today?' Susan asked.

George looked down and wiggled his toes. Eustace looked proudly – almost defiantly – at his teacher.

'My father had to pawn them,' Eustace said.

George looked at the floor. 'Mine fell apart in the flood,' he said.

The streets of Northam often flooded, sometimes up to the stairs of the houses. Being so near the sea brought its risks.

'Well, we can't have that, can we?' Susan said. 'You go home now and I will see what I can do.'

The boys nodded.

As she watched them walk away, Susan bit back tears. She'd grown up in this poverty. She knew how long a pair of boots had to last. But somehow, her parents had managed. Not anymore. Not in 1912. People were no longer poor, they were destitute. The wretched coal strike affected everyone.

People couldn't afford to eat, let alone kit their children out with boots.

She got up suddenly, grabbed her overcoat and set off. She left the school, ran through the puddles in the street, down roads where children usually played but today a deathly silence prevailed, past the church and ended up at a building. The Salvation Army.

She stepped inside. A woman and a man were having a cup of tea.

'Can I help you?' the woman said, stepping forward.

'Yes,' Susan said, breathlessly. 'I need shoes so my pupils can get to school.'

An hour later, Susan left the Salvation Army building with a smile on her face. In a bag, she carried something. She set off, down the streets, back past the church, over the puddles and back to the neighbourhood she knew. She had written Eustace and George's addresses down on a scrap of paper. First, she read out Eustace's. *Peel Street.*

She wandered along, dodging children playing with hoops, ignoring the scowls of women who sat outside their doors, holding their mops. She came to the address. She knocked on the door. She waited some time before a man came to the door. He opened it and Susan stepped backwards. The man was so frail he was almost paper thin, like a ghost.

'Is ... is the lady of the house here?' Susan ventured, instantly feeling foolish.

The man laughed, holding a hankie to his mouth to stop the phlegm that came with laughter. 'She died four year ago. Drink. Why?' he said.

'Does Eustace live here?' she said.

'Right 'o he does,' the man said. Then she saw a dark-haired skinny lad peering behind his father. Eustace.

'I'm his teacher. I've brought him ...' her voice trailed off. 'I've brought him a book he forgot at school.'

The father shrugged, coughed and wandered off, pushing Eustace forward to his teacher.

Susan stepped nearer, smiled and opened up the bag

she was carrying. She showed Eustace and his face lit up.

'Boots, Miss?' he said.

'Yes, for you.'

'But where, Miss …?'

'That doesn't matter,' Susan said. 'They're about your size. I want to see you at school tomorrow in these, nicely polished.'

He grinned and held them up, eyeing them from all angles.

'Thank you, Miss,' he muttered. Then his father coughed loudly and he blinked.

'Go, go,' Susan said.

The boy closed the door.

A few streets away, Susan knocked on another door. A woman, heavily pregnant, answered.

'Does George live here?' Susan asked.

'Yes,' the woman replied. 'You're his teacher.'

'I am,' Susan said.

'Has he done something wrong? If he has, I'll clout him one,' the woman said, pushing back two other dirty-faced children from the door.

'No, he's done nothing wrong.' Susan had to play this carefully. The woman had a strange air of pride about her. Despite the dilapidated house, the door that was hanging off its hinges, this woman emanated an angry sense of self worth.

Thinking quickly, Susan said, 'We held a contest today. A spelling contest.'

'Oh?' the woman said.

'Yes, George won. And the prize was a pair of shiny boots.'

She handed the bag over. The woman took the bag, looked inside and raised her eyebrows. 'George!' she called out.

Moments later a boy came to the door. He smiled, recognising his teacher.

'Seems you won a contest,' his mother said.

George opened his mouth to protest but Susan gave him a stern look. 'The spelling contest,' she said, nodding at him.

'Oh … yes … that, Miss,' he said.

'Well, the prize is here. New school boots!' Susan said.

George looked in the bag and pulled them out.

His mother rubbed her burgeoning belly and seemed not to think anything was amiss. George looked at the boots, feeling their laces.

'Thank you, Miss,' he said.

Susan smiled and stepped backwards. She felt an ache in her throat and longed to cry. She didn't. Instead, she made a stern expression and said, 'I expect to see you bright and early tomorrow morning. Don't be late.'

George nodded.

The mother slammed the door.

Stepping away into the puddle-strewn street, Susan wandered. She didn't know where to go. She didn't want to go home to her mother and father and brothers. She didn't want to see anyone. She was angry, so angry, and so hurt and so saddened. Why had God deemed it so that some fortunate souls lived in splendour with everything they could wish for while others, even little children, lived the way they did?

Why did parents feel they had to make the choice between putting a meal on the table and giving their children a pair of boots to go to school?

She walked on, past a pub where loud voices were yelling inside, past a boy playing in the road with a ball, past the fish shop and the horse and cart selling manure. It was only when she got around the corner, onto a back lane where no one was, that she allowed herself to weep.

Life, society, the world simply had to change. She'd been so angry about women's rights for so long she'd forgotten about the rights of those around her. The rights of the poor to have the dignity to own shoes. The rights of the children to learn without their stomachs burning with hunger.

She looked towards the docks to the empty skies where in just a few weeks a great, opulent, mega-ship would pull alongside. *Titanic* would be a godsend to so many, bringing jobs, earnings, money. She was only a ship – a huge mass of metal, wood and steel.

But she represented hope, escape, a future. And she couldn't have been coming at a better time.

# Chapter Seven

**Catherine**

The weight of him almost made Catherine fall into the gutter several times as they staggered away from the King's Arms.

'Hold him tighter,' her mother gasped, wrenching him up onto her shoulder. Catherine took a deep breath and heaved her father up so he was able to stand and together the women half-dragged, half-carried the inebriated man home.

When they reached the front door, Catherine's mother kicked it open and threw their load onto the hallway floor. She gave him a kick in the stomach for good measure then stepped over him.

'Right, , great lump, get up!' she cried.

'Owwww, ohhh, leave me, woman,' Catherine's father cried.

'We got a visitor coming soon, so you get up, I say!' cried her mother again, coming back and kicking her father in the other side of his abdomen.

He reached a hand out to Catherine and she managed to pull him upright. 'Please, Father, Percy is coming over today and he wants to ask you something,' Catherine said.

Swaying, the man nodded and smiled. 'My little girl, my dear little miss,' he slurred, trying to touch her face but missing.

She manoeuvred him to the chair and he collapsed into it.

'Pour this on him,' her mother said, bringing a jug of water.

Catherine gaped. 'Pour it?!' Catherine said.

'Oh, give it here, I'll do it,' she said. Catherine gasped and laughed as her mother poured a full jug of water over her father's head.

He cried out and inhaled fast and sharply, before standing upright. It seemed to work. He didn't look angry, just awake at long last.

'Yes, right, where is he?' he asked, blinking through his wet eyelashes.

'He's coming soon, so wash up, change and be ready for talking,' Catherine's mother yelled.

Like an oversized lamb, the man dutifully went off to wash outside. Not long after, he came back – looking no different except for soapy water dripping off his chin – just in time to hear the front door rattle.

'It's Percy!' Catherine said, quickly glancing in the mirror and licking stray tendrils of dark curls and pushing them off her face.

'You. There,' Catherine's mother said, pushing her husband to one corner of the room where the semi-darkness hid the fact that he looked like he'd been sleeping rough. Catherine looked at her mother. The woman smoothed down her pinafore, brushed some dust from the kitchen table and nodded as if to say, 'Now girl.'

Catherine nodded back and pulled the door open. There Percy stood in the street, wearing his best grey wool jacket and trousers.

'Come in,' Catherine said, looking at her feet in the coy manner she adopted around Percy.

Percy stepped inside. Catherine's mother came and ushered him to the parlour– the 'best' room that never was sat in.

'You come and sit in here, my dear,' she said, opening the door to the best room. She lingered, watching Percy take in the two ornaments, the tablecloth, her best things on display.

Catherine entered, feeling as nervous as Percy. The parlour was never used. A small round wooden table sat in the centre covered with a lacy off-white tablecloth. Two cheap ornaments of birds sat on a woodworm-ridden sideboard. There was a wooden cross on the wall.

This was hallowed territory. If her mother was letting her and Percy sit in the parlour , she meant business.

'I shall go and make us a pot of tea,' her mother said, smiling and retreating backwards.

Percy took his cap off and fingered it. 'Where is your father?' he asked.

'Here,' came the voice, as Catherine's father came in. He was so large he filled the small front room. 'Well?'

Percy cleared his throat. 'I wish to ask you, sir, for your daughter's hand.'

The words echoed around the room. Silence. Catherine stared at her father. He was staring out through the window, looking at a view no one in the family ever really saw – the 'parlour window view'. Catherine held her breath. Surely, he wouldn't need to think about it? He barely knew she existed. Just one more daughter hanging around. She gazed at her father. His eyes squinted and he looked thoughtful.

Catherine followed his gaze and then realised. He wasn't thinking. He wasn't pondering. You could see the King's Arms from here. This window was so barely looked through that her father was staring at the view as if at a new, beautiful vista he had never seen before. Wistfully, her father gazed at the front door of the pub. Catherine knew now was the moment to strike, while he was weak.

'Father?' she said, clearing her throat.

Shaking his head, as if drawn back to the present after a trance, Catherine's father grinned a grin that showed how many teeth he was missing.

He stepped forward, shook Percy's hand and said, 'My son.'

Then he staggered from the front room, grabbed his hat and set off across the street to the pub before Catherine's mother could work out where he had gone.

'Was that a yes?' Percy said, hurrying to Catherine's side.

She smiled. 'I believe it was,' she replied.

Percy bit his lip and blushed furiously. 'So, we'll be married?' he dared to venture.

'I reckon so,' Catherine said. 'But you know we need to wait.'

'Wait?' Percy's face fell.

Catherine looked at the lacy tablecloth and fingered its edges. 'Yes, let's see that you get that steward job on *Titanic* and get all those tips we spoke of,' she smiled, reaching for his hand and sending a bolt of electricity through him.

He smiled now too and nodded. 'Yes. I will,' he said. 'I'll be a steward, you'll see. I'll come home with enough tips for us to have a life. A proper life.'

She smiled now and he hovered near her. She knew what he wanted. Nice, nasty, rich, poor, kind, cruel – all men had the same look when they wanted this.

But instead of turning her lips to his, she proffered her cheek. Percy laid his lips on the soft roundness of her face and lingered, breathing in her smell. The scent emanating from her was of carbolic soap and soda crystals but, to Percy, she smelt like a princess.

'I will give you a wonderful life, Catherine,' he said, looking at his hands again and blushing.

She stared at the wooden cross on the wall and dared to hope.

# Chapter Eight

**Lucy**

In six weeks, Lucy counted, Joseph had had three black eyes fighting for a day's work at the docks. He'd managed to get a half day here, a half day there. He'd even managed to get a ten-day stint on a coal transportation ship as coal began to trickle its way back into the city. But it wasn't enough. They went from mutton to boiled vegetables. From fresh bread to stale loaves the baker was giving away cheap at the end of the day. As she put the screaming baby down for a nap, Lucy tidied some of the things lying around on the kitchen table. Under a pile of rags that needed washing, she found a neatly folded up newspaper sheet.

She opened it and saw an image. It was of a strange contraption that looked like a boat on wheels. Ten or so people sat inside the 'boat' shape and were smiling. It was the charabanc Joseph had spoken of. 'With its internal combustion engine and five rows of comfortable benches facing forward, including space for luggage, this is the new way to travel. Travel at 15 mph to visit the coast, the countryside …'

Lucy traced her finger over the passengers in the charabanc. Some were ladies in fine hats and gloves. The men wore hats and smiled. It was another world. Could they really be a part of it?

A knock at the door made her jump. Her stomach lurched at the thought of the baby waking. She went to the door, silently, desperately trying not to creak a single floorboard. Susan was at the door with Catherine.

'What?' Lucy said, stunned.

'My half day,' Catherine said, by way of explanation.

'Mine too,' Susan chipped in.

'May we?' Catherine asked.

They stepped past Lucy and into her kitchen. 'We have a lot of news,' Susan said. 'Is Joseph not back yet?'

Lucy shook her head. 'No, he got half a day at the docks,' she replied.

'So you don't know?' Susan asked.

'Know what?' Lucy asked, wide-eyed, staring at them both for an answer.

'White Star is taking people to sign on from today,' Susan said.

'Sign on?' Lucy asked. Her mind was bleary from another morning of endless screaming from Florence.

'To *Titanic*!' Catherine screamed.

'Shh! You'll wake the …'

An enormous scream erupted from Lucy's bedroom. She rolled her eyes and shot Catherine a dagger look.

'Sorry,' Catherine shrugged.

Lucy trudged off to get the baby. When she returned, both women were still as excited-looking as when they'd first arrived.

'My father and two of my brothers have got work,' Susan said. 'They've just signed on.'

Catherine sat straighter and added, 'And Percy will find out today if he's signed on as a steward.'

Lucy stared at the door, the very door Joseph had walked through that morning to get some work at the docks. He hadn't said anything about signing on to *Titanic* that day. He hadn't mentioned it at all.

'Have you heard anything from Joseph?' Susan asked.

Lucy shook her head.

Catherine smiled and couldn't resist. 'Secrets already, lovebirds?'

Susan hit her in the ribs.

'Maybe it's a surprise?' Susan said kindly.

'So, where are your father and brothers now?' Lucy asked.

'Guess,' Susan replied. 'Celebrating. The pay is low, but they've heard rumours *Titanic*'s an easy ship and they'll be steaming easy. It'll be nothing to them. My father even joked he'll put his feet up down there!'

'If Percy gets his position there won't be any rest,' Catherine said proudly. 'He will be in first class and it's endless but the tips, I hear, are enormous. Two years ago, Albert Raynes from down Percy's way came back and rented a house for a year with his tips from just one sail!'

Lucy smiled and nodded. 'Well, I hope Percy signs on,' she said.

'Oh, he will,' Catherine said.

'He will,' Susan added, 'or madam here won't marry him!'

Catherine smiled like a cat about to get a huge bowl of cream.

Susan grabbed Lucy's hand. 'Just think, though, if Joseph does this one last trip, that's it for you. Things might change. Things might change for all of us,' Susan added, pulling a paper leaflet out of her bag and pushing it across the table to Lucy.

*'Equality for women. A meeting.'* She read.

'In two days' time,' Susan said. 'I'm going.'

Catherine rolled her eyes. 'And I'm not,' she said. 'I don't want the vote.'

Susan looked horrified. 'Of course you want the vote!'

'No, I want Percy to have the vote and he can do my bidding,' she said. 'I don't care about the vote. I just want to not clean doorsteps and ovens no more.'

'But don't you see, the vote can help you stop doing that?' Susan said, exasperated.

'It's no good,' Lucy laughed. 'She wants to be lady muck and that's that!'

'What about you?' Susan asked, pushing the leaflet back at Lucy. 'Can you come?'

'And leave the baby? Not likely!' Lucy said.

Susan rolled her eyes. 'So it's just me, fighting for you two and your future,' she sighed. 'And even your future,' she cooed, leaning in and tickling Florence's chin.

Just then the door opened and Joseph walked in. His shoulders were hunched and his head hung.

He saw the women at the table and forced a smile.

'Joe,' Lucy said, getting up. 'What's wrong?'

Susan and Catherine exchanged glances. Susan suddenly felt terribly guilty. If her family had jobs on *Titanic*, and Joseph didn't … life could be very awkward for a while.

Joseph wandered to the kitchen and fetched a cup of water from the jug on the side. He gulped it down, wiped his mouth and sat at the table with the others.

'Bad news, I am afraid,' he said, putting his fists on the table top.

Lucy's whole world seemed to shrink. The tiny room, the mould covered ceiling, the crying baby, the smell of soup she was trying to create from nothing, all combined to form a strange, dreamlike, nightmarish room she felt suffocated in.

If he didn't have work on *Titanic*, they would starve. This was the chance of a lifetime. This was their way out.

She felt dizzy, faint. Her hearing went first, just a whistle remained. Then everything went black. A thud was the last thing she heard.

When she opened her eyes, three faces stared down at her.

'Lucy, Lucy,' Susan was saying.

'Lucy, come on,' Catherine said, slapping her cheek.

'Not so hard!' Susan shrieked, pushing Catherine aside.

'Luce … Luce …' came a voice she loved.

She managed to open her mouth.

'What … what happened?' Lucy croaked. Her voice felt strange, as if it belonged to someone else.

'You fainted,' Catherine said brusquely. 'Although I have no idea why …'

'Catherine,' Susan hissed, elbowing her.

The three of them helped Lucy up off the floor and

onto the only arm chair in the room. She sank into it gratefully and felt the blood rush back to her head.

Then she remembered. The awful news. Everyone seemed to have got work on *Titanic* except Joseph. Tears sprang to her eyes.

'It's my fault you fainted,' Joseph said, smiling. 'I'm so sorry my love. I wanted to play a trick on you. I was pretending to be downhearted … It was an act.'

Lucy frowned. 'An act?'

The two women grinned, smiling at her now and taking one hand each.

'Lucy, I did get work on *Titanic*. As a stoker. Six pounds a month and to New York and back. It's an easy ship, new and we'll steam easy. It'll be like a bloody holiday! I've got work and when I get back, we're done! We can get out of all this!'

Lucy looked at Florence, sitting so happily on her blanket on the floor, she had suddenly grown more hair now, brown like her father's. The baby gurgled and her little mouth began to curl upwards. It was as if the child understood what her father was saying, for she smiled back at her mother for the very first time ever.

'Oh, thank God,' Lucy gasped, thudding her head against Joseph's chest and squeezing her two friends' hands for dear life.

Just then the door banged and Lucy went to it. Percy ran in with her, his face flushed and his eyes twinkling.

'I've been looking everywhere for you, Catherine!' he cried. 'They told me they'd seen you coming here. Pardon the interruption,' he added, taking his hat off and nodding at Joseph. 'But I had to come. I just had to! I've some news!'

Everyone stared at Percy now as he stood in their small house, cap in hand, his pulse visibly pumping in his neck.

'Well?' Catherine said.

He held up a piece of paper. 'Signed on. First Class Bedroom Steward. Three pounds a month!' he cried.

Joseph got up, walked over and shook Percy's hand.

'Then we'll be at sea together,' Joseph said.

Lucy felt tears fall down her face. For the first time in

months, she felt hopeful. Life – for everyone – was finally looking up.

# Chapter Nine

**Susan**

The first thing she noticed was that not everyone looked the same as her. Naively, Susan realised, she had thought every woman at a suffragette meeting would be like her – young, healthy, reasonably intelligent. Instead, she was met with women from all walks of life. It was the sixth of April, 1912. Susan looked around and saw older women, younger women, women with wedding rings on, women without, women who were robust and walked like men, women who were delicate and feminine and quiet. She found a seat and sat down and then clapped as the audience erupted into applause.

A speaker walked on stage. She began her speech. Susan listened avidly.

'Women are tired of languishing at home, at the stove, at the hearth, at the dolly tub. Poor women are worked to the bone, before returning to a home where they must work all over again. A vote for women is a vote for humanity and a future …'

The crowd applauded. Susan clapped until her wrists ached. Two hours later, she emerged, heart racing, bag stuffed full of paper leaflets.

Back at her home, she raced past her angry mother, past her celebrating father and two brothers and into her bedroom. She threw the leaflets onto her bed and read them, devoured them. Then her eyes fell upon one in particular.

*'Night-time protest. 10pm. Thursday.'*

Her hands shook. Night-time. So women protested at night? How? Still a flicker of excitement began inside her. The thought of joining other women, these sisters of the same cause, at night, protesting, thrilled her. She had to do something. She had to act. She reached under her bed, pulled out a wooden sewing box, lifted the scraps of fabric and cloth and stuffed the leaflets underneath. Then, she smoothed her hair, crept back downstairs to join her family celebrating.

'You're back then, Missy,' her father said.

Susan sat at the table as her mother dished up the dinner. There were dumplings, she noted. Must have been a special occasion.

Her brothers Jack and Ernest began wolfing the food down.

'Got to get some meat on them. Want to make a good impression on *Titanic*, don't we lads?' her father said.

Both brothers nodded.

Susan smiled, taking in their youth, their excitement. They were her younger brothers and she'd always been protective of them. She saw her mother wolf down a dumpling whole and wash it down with a glass of sherry.

Sherry was Susan's mother's 'little helper' – but it was something she kept hidden, the bottle stashed at the side of the range. But to share sherry with the family and toast openly - .this was a celebration.

'To the *Titanic*, the unsinkable ship,' Susan's father said, raising his ale glass.

'To *Titanic*, the unsinkable ship!' the family chorused. Susan drank her morsel of sherry and felt its warmth course through her. She felt happy. Happy for the first time in months. *Titanic* was coming and would bring jobs, prosperity, new beginnings. The coal strike was over. People were moving again and working. All the children in her school had boots this week. And she was going to attend her very first night protest with the suffragettes. The whole world seemed on the brink of a new era.

It was the next day that Susan came downstairs before setting off to work that she saw her brothers and father lined up in front of her mother.

She pulled her boots on and laughed as her mother spat on her hankie and wiped breakfast from her brothers' mouths.

'Still babies,' she tutted, scraping butter off their lips.

They blinked back at her, dwarfing her, towering over her, but still in awe of her. Next came the 'goodbye' to her father.

'I'll be seeing you,' she said, handing him a flask. And that was that.

As Susan grabbed her school bag to set off, her brothers and father filed past her to go down to the White Star Line and board the ship.

'Stay well sister,' Ernest said, flicking her ear as he'd done when they were children.

'Stay safe,' said Jack, winking and nodding.

Jack, she was sure, knew about her suffrage leanings. She blushed and chose to ignore him.

Then her father came. He looked at her, then stopped. For one strange moment Susan felt she had slipped into another dimension. Her father was never demonstrative. Never a hug or kiss type of man. But suddenly he dropped his kit bag, leaned in and enveloped his daughter in a hug that smelt of tobacco. He said nothing. He hugged her for a few moments. She felt his back under her arms. He looked like a burly stoker but when she touched him, she realised his bones stuck out from his back. The years of stoking fires, lifting shovels, toiling in 50 degree heat had taken their toll.

'This'll be my last sail,' he murmured into Susan's hair.

'Yes, father,' she said.

He pulled away then and, without looking back, stepped out into the street with her brothers. Her mother joined her at the door as they watched them walk away.

'I had a dream last night,' her mother said, folding her arms over her pinafore and watching the three men cross the street, kit bags over their shoulder.

'Oh?' Susan said, readying herself for the walk to work.

'Yes. It was of a hive of bees,' she said, 'the hive was buzzing so loudly. Then a huge wind came and knocked it sideways. The bees were still buzzing, they were angry buzzing, you know, like they were trapped. They buzzed and buzzed and buzzed, trying to get out. In my dream I could look inside the hive. I didn't get stung, the bees didn't see me. They were there, crawling, desperate, trying to get out. They couldn't. They was trapped, you see. Then the hive went silent. I woke up.'

Susan smiled and hugged her mother.

'Well you can get a good nights' sleep for a few days with them three away,' she said. And she set off down the street for the school. As she walked down their road, past the bakery, past the butchers, past Percy's cobbler's, she suddenly stopped.

It was there. On the horizon. Towering over the houses like an invader from the future. Four yellow funnels stood aloft majestically.

'*Titanic*,' she whispered.

She looked at the clock outside the post office. She still had time. She took a detour, past the fishmongers, down a lane and towards the sea where the children played in marshland. From there, she turned a corner and then she saw it in all its glory.

The ship was the biggest thing she'd ever seen. A long, yet tall, elegant, yet bulky, beauty of a thing. The four funnels were spewing sooty smoke already, preparing, as if to say; I'm ready. The paintwork from the sides glistened in the April sunlight. Susan knew about ships. Her father and brothers never stopped talking about them. She'd never seen them as beautiful, though, just a workplace where the men in her family went to earn some meagre pay. But now even she stood, gaping in awe at this beautiful creation. *Titanic*. It meant huge, big, massive, enormous. Her schooling taught her that the Titans were the pre-Olympian gods, the children of heaven and of earth. This ship looked godly. Imposing. Perfection. Yet terrifying. All at once.

Two children skipped past her. They ought to have been at school but carried buckets looking in the marshy water for fish or cockles.

They stopped too, now, staring at the awesome spectacle docked ahead of them on the horizon.

'Is that *Titanic*, miss?' one asked.

Susan nodded. 'Yes, it is,' she replied.

The other child didn't even look up, just began rummaging around in the marsh with his hand.

'It's cursed, that boat, my grandmother says,' the boy said, swishing his hand in the muddy water.

Susan suddenly felt very cold. 'Cursed?' she said, laughing a little. 'I don't think so!'

'Oh, it is,' came the reply. The boy looked up at her now, seemingly refusing to look at the vessel at the docks. 'No good will come of her.'

# Chapter Ten

**Lucy**

'Now, you're certain you have everything?' Lucy said, fussing about Joseph and checking his kit bag.

He laughed, finishing his chipped mug of tea and slamming it down on the table, a noise that made their baby daughter giggle, not cry. 'I am all set!' he cried, grabbing Lucy by the waist and spinning her around their tiny room.

She laughed now but as he set her down, dizziness hit her. She'd felt funny all night, unsettled. The room span a little now and she sat down at the kitchen table.

'You all right, my love?' Joseph asked. 'Did I spin you too hard?'

She laughed. 'No, I'm all right,' she replied. She stopped then, before reaching for his hand. 'I shall miss you, that's all.'

He bent down and kissed her head. 'And I shall miss you,' he said. 'But, we both know this is my …'

'One. Last. Trip!' Lucy giggled.

'Exactly,' he said, grinning back at her. He went to his kit bag and rummaged inside it, before pulling out a slip of paper and handing it to her.

She read the top of the slip. 'Royce's Pawn Shop? What's this?' she asked, frowning.

'Well, a few of the lads did the same thing and we took our shoes to Royce's. I took mine - here's your money to keep you tided over 'til I get back.' He handed her envelope of coins and notes.

'Money? For shoes?' she said.

'Yes. My best ones.'

'Your only ones!' she said.

'So,' he shrugged. 'I won't need them where I'm going! Take the money, feed up Madam here, and I'll pick them up when I get back with my pay. I'll be needing them when I am a charabanc chauffeur!'

He mimed holding a steering wheel and made his way around the room, beeping an imaginary horn. She laughed at his charade, but sadness gripped her. She thought of all the other men – fathers, husbands, sons – who had taken their shoes to the pawn shop. She tucked the Royce's slip away in her pinafore pocket.

'Now I want to hear of no scrimping whilst I am away,' he said, picking up Florence and kissing her chubby face. 'I want the best, most warmest, most puffiest, densest bread, the creamiest, thickest milk, the freshest eggs and the best cuts of meat for my two girls.'

Florence erupted into happy giggles as he play-bit her neck.

The clock chimed.

Lucy looked at it. Joseph too. Their eyes met and for one moment, they seemed suspended in time. They both knew this was it. He was leaving her now. Oh, he laughed and joked at home, but she knew how hard the work was. How horrendous the days were – one long endurance challenge of heaving coal onto a shovel, throwing it into a fire that seemed surely hotter than the fires of Hell, wiping sweat off his brow that would reappear seconds later, only to repeat the whole process again and again and again. She knew how the men came off the ship stones lighter, so dehydrated their veins showed through their skin. She flung herself at him then, wrapping her arms around his neck and covering him with kisses. If she could make a spell to stop him going. If she could work it so that they could get away and he'd never have to go to that boiler room again.

'My love … my love …' he gasped, coming up for air and releasing himself from her grip. 'You'll choke me before I choke on the soot!'

She pulled away and he saw tears in her eyes.

'There, there, this is an easy one,' he said, touching her face. 'She's a new ship. She'll steam so easy we'll all be sitting with our feet up!'

She laughed then, wiping her face with the back of her hand.

'Then let's go,' Lucy said.

She lifted the baby and placed her in her pram, bundled her up with blankets and put on her own overcoat. Joseph grabbed his coat too, his cap, and slung his kit bag over his shoulder.

'You're coming with me?' he grinned. 'I can't see Madam here doing a four-hour shift in the boiler room.'

'We'll come and see you off,' Lucy replied.

As they walked down the street, past the shops they knew, many shopkeepers came out and doffed their caps to a *Titanic* stoker walking past.

Usually stokers were the lowest of the low. But not today. Getting a job on *Titanic* after months of a coal strike was like scooping a winning jackpot ticket.

'I feel famous,' Joseph said, smiling.

As they reached Oxford Street, they passed The Grapes pub. The loud laughter and yelling of excitable men could be heard from outside. Joseph waved at a man he knew through the window.

Just then Lucy saw a man she recognised. He was wearing his very best coat and had done something to his hair, slicking it all down to one side.

'Percy?' Lucy said.

'Oh, hello,' he said, instinctively smoothing his hair. 'I'm going to board today.' He kept looking around him. 'I had thought Catherine might come and say goodbye but…' His voice trailed off.

Lucy knew Catherine cared for no one but herself, but she longed to spare Percy the misery, so she said, 'She'll be working hard at the big house. She's very hardworking. Like you, Percy. Just think of the life you can set up when you return.'

Percy smiled then and his shoulders relaxed. 'Yes, you're right,' he said.

'Jo-seph, Jo-seph, Jo-seph!' came some shouts from the doorway of The Grapes. The other stokers and greasers were beckoning him, already drunk, holding tankards of ale and slopping the beer down their stoker uniforms.

'Join them if you wish,' Lucy smiled.

'You're sure?' he said.

'She wears the trousers, she wears the trousers!' came the sing-song shouting from The Grapes.

Joseph simply laughed.

'I should see them. This is my last trip after all,' he said.

'You go, my love,' Lucy said.

Joseph leaned over the pram. The child was sleeping, despite the noise and revels from the pub. 'I swear she's a mini stoker like me,' Joseph laughed, stroking Florence's soft cheek.

Lucy felt her throat ache with tears that she knew she must now allow to come. She gripped the bars of the pram harder, forcing herself not to cry.

'You'll have me back before you know it,' Joseph said, holding her hand. He traced her wedding band under his fingers. 'You'll be cursing me in a few days' time, plunging my black clothes into that tin bath again …'

He looked at her then. His smile faded. She blinked and a single tear fell down her cheek.

'Goodbye, Joe,' she said, forcing herself to swallow a sob.

'My love,' he murmured, holding her head to his chest and kissing her ear, her hair, her forehead.

She didn't know why she said it. She'd never said it before. She heard herself say some words and had no idea where they had come from. 'Be careful, Joe.'

He nodded. 'I will.' Then he kissed his own fingers, placed them on her lips to press his kiss there and grabbed his kit bag once more. He walked off, into The Grapes to the cheers of the other stokers 'Jo-seph! Jo-seph!'

Then the door swung shut behind him.

Lucy turned the pram and was set to go home. But something told her she should not. Instead, she walked past the shops, past the bakery, past the news stand where the boy always shouted, past the butchers.

She didn't want to go home yet.

So, she turned back on herself. She walked past The Grapes, fighting every ounce of her being to run inside and kiss Joseph once more, and down to the docks. There, she was stunned to see hundreds of other people had decided to do the same.

There were men and women with flags, children being held on their fathers' shoulders to get a better look. Lucy struggled to push her pram through the crowd to get a glimpse, a better vantage point. Then she found it, between a large man with a child on his shoulder and two older matrons who were already sniffing behind handkerchiefs.

She waited. She had no idea how long had passed. But then she saw movement. Something was happening. Some enormous noises erupted from nowhere and she realised, stunned, that *Titanic*'s funnels were blaring as soot and smoke erupted from them. Joseph was down in that boiler room. He would be stoking that fire that made those funnels erupt.

She craned her head to see better. It was twelve noon. She saw *Titanic* being towed out from its berth at the docks by tug boats. The majestic ship had been berthed next to the SS *New York*. Now, as she passed the other ship, Lucy heard gasps erupt from the crowds.

Her heart hammered. A head was in front of her. She couldn't see.

'What is it?' she asked the big man next to her.

He stood on tiptoes.

'Looks like *Titanic* just nearly collided with the *New York*!' he said.

Down in the docks, the *Oceanic* was also berthed, a ship Joseph had sailed on before. As Lucy stretched her neck to see what on earth was going on, she tried to make sense of it.

It appeared the *Titanic* had sailed away from her position next to the SS *New York* and the power of her moving had caused the *New York* to break away from her position. The *Titanic* had narrowly missed colliding with the SS *New York*.

Lucy stood there with the crowd, as the huge vessels remained motionless on the water. It appeared nothing was amiss, checks were done, the *New York* was safely reberthed and *Titanic* could now set sail once again.

Again, the horns went off. Again, smoke chugged out in plumes from the funnels. Lucy stood on tip toes and watched as *Titanic* began to move. She was huge – the most enormous vessel she had ever seen – and yet the ship seemed to glide rather than sail. She had an elegance about her Lucy had never seen on a ship before in Southampton.

As *Titanic* steamed down the Solent, all the while getting smaller and smaller, the crowd cried out and waved their flags. As the people standing in the crowd next to her began to wander away, to go home, Lucy stayed there until the last. There were a few hundred still there but now she could get a better look.

She watched as the mighty *Titanic*, sailing on her Joseph's muscle power, became smaller and smaller on the horizon. She stood there, ignoring Florence as she grizzled to be fed, watching. She watched and watched until the great ship was no more than a tiny sliver of white on the horizon.

And then *Titanic* vanished.

# Chapter Eleven

**Susan**

The feeling of hope everywhere was so thick you could cut it with a bread knife. Everyone seemed more buoyant since *Titanic* had set sail. The whole city, which had for months been in the grip of the coal strike and huge unemployment, seemed to be booming. Haberdasheries who had made *Titanic*'s uniforms advertised the fact outside and now had queues of women jostling to buy fabric. Butchers who had provided fine cuts of meat to the ship's chefs were in demand by housewives from all over the middle-class areas of Southampton. Even Susan's mother seemed happier – and not just because she had no men to feed for a few days.

At the school, children spoke of nothing else other than *Titanic*. Or 'the big ship' their fathers had gone to work on. For the first time, Susan felt change was possible. But of course, there was still so much to do. She still had the words from the leaflet in her head, about the night protest. Tonight was the night and Susan wondered; should she risk it and go? Was it the right time? Everyone seemed so happy, so full of hope. Was now the right occasion to start throwing a cat amongst the pigeons? She worried all day, through every lesson and every 'hands up' she shouted at the children in her class. Even after she ate her dinner at home with her mother,

The Titanic Girls

she wondered; what was the right thing to do?

It was only as she saw her mother's hunched back in the kitchen, exhausted by years of drudgery that her mind was made up. She was going.

'Mother, I am going off up to bed early,' Susan said, yawning obviously.

'Now?' her mother said.

'Yes, I had a very difficult day with some children today,' Susan replied. 'I'll see you in the morning.' She kissed her mother and went up the thin, creaky wooden stairs to bed.

'Up the wooden hill!' her mother called after her.

Susan shut her door. She knew what would happen – the same as happened every night. Her mother would do the chores she needed to – tidy up the kitchen, hang any wet clothes up on the wire in front of the fire, then she'd sit down and sip on her never-ending sherry glass by the fire until she fell into a stupor. This usually only took two hours. Faster, when the men were away because there was no one to judge or interrupt her.

An hour later, Susan dared to check. She opened her door, winced as it creaked and then waited. When no sound came, she padded down the stairs and looked over the banister. Her mother was making a soft regular snorting sound in front of the fire. A sherry glass hung precariously from her fingers, about to drop. Susan hurried over, took the glass and put it on the table. Her mother didn't stir.

Now was the time.

Susan grabbed her leaflet, put on her overcoat and hat and unlocked the front door. She stepped out and closed the door behind her. She took a gasp of cold air. It was April but it was still so chilly at night. She read the address again on the leaflet and set off, hearing her boots making clip-clop noises on the empty pavements.

With all the men away on *Titanic,* the pubs were empty. There was no one around. Was this a good thing or a bad thing?

She walked on, seeing her breath making clouds in the cold night air. Then she saw them, a group of women in dark overcoats gathered by a row of shops. She hurried over, saw a woman from the previous meeting and smiled.

The woman didn't smile back. Instead, she averted her eyes and looked away. Susan reached the group and became enveloped in them. She heard whispering from the main speaker from the other night. She craned her ears to hear better. Would they be marching? Putting up leaflets or posters?

She heard some words and saw some heavy items being dished out.

Bricks.

Her heart hammered.

She looked at the woman next to her as she wrapped her hand around a red brick. 'What … what's going on?' Susan asked.

'You'll see,' the woman replied, her eyes glinting in the streetlamp.

The women walked, then their pace quickened, soon they were running along the row of shops.

'Now!' someone yelled.

In an instant, Susan heard the shattering, piercing sound of breaking glass. She turned quickly to see the women from the other night – the well-to-do, respectable women, arms aloft, fists straining behind them, throwing bricks through the shop windows. One woman, a larger woman who had been silent during the meeting, threw one, then another. She was trembling, laughing madly.

'Votes for women!' she suddenly screamed, shrilly. 'Votes for women!'

Susan exchanged glances with another woman. Up above, two windows' lights went on. A pair of curtains twitched.

From nowhere a whistle sounded.

'Oh, God, it's the police!' someone cried.

Susan darted from one side of a shop to the other. She still had a brick in her hand. A whistle went again, and she saw the women scarper in all directions, like pigeons scattering in a square. Susan was frozen to the spot. She heard the heavy thud of boots on the ground.

'Who is there?' male voices yelled.

The boots got nearer.

'Oh, God,' Susan muttered.

The other women had vanished. They'd done this before.

Heart hammering, Susan dropped her brick into a gutter and ran. She ran down an alley, behind the ice cream shop. The thud of boots quickened their pace behind her.

She looked this way, then that. There was nowhere to hide. She came to a dead end and hung her head, knowing it was all over. She was trapped.

Then a back door to a shop opened. A dark-haired man wearing a white apron dropped a pail of rubbish outside and saw Susan standing there.

Her look of sheer terror must have registered with him because he looked to the left, heard the thud of the boots from the police , grabbed Susan, and dragged her inside the shop before slamming the back door behind them.

Susan stood there, heart hammering, hearing the din of voices the other side of the door.

'There was one of 'em here, I swear it,' came a voice.

'Go that way, she's probably run off down there. Bloody bitch …' another said.

The voices grew fainter.

Then the boots.

Then silence.

Susan closed her eyes. She felt that her heart would hammer its way out of her chest. When she opened her eyes, the man was still there, staring at her, a quizzical expression on his face. She looked around her. She appeared to be in some sort of kitchen – pristine, the smell of delicious sugary sweet treats all around.

'Where … what is this place?' she finally said.

'My ice cream shop,' the man replied. He had an accent. Spanish? He read her mind and said, 'Italian. My name is Angelo.' He walked to the counter, rolled a cigarette and lit it. 'You want one?' he said.

He passed the cigarette to her. Susan had never smoked in her life. Catherine did but it had never appealed to her. Now, her heart still racing, she grabbed the cigarette gratefully and puffed on it, feeling the smoke hit the back of her throat, and coughed wildly.

'Your first time?' Angelo grinned.

'No,' she lied.

He smiled. 'What is a young woman like you doing in an alley way being chased by the police at night?' he asked.

Susan shrugged. 'If I told you, you would never understand,' she said.

He took off his apron and grabbed a set of keys from a hook above a churning machine. 'I have to lock up now. I can walk you home?'

She nodded, gratefully, handing the cigarette back to him.

She watched as Angelo opened the front door to the shop, escorted her out and then locked the door. The street was empty.

They walked in the other direction from the vandalised shops, past the little church and towards Susan's road.

'This is where I live,' she said.

He nodded. 'Very well,' he said.

'Thank you so much for escorting me,' Susan said, in her best respectable school teacher voice.

Angelo grinned, looking at her, or rather through her. 'I think I know exactly what you were doing,' he said, eyes narrowing shrewdly.

'Oh?' she said. The way he looked at her unnerved her. He seemed to know what she was thinking. She felt a blush creep up her chest and over the top of her high collar.

'Yes,' he said. 'And let me tell you. I may be a man, but I am all for the right for women to vote.' Then he smiled, waved, and walked away.

# Chapter Twelve

**Catherine**

If there was one thing Catherine hated, it was the early morning starts. She seemed to get up earlier than anyone else in the street. It had been six days since the *Titanic* had set sail. The streets were even emptier than usual with all the men away on the ship.

As she heard her footsteps echoing along the cobbles, as she dodged puddles and horse manure, she could have sworn she was the only one alive. Her breath made plumes of what looked like smoke in the cold early morning sea mist. It was April 16 but might as well have been December.

'Brrrr,' she muttered, rubbing her hands together.

She walked along, seeing the bakery opening up and the baker's son loading his bicycle basket with loaves and rolls. Her stomach roared with hunger as she saw the steam rising from a round, plump roll hidden under a tea towel.

'Hey, sonny,' she said, flickering her eyelashes and putting on her best smile. 'Which way to the docks?'

The boy, dazzled by this woman's beauty, stammered and turned and pointed over his shoulder. Catherine swooped in while his gaze was averted, grabbed the freshly baked roll from under the towel and shoved it into her pinafore pocket.

'Thanks, my love,' she said.

When she turned the corner, she grabbed the roll and stuffed it into her mouth. Her teeth tore at the hot doughy goodness of it and she gulped a mouthful down. She was just enjoying the taste of warmth and comfort, when she saw it. She had to blink. She looked again. No, she had really seen it.

She wandered over. On the corner where the newspaper boy always stood, was a placard. It was leaning against a wall. A pile of first edition newspapers, the ink still wet, was bundled up in string beside it.

She went nearer, re-read the headline on the placard for the tenth time and then stood there. She dropped the remainder of the hot roll into the gutter.

*Titanic sinks … Great loss of life …*

The young boy emerged from the shop. He bent to untie the string holding the pile of papers together.

'I … haven't any money. Can I have a read though?' Catherine asked.

The boy – seemingly stunned too by the news – nodded. Silently, he cut through the twine with his penknife and handed Catherine the top newspaper, an early edition of the *Daily Echo*. She saw a step outside a sweet shop and staggered to it. She felt herself sit down. She felt the cold, the damp, coming up through her dress into her bottom. She didn't care.

She read the article.

> *Titanic Collides with Iceberg in Mid-Ocean: Olympic and other ships to the rescue. The White Star liner Titanic, the world's largest and most luxurious vessel which left Southampton on Wednesday last with over 2,500 souls on board collided with an iceberg last evening in mid-Atlantic.'*

Further down, the headline read:

> *'All the passengers safe. A wireless message to Halifax states that all the passengers were safely taken off the Titanic at 3.30 am. The White Star Company emphasises their claim that Titanic is unsinkable.'*

Catherine looked at the placard the boy was now holding. 'Why does that say "great loss of life" while this article says everyone is safe?' she said.

He walked over, holding the placard over one shoulder.

'That was the first edition, from last night,' he explained. 'A second edition is on its way. People died.'

Catherine got up and grabbed the newspaper. She didn't go in the direction of the big house. Work could go jump today. She hurried past the shops, saw that many of them had been boarded up after some kind of vandalism, and hurried on to Lucy's house.

It was five thirty in the morning. Too early to knock at doors. Catherine didn't care. She ran to Lucy's door and hammered on it with the flat of her hand.

No response.

She hammered again, this time with a curled fist.

She heard the tell-tale noise of an angry baby crying. Florence. Moments later, an exhausted looking Lucy peered round the front door. Her fair hair that was usually twisted off her face, fell about her shoulders. In her white nightdress, she looked like a mere girl.

'Catherine?'

Catherine pushed past her, into the kitchen and slapped the newspaper onto the table. Lucy pulled her nightdress tighter around her and looked at the front page.

She clapped a hand to her mouth. '*Titanic* sank?'

Catherine nodded. 'An iceberg. So the boy says on the corner.'

Lucy read the article as fast as she could. Her eyes were looking not at sentences but individual words. *Passengers ... safe ... no lives lost ... unsinkable.*

Relief flooded her.

'So everyone is all right, Catherine!' she gasped. 'Oh, God, thank God, thank God ...'

Catherine gripped Lucy's arm tight. 'No,' she said. 'That's the first edition. Another one is coming out. People have died. People are drowned.'

Lucy blinked at Catherine. She looked like a doe about

to be shot.

Catherine felt an emotion she wasn't familiar with. Pity.

'Come on, get dressed, we'll go out and see what we can find out,' she said.

Lucy hurried upstairs. Catherine waited in the small kitchen. She drummed her hands on the table, her fingers forming an agitated tattoo.

Strangely, she didn't think of Percy, of her fiancé. She thought of Lucy and Joseph ... and Susan and her brothers and father. That was real love. That wasn't calculated. She'd cope if Percy was gone. But what about her friends?

Lucy came down, hair thrust up into a maidservant's style bun and a dress haphazardly put on. 'I'm ready,' Lucy said.

Lucy grabbed her baby, placed her, crying, into the pram and put on her overcoat.

'Where will we go? Who will know?' Lucy asked.

'The White Star Line,' Catherine said. 'The horse's mouth.'

Both women were out on the street. It was not long after dawn. They had felt sure they were the only people on earth who knew. But now, they saw that wasn't true. Lucy walked briskly , pushing the pram, watching as woman after woman, mother after mother, came rushing out of her home. She watched as young boys ran, knocking at doors, before running on to the next door, before seeing another mother, or daughter, or sister, stagger out of their homes into the street. Some cried. Some looked shocked, too stunned to ask questions. Lucy saw one older woman holding her stomach and bending over, sobbing and crying. 'Oh, it aches ...'

She thought at first the woman was in pain from something physical but as they hurried past, they saw the woman closer. She was gripping her womb area, her face contorted into spasms. 'My son was a bellboy on the ship ... he's only 15 ...' she wailed.

Lucy couldn't stop. Catherine gripped her arm and tugged her onwards. The women half-walked, half-ran, their boots splattering through April puddles and the muck from the manure dropped in the street.

When they reached the White Star Line offices, they could barely move.

'We're not the first here,' Catherine muttered.

Lucy craned her neck and saw dozens, no, more than a hundred people all standing outside the White Star Line offices. Some were young mothers like her, pushing their babies in prams. Some had other children hanging on to their petticoats. Some were older mothers, sniffling into handkerchiefs, desperate to know if their son was gone.

Catherine had no idea how long passed. Was it minutes? Or hours? She was supposed to be at work, scrubbing that godforsaken, permanently mucky front door step at the big house. She didn't care now. She looked at Lucy. She wasn't crying. She wasn't even speaking. She saw her friend's knuckles gripping the baby's pram. They were white. She was holding on for dear life.

Suddenly both women heard a voice they knew and turned.

'Catherine! Lucy! I came the minute I heard!'

It was Susan. She was holding a second edition of the local paper. She looked at Catherine, gave a knowing look, and tried to hide the paper behind her skirts. It was too late. Lucy saw it.

'Please. Show me,' Lucy said. She didn't say it in her usual voice. Her voice was normally like a bird's, a sweet sing-song voice. Now she demanded it with the voice of a woman much older than her years.

Silently, Susan handed over the paper.

Lucy read the front page. *'Titanic sinks. Great loss of life...'*

The crowd began to shuffle forward. The women stepped forward too, close enough now to see a piece of paper, scrawled upon in erratic, rushed handwriting and stuck up outside the White Star Line office. It read:

*'Titanic foundered about 2.30am April 15. About 675 crew and passengers picked up by ships boats of Carpathia and California. Remaining and searching position of disaster. Names*

*of those saved will be posted as soon as received.'*

Susan's stomach lurched. Lucy gripped the handle of the pram harder. They gazed at each other now, each afraid to say what the other was thinking.

It was Susan who finally spoke. 'There were over two thousand passengers on *Titanic*. And nine hundred crew,' she said, her voice a hoarse whisper. 'If only six hundred and seventy-five crew and passengers have been picked up …'

Lucy nodded, her face vacant, lost. She stared straight ahead.

'Then most people are dead.'

# CHAPTER THIRTEEN

**Lucy**

It was the soft amber light Lucy remembered most about their life in the countryside. The way the evening sun shone through the trees, causing a dappled effect of dancing shadows of leaves on the freshly-cut hay and wheat. Her father worked on a farm, his father before him, and his before him. Women of her family all ended up helping on farms as well, until they married.

That was when she'd first seen him. It had been evening time after a full day's work in the heat. He'd been baling up some hay and he'd turned and wiped his brow. She'd been sitting on the ground with the other women, having some water. He'd smiled at her. She'd turned to her left, then right, to ensure he was smiling at her and not someone else.

But he was.

She remembered how he'd come over and started talking. What had they talked about? She struggled to remember now. All she knew was that he had offered her his hand to help her up, then they'd talked about how warm it was and he had offered her some of his own water. Her hand has brushed his as he'd handed her his flagon. She remembered how that evening the sunlight had caused his brown eyes to have amber flecks in them too. He looked like the lost son of a Greek god, wandering the earth …

Their courtship had been fast. All life was fast. If you didn't act in the present, something could always come and scupper things for you. Diphtheria, consumption. So they'd courted in the fields, walking coyly side by side. Then Joseph had asked Lucy's uncle for her hand because her parents had already both died. Her uncle had obliged and just eight weeks after they'd met, they said their vows at a country church on Christmas Day, the only day they could get time off.

She remembered their vows, the fumbled giggles of their wedding night, the love she felt for him. She remembered how ambitious he was for a better life for them and how it had been his idea to leave the country.

'Tractors will replace us before long,' he kept saying.

And so she'd followed him, off to the biggest city nearby; Southampton. He'd found them a tiny two-up, two-down and promised this was a short stop in the great scheme of things. Florence had soon followed, and Joseph had got jobs on the great liners sailing between Southampton and New York.

He'd become part of the Black Gang which they laughed at behind closed doors. Lucy knew how the local people either looked down at the Black Gang or were terrified of them because of their reputations for hard drinking and even harder brawling. But Joseph was nothing like that. He'd been a breath of fresh air …

'Lucy, Lucy,' Susan was saying.

Lucy gripped the pram's handles. She was brought back to reality with the piercing shriek that could only be coming from Florence

'I think Florence wants feeding. We've been here hours. You should go home,' Susan said.

Lucy looked around her. Catherine had long gone; her mistress would not care whether *Titanic* had sunk or not. She still must work. But Susan had stayed in the queue, with Lucy and all the other mothers, wives, daughters and fathers, all waiting for resolution, to see their loved one's name on either the list of the survivors or the list of the dead.

Five times Lucy had reached the front of the queue,

checked the list of survivors and the list of the drowned.

Joseph's name had not appeared on either.

Each time she pushed the pram back to the rear to start the process again she was filled with hope. His name was not on the list of the dead. There was still a chance.

Susan was doing the same, looking for her father's name and those of her brothers Jack and Ernest.

'I really think you should take Florence home and come back later on,' Susan said. 'I can stay here and I will run back and fetch you the moment I see anything.'

Lucy nodded, like a dumb thing. Her baby was crying louder now, attracting glances from mothers nearby. It normally instilled the desire to grab the child, to feed her, to soothe her, to do anything to stop the crying. Now she felt nothing. The baby could cry. Why shouldn't she? Her father was missing.

Numb, Lucy nodded again. Before she set off, she touched Susan's arm and gave her a look. 'I hope your men are on the saved list,' she whispered. She pushed her way back through the crowd, registering other women like her, biting their nails, hands over their faces, some already fainting or too weak to stand. As she walked on, she saw some women staggering back from the front of the queue.

'Tom's sure to be all right,' one woman said to the other. 'He was always one of the lucky ones.'

The other woman shook her head sadly, but with a gesture of pride. 'I know he's gone. But I know my Tom would do his duty …'

Back at home, she opened the door and closed it again. Duty … duty … The word rang out in her head. What duty? Did her Joseph sign on to *Titanic* to die? Why was it their men's 'duty' to drown?

She sat down, exhausted. It was silent. She usually heard the cry of children playing in the street during their lunch hour from school. Now there was nothing. She peered out through the window. Hoops and balls lay in the street, discarded. Across the street, all the curtains of every house were drawn. Drawn in mourning.

Lucy swallowed hard, got the baby out of her pram

and fed her. She sat there, giving her milk to her baby, watching the child feed and soothe and still Lucy could not cry. Her eyes fell on the door, the space next to it where Joseph always threw his kit bag. She looked at the table where he'd sat just days earlier, promising this was the last trip, that they'd start a new life.

Florence came off her breast now. She usually erupted into a cry again unless Joseph was home. But it was as if the child knew something was amiss. She didn't cry or scream. She sat up, reaching out for her mother's collar.

'You know, don't you?' Lucy whispered.

The baby gurgled. She held her tightly to her breast and willed herself to weep. She knew that would make her feel better. But tears would not come. Something was stopping them. It was only as she felt the slip in her dress pocket that she knew why she could not cry.

She took it out and unfolded it. Royce's Pawn Shop. Joseph's shoes were there. Part of him.

She knew if she cried now, it was as if she were accepting he might be dead. She could not do that. She must not.

'Come on,' she said, dressing herself and getting the baby back into her pram. 'Let's go on a little walk.'

She left the house and walked down the street. It was deathly silent. When she came to the corner, she saw people all walking in the direction of the White Star Line offices. Some were sobbing. Some men walked with their hand scrunched into fists, a look of anger on their faces. Children ran alongside their mothers' skirts, oblivious.

Lucy turned another corner and came to a row of shops. She stopped at Royce's Pawn Shop. The door was closed and no one was inside. She looked in the front window. There were pocket watches, clocks, umbrellas. And shoes. So many pairs of shoes.

She felt overwhelmed suddenly. Her breath seemed short. She cast her eyes across the shoes. They all looked the same – black, polished, 'best' shoes. Her heart quickened. She'd thought she'd find Joseph's straight away but every pair was identical – all the best shoes of stokers and greasers who had pawned them to give their wives some money to survive on while they were away.

Her breathing quickened. Her corset suddenly felt too tight. She needed to … had to find his shoes. Which were his? She knew they were black. But he so rarely wore them she couldn't remember what they were like. She made a foolish, ridiculous bargain with herself. *If I find his shoes … then he will be on the survivors' list … he will make it …* The shoes were dancing before her eyes now. Pairs and pairs of them, all the same.

She felt she might die or faint there and then when suddenly a hand touched her arm. 'Lucy,' Susan said.

She turned and saw Susan's eyes were red with crying.

'I've got some news about my family.'

# Chapter Fourteen

**Susan**

Lucy and Susan opened the door of Susan's house and stepped inside. Susan's mother was in front of the fire, beating the dolly in the tin bath so hard it appeared she might smash through it and cause a flood of dirty laundry water all over their tiny two-up, two down.

Susan saw her mother's face. She knew. Someone must have already told her. Their father's name Thomas Jarvis was on the drowned list. The two brothers' names were still nowhere to be found.

'No use cryin' over it,' she was saying, twisting and bashing the dolly over the rags of clothes in the bath. 'No point. Can't bring him back.'

Susan sat there, numb, her eyes so dry from sobbing that no more tears would come.

'The boys will come back, of course,' Susan's mother said, sighing and standing up straighter. 'The boys will return home, you'll see.'

Lucy sat at the table, too afraid to say anything for fear of offending. She knew Susan's mother was hard, as an old stoker's wife had to be. But she didn't seem distraught in the least at the death of her husband. Lucy could not understand why.

Susan did understand why. She knew her mother. And

she knew this abuse on the tin bath was her mother's way of coping. It was also a generation of women who knew all too well about death and how fragile life was. Susan's mother had lost all three of her siblings to diphtheria. She'd lost two children before she'd had Susan and her brothers. Death wasn't something far away or distant, it was always present, ever here.

'Are you ... are you sure about your father?' Lucy ventured, quietly.

Susan nodded. 'I got to the front again and read the notices. Father's name was on the drowned list. Thomas Jarvis, stoker. It's certain. We will get a letter in a few days from White Star ...'

Lucy stared at her lap. The baby was asleep in the pram, thankfully. Susan stared down at Florence sleeping and felt her throat ache with emotion.

She had lost her father, yes. But she was a woman now. If Florence were to lose her father ... if Joseph was dead ... what then?

Susan looked at Lucy. She too looked stunned and exhausted. A husk. She knew Lucy could never survive without Joseph. She was a country girl. Too soft. Too weak. Her thoughts were torn apart by a loud scream.

'Arghh, wretched thing!' her mother cried out. She'd tipped the bath so hard the water had erupted from it and gone all over her dress, her feet, the floor.

Susan hurried over.

'Here, Mother, let me,' she said, taking the dolly from her.

'No!' her mother cried out. She gripped the dolly hard and yanked it away from Susan, pushing her away at the same time.

'Mother,' Susan stammered, falling backwards. Lucy stood up.

Susan's mother slammed the dolly into the fireplace with an almighty crack,.

'Mess and dirt ... only ever been mess and dirt!' her mother muttered, slamming the stick against the hearth again and knocking a candle holder over.

'Mother!' Susan yelled, grabbing her and trying to restrain her.

Her mother's body felt hard and rigid. Like an insect with a hard shell. But as Susan wrapped her arms around her, she felt her mother's body soften, as if it were melting. She felt her mother lean her head against her neck and heard the strangest mewing sound. For a moment Susan had no idea what this noise was. Then she realised.

Her mother was crying.

Susan stood stock still. Her mother had never shed a tear in her life. She was hard. Cold. Stern. Straight-talking. For a moment, Susan had no idea what to do. Then, without thinking, she felt herself raise her hand and shakily touch her mother's hair. The hair was grey, thin and brittle as a wire brush. She touched it, lightly, and felt her mother's wet sobs streak into her neck.

'Oh, Susan ... Oh, Susan ... what are we to do?' she wailed.

Susan guided her mother to the kitchen table. Lucy moved aside, pulling a chair out for the woman with one hand.

Susan's mother collapsed onto the table and folded her arms into a pillow for her head. Her body was racked with sobs. Susan looked at the floor, strewn with dirty washing and filthy water.

'Mother, it'll be all right ... it will be all right ...' Susan heard herself saying. She didn't believe a word of it.

'What'll we do? What'll we do for bread? And the rent's due in a week! Oh, God ... that wretched boat and its wretched rich and cursed White Star ... Oh, God ...'

Susan suddenly felt very cold. She remembered a conversation. Something about a curse. She felt herself shiver. Who was that conversation with? Then she remembered. That boy down by the water. He'd been too afraid or superstitious to look in *Titanic*'s direction. But he had said it was cursed and no good would come of it.

Susan pinched the top of her nose and blinked hard. Her head was banging with the worry and pain of it all.

Curse or not, her mother was right. How would they

manage? How would they make rent? How would they get food? True, she had work as a teacher but that wasn't enough to keep her mother as well. They all relied on her father and brothers' earnings.

Suddenly her mother sat bolt upright and scowled at Susan. Her tears vanished and a stern, cold look returned.

'And you! If you'd married, we wouldn't be in this mess!'

'What, Mother?' Susan gasped.

'I said if you'd married, and not been a hoighty toighty miss wantin' to be a teacher, if you'd got yourself a husband, he'd provide for us now. But no, you couldn't do that! You want votes for women – I tell ye! Votes won't pay our rent!'

Susan put her head in her hands. She felt adrenalin rushing through her. How would her mother survive? She was waiting for her father and brothers to bring home their pay from the Titanic sailing. There was no other money.

'We'll find some money,' Susan heard herself pronounce.

'Where?!' her mother yelled, bashing the table with a fist. 'On that tree outside the church? I got nothing!' she screamed, standing up and turning her pinafore pockets out. 'Nothing!'

Susan felt anger rise up into her neck. She felt her flesh burn. 'And is that all you think about, Mother? Money? What about the man you married, your husband? He's laying dead at the bottom of the sea! Have you even mentioned HIM yet?'

The force that hit Susan's head was so hard she felt saliva erupt from her lips and fly across the room. Suddenly her cheek burned and tingled as she turned her slapped face back to look at her mother.

'Shut up, missy,' her mother spat, walking away to the scullery. She bent down to the side of the range and grabbed her bottle of sherry. She didn't even pour it into a glass this time. She raised the bottle to her lips and Susan winced as Lucy and she heard the chug-chug of her mother downing its contents.

Susan breathed hard. She felt her face, still burning,

stinging from her mother's slap. 'I'll get us some money … some food,' she muttered, one cheek burning crimson. She stood up. She paced the floor and bit her lip. There'd be compensation, surely? There'd be money coming from the death of their father? And people were good. There'd be charity. People would donate things. In time, Susan reasoned, there'd be court hearings and pay offs and discussions about who was owed what. But now it was too soon, too early. They still didn't truly know how many passengers were dead or saved. And what of her brothers? Their names had not been on any list. They must be all right. They had to be.

Susan looked at Lucy, now cradling her baby who was sobbing after hearing the slap on her face. Susan scuffed at the threadbare rug covering the wooden floor and then she remembered.

The boots for the children at school. The Salvation Army. Suddenly buoyed by hope, she grabbed her coat and made for the door.

'And where do you think you are going now, missy?' her mother drawled, holding the bottle at her hip.

'To the Salvation Army,' Susan replied. 'If we're in this bad a state, then hundreds of other families here will be too. We have to … *I* have to do something …'

And she slammed the door behind her.

# Chapter Fifteen

**Catherine**

The pair of boots that stood beside her were shiny and clean and the skirts that fell over them were freshly laundered and smelt of something vaguely floral. Catherine looked up from her place at the fire where she'd been cleaning and met the eyes of her mistress, Mrs Welch.

'Did you know anyone on it?' the lady said.

'On what?' Catherine said, putting her wire brush and rag down.

'On *Titanic*,' the lady said, rolling her eyes.

Catherine sat back on her haunches on the floor. She wiped her brow and swallowed. 'Yes, matter of fact, my …' her voice trailed off. What was he? She had no ring. But it made her sound proper and her vanity made her want to say it. 'My fiancé was on it,' Catherine said.

Mrs Welch nodded sadly and then shook her head. But Catherine was sure she saw it – a flicker of enjoyment at the drama of it all in her eyes.

'Anyone else in your family? I know many from Northam work on the ships,' Mrs Welch said, digging for more.

'My father's a stoker but he didn't go this time. He couldn't get signed on,' Catherine replied, remembering how her mother had chastised him for being too drunk to get there in time. 'You missed a bloody trick there, you idiot!' her mother had yelled when he hadn't gone. Now Catherine thanked God her father's constant state of inebriation had stopped him going. His love of ale had saved his life.

'And do you know anything yet, about your fiancé?' Mrs Welch asked, her eyes twinkling and a tiny pulse flickering above her collar in her neck.

Catherine sighed. This was more conversation than she had ever had with this woman in a year of working for her. Usually, she was invisible. Then someone knocked on the door and the maid called Mrs Welch. She had some visitors, some women from the church. Mrs Welch hurried off to greet them and Catherine overheard her saying 'Have you heard about it? Yes, it sank! My charlady had a fiancé onboard! Can you imagine? Yes, it's tragic … tragic …'

Catherine bent back down and carried on scrubbing. What was the end of the world to people like her was gossip and excitement for those who didn't work the ships. Catherine didn't know how to feel. She felt immense relief that her drunk of a father was safe, not so much because of any love for him but because of the coin-shaped hole he would leave in her mother's life if he'd drowned.

But what of Percy?

Catherine scrubbed a particularly stubborn stain of soot next to the fireplace and thought of him. His frail shoulders, his cough, his earnest expression and slicked down hair. He was due to be her husband. So why did she feel nothing?

When she finished her day's work, she pulled on her overcoat and set off for the walk home across the city. It wasn't like other days. A hush had descended. She noted that most houses had their curtains drawn. The children who usually played in the streets she walked past were kept indoors. Before turning into her street, she saw Percy's family's cobbler's. The door was open. She was about to walk past when she saw a woman pop her head out. The woman saw Catherine and stared at her. Catherine stared back. Then the woman smiled and beckoned Catherine over.

She stepped across the puddle-flooded road and to the

shop.

'You must be Catherine,' the woman said.

Catherine nodded.

'I'm Percy's mother; he spoke of nothing but you,' she said, smiling. 'Won't you come in?'

Catherine wanted nothing more than to get home and eat a meal. But she saw the woman's desperation behind the smile and walked inside.

Around the walls were shelves and shelves of shoes. Mostly men's working shoes. Catherine felt her own wet boots from walking through puddles and longed to take them off.

'Percy was going to bring you to meet us but there wasn't time before he signed on to *Titanic*,' his mother was saying. 'But he spoke of you. He was … he is … so proud you are going to be his wife.'

Catherine nodded. His mother looked strangely ecstatic. Her eyes looked wide, mad, like a woman who had not slept for weeks. 'I've heard nothing of Percy yet. I am going back down to White Star tonight. There's to be a vigil. Will you come?' she asked.

Catherine stifled a yawn. She'd worked since early morning and just wanted to sit down. But this woman seemed to implore her. 'I'll come along with you, then,' she said.

The woman locked the shop and linked Catherine's arm in hers.

'Where's Percy's father?' Catherine asked, as they stepped through the puddles to the other side of the road.

'He is already down there. He's been waiting all day,' she replied. 'He won't come home. I took him a parcel of food earlier. Many of them have stood there all day.'

Catherine felt the woman's tiny hands grip her arm with a strength she didn't know older women could possess. She glanced at Percy's mother. She was staring straight ahead, even smiling occasionally. She had a fiercely determined look on her face; the look of a mother who knew with certainty that her son was alive.

When they reached the White Star Line building, they could barely move for people. Women with prams blocked the road. Police were there now too, moving people aside and controlling the crowd. Catherine heard a man cry out 'Where's the new list? Where's the names?' She saw a woman staggering back through the crowd from the front of the queue, being held up by two younger men.

'He's gone ... he's gone ...' she wailed, hitting herself in the chest with her fists.

Percy's mother did not look at her. She looked straight ahead, squinting over the heads of the crowd, trying to read the latest list of survivors and those who had drowned.

Glancing around her, Catherine saw women of her age. Some had babies or young children. Others stood alone, fingering their wedding bands nervously. Many had tears streaming down their faces.

'Why do I not feel like them?' Catherine asked herself. 'Why am I not sobbing?'

The truth was, Catherine felt nothing. Nothing at all. She thought of Percy. His face so desperate to please her, his yearning expression. It instilled nothing in her whatsoever. Not even pity and certainly not love. She tried to imagine him jumping from the great ship and swimming. She simply could not see it. Percy was weak. Afraid. Catherine could imagine Joseph or Susan's brothers fighting for their lives. But not Percy somehow. She closed her eyes and tried to imagine Percy in the water, kicking, screaming, gasping for air. Horrified, she realised that still no emotion came.

'We're nearly there,' came a voice. It was Percy's mother gripping her arm once again with those bony, skeletal fingers.

They shuffled forward. The two large lists pinned up outside the building were getting more and more into focus. Catherine watched as women reached the front, came away either crying or elated. It was like some strange, horrific game of chance. She saw one young pregnant woman collapse in tears as she came away from the front and thanked God she did not love anyone enough to hurt this much.

They shuffled onwards. There was one man in front of them and two women. When they had seen the names they were searching for, they moved aside.

'We're here,' Percy's mother said.

An employee of the White Star Line was trying to control the crowd.

'Step forward ladies,' he told Percy's mother and Catherine. 'List here is those found safe. List here is those drowned.'

Catherine watched as Percy's mother scoured the lists. She reached out a gloved hand and even though she could not touch the lists, she was rolling her finger down the list of names in the air.

Catherine suddenly felt very hot and tired. She was about to try and loosen her pinafore and the collar around her neck when she felt the bony fingers come away from her arm at last and the blood flow back into it.

'Oh, oh, God, oh, God, oh, Jesus,' Percy's mother was saying. She reached out a hand to the bemused employee of the White Star Line standing at the front of the crowds and said, 'He's there! He's there! Just look! Just look!'

Catherine looked straight ahead and, on the list of those saved, she read a name.

Percy Waite.

# Chapter Sixteen

**Lucy**

Next day, Lucy poured the tea into three cups and sat down at the kitchen table. Susan lifted hers to her lips and drank. Catherine stared straight ahead.

'I thought you'd be thrilled,' Lucy said, trying to keep the bitterness out of her voice.

Catherine stared at her cut and blistered fingers. 'I'm pleased, of course,' she said. 'I just ... we didn't love each other, did we? What am I supposed to do now he's coming back, do a jig?'

Susan scowled at Catherine. Lucy saw her look and shook her head as if to say; *It's all right.*

'You've still heard nothing then?' Susan asked Lucy. 'About Joseph?'

She shook her head. 'Nothing. I've been every day. I've been to the Seafarers' Union too. Nothing. He's not on the list of the dead or the saved. They reckon he's missing.'

'What does missing mean?' Catherine asked.

'Missing,' Lucy replied, getting up to get more hot water.

Susan shot Catherine another look.

'He'll be all right,' Catherine suddenly said, spurred into action by the jolt Susan gave her knee with hers beneath the table. 'If anyone can come back from *Titanic*, it's Joseph.'

Lucy poured more hot water in the kitchen before bringing the pot over. 'I'm holding on to hope,' Lucy said.

And she really was. At first, in the hours after *Titanic* had sunk, Lucy had despaired. She'd still been unable to cry, even now four days later, but every day that she didn't see Joseph's name on the list of the dead, she was bolstered with more hope. Ten days had passed. If his name was not there on the 'drowned' list, then there was still a chance.

'Talk to me about you and Percy,' Lucy said, trying to sound bright. 'When will he be coming home?'

'His mother says he's having to stay put in New York for now. They're doing some investigation,' Catherine explained. 'He has to stay there and answer questions. They'll be looking for blame, no doubt. They say it was an iceberg, but some say they were going too fast. Who knows what they'll drag up. Anyway, once that is over, then they're going to get a ship to bring everyone home again.'

Lucy suddenly felt her breath leave her body. 'When?' she asked.

'Don't know,' Catherine shrugged. 'Once the inquiry's done I'd wager.'

Lucy stared into space. Then Joseph had to be found by the time the Inquiry ended or else … or else how would he get home? She thought of a huge liner picking up all the poor souls who had survived the sinking. She thought of its huge funnels pumping out smoke and steaming out of New York harbour, without her Joe on it.

She fought the sudden urge to be sick. It was impossible. She ran to the outside toilet, slammed the wooden door open and retched over the lavatory. She bent over, heaving nothing but hot tea and bile into the bowl.

'You all right?' Susan asked, running out to her.

Shaking, Lucy wiped the back of her hand across her mouth. She stood up, trembling. Susan helped her.

'I don't know. I feel so unwell since …'

'Since April fifteenth,' Susan finished for her.

'Yes,' Lucy nodded.

She grabbed a handkerchief and cleaned her friend's pretty face. 'There. You're a picture again,' Susan smiled.

But Susan's smile was not the smile she had once owned. Her mother had received a confirmation letter just a day earlier that her father had, indeed, died on *Titanic* and his body had been buried at sea. Her mother had kept the letter neatly folded on the mantel, as if it were somehow too final to put the letter away.

Susan helped Lucy back to her seat.

'Tell me of comical things,' Lucy said, wiping her chin and trembling. 'Cheer me up a little.'

Susan nudged Catherine. 'Being comical's your job,' Susan said.

Catherine put her teacup down and leaned in. 'Well, a day ago, I saw Mollie Crabb coming out of her house with her lover looking pleased as punch. You know, Tommy Watson?'

'The one with the lazy eye?' Susan asked.

'Yes, him. Well, she'd been carrying on with him while her husband was away on *Titanic*. Then, the other day, they told her her husband was drowned. She was all set to move lover boy in when the man at White Star told her he'd made a mistake, putting her husband's name on the wrong list. Turns out he is alive and coming home – and her new man's boots are next to her bed!'

Lucy tried to smile. She really did. She watched as Catherine erupted into wicked peals of laughter, banging the kitchen table. But Lucy noted Susan was only half-smiling too. 'Ah, I tell you,' Catherine sighed, draining her cup. 'Mollie'll have a lot of explaining to do when he gets home. If she 80oesn't talk, the street will. I reckon she's in for a bit of trouble …'

Lucy stared at Catherine's face, grinning and laughing. She suddenly felt the flame of anger lick at her neck and she blurted out, 'So, are you to wed Percy when he gets back?'

Susan and Catherine both stopped, unused to Lucy's voice being so curt and low.

'I … I don't know,' Catherine said. 'Might do, might not. Depends what he brings back.'

'Because you owe him that much,' Lucy said, trembling a little. 'You owe him. You made him think you love him. I've not seen a single tear – not even when you thought he might be dead!'

'Lucy,' Susan interrupted, placing a hand on hers.

'Get off!' Lucy cried, getting up. 'I'll speak what I feel. You,' she spat, pointing at Catherine, 'you who get men wrapped round your finger. You chose him – an innocent! And when he was thought to be drowned and was your fiancé you didn't care one jot! Not one!'

'Lucy it's not …' Catherine said, rolling her eyes.

'Don't you make that face at me!' Lucy yelled, her whole body shaking. 'Rolling your eyes! Why do you get your man back? Why do you get a man back who loves you? Why do you get a fiancé, a life, a future when you don't care if he was alive or dead? Why is your man coming home while mine is lost – dead or drowned? I hate you! I hate you!' She collapsed back into her chair. She was sweating and shaking. Still, her eyes remained dry. It was as if she'd forgotten how to cry.

Catherine stood up with as much feigned elegance as she could muster. 'I'll take my leave I think,' she said.

'That is wise,' Susan said.

'Yes, you get out,' Lucy spat. 'You're nothing but a slut anyway. Go and parade down the high street. Go and wait outside the union to see if any other men come out who take your fancy, anyone better than Percy!'

'Lucy, come on,' Susan said.

'It's all right,' Catherine said, smiling. 'I think Lucy has made it clear her feelings for me.' She opened the front door and was about to walk out when she saw a woman standing there, holding a letter in an envelope.

'Pardon me,' came the voice. 'Does a Mrs Williams live at this address?'

Catherine stood to one side. All trace of the anger on her face had vanished. 'Yes, she's inside…'

The woman peered around the door frame. 'May I come in?' she called.

Lucy and Susan stood up at the table. Susan reached for Lucy's hand and squeezed it.

Lucy swallowed hard. 'Come in,' she managed.

The lady entered the tiny kitchen. She looked up and saw the mould on the ceiling and felt the damp immediately enter her lungs.

Lucy noted the envelope she held in one hand. It looked official with a special stamp. She dragged in a ragged breath. The room suddenly felt very small, smaller indeed than it had ever felt. She looked as she saw Catherine come back into the room, standing by the front door, her face pale. Susan, Lucy saw, was holding her breath.

'I have a letter here. A telegram,' the lady began.

Lucy was breathing so fast she felt her ears ring. She began to lose all sensation in her hands, her wrists. She looked at her fingers. They had gone stiff where she was hyperventilating so hard. She couldn't move her hands. Why couldn't she? Still, she needed to breathe. She breathed in, then out.

'Deep breaths, Lucy,' Susan said.

She felt Susan take her hand. She looked, shocked, as Catherine took her other. They sat her down on her chair as the woman, this official-looking stranger, handed her the envelope.

By now Lucy's hearing had vanished almost entirely. All she could hear was a loud ringing in her ears. She heard, as if from underwater, a voice say, 'Open it, Mrs Williams. Open the letter please.'

As if a puppet on a string, Lucy watched as her hands tore open the envelope. She unfolded the paper and tried to take in the mess of black typed small letters across the page. From nowhere, inside her, she felt sure she heard Joseph's voice say, 'It's all right, my love, this is where you find out. This is where you will know …' She read the words on the page. She read them again. She shook her head.

*Joseph Williams, stoker, age 27, drowned…*

In slow motion, Lucy saw Susan clap a hand to her mouth and stifle a cry. She turned to Catherine. She saw her dark-haired friend, so cocky moments earlier, bow her head with a hushed reverence and look at the floor.

Lucy began to say 'No … I … can't …'

Then everything went black.

# Chapter Seventeen

**Susan**

Susan had slept fitfully the night just gone. She couldn't get Lucy out of her head. She'd helped her up after she had fainted, given her a brandy she'd fetched from the union and put her to bed. Now, Susan was standing in a room with tables were so laden with donations that some of them were bowing in the middle. In one area, there were shoes, clothes, overcoats, dresses and hats. On another table there were warm blankets, tins, some fruit cakes and preserves. Susan wandered across to a teacher she knew from the school and said, 'Here I am. How can I help?'

It had been twelve days since *Titanic* sank and hours since Susan had seen the horror of Lucy falling and hearing Joseph was dead. She felt so helpless doing nothing. So here she was.

The woman smiled. 'You can start by sorting what's got holes in and what's not over there,' she said, pointing to a table strewn with boots. There were adult boots, women's small boots, children's boots.

'Some of the children whose fathers have died on *Titanic* don't have shoes,' the woman explained. 'So if you sort out which have no holes and can be reused, place them over there on that table,' she added.

Susan nodded. She knew of this predicament all too

well.

'Right,' Susan said. She looked around her. Everywhere there were people buzzing – volunteers, Salvation Army workers, old ladies, younger girls, even fathers who would usually be found lurking in the local pubs were there offering to help.

As she sorted through the boots, checking for holes in the soles, Susan looked over at a table where fresh and tinned foods were being put into boxes.

'What's going on over there?' she asked the man next to her.

'Nourishing food parcels,' came the reply. It was an accent she recognised. Italian …

'Angelo!' she said, looking up at him.

He smiled.

'What are you …?' she said.

'Helping, just like you,' he said. 'My mother knows several of the wives who would come into the ice cream shop. They've lost everything. Some of them haven't eaten since the ship sank, giving everything to their children. They're malnourished …'

Susan nodded. 'Women can't eat … children have no shoes. It was bad before on account of the coal strike, but now …'

Angelo continued for her. 'Now it's much worse,' he said.

She smiled. Quietly, she said, 'I should thank you for letting me run into your shop the other week. I'm not a criminal, honestly.'

Angelo looked at her. 'You are the least likely looking criminal ever,' he said. 'But I know what you were doing. And, as I said then, I agree.'

Susan frowned and stopped her boot-checking. 'You – a man – agree with votes for women?'

He nodded. 'We sell ice cream here,' he said. 'But back in Padova my mother was an academic. The only woman in her city to get university place. She is for women's rights. Trust me, she may dish out sweet ices, but the woman is all for Signora Pankhurst.'

Susan couldn't help but smile. And as she did, her face ached because it had been so long. Then she remembered her father and brothers and her face fell once again.

'You lost someone too?' Angelo said, folding up another box of shoes.

Susan nodded. 'My father drowned,' she replied. 'We still don't know about my brothers. Everyone seems to get telegrams but not us. We have no idea if they're alive or dead. Nothing.'

Angelo nodded thoughtfully. 'How you say, no news is the good news?' he said.

She smiled. Angelo seemed to know just the right thing to say at just the right time.

'Listen everyone, look lively!' came a voice of a woman in a Salvation Army uniform. 'Thank you to all for coming today. We now need distributors to take these nourishing food parcels out to the widows. Volunteers?'

Angelo shot his hand up. Susan followed. They walked over and were given boxes of food and addresses. As they emerged from the building, blinking in the late April sunlight, they began their walk. As they crossed the street, Susan saw a newspaper boy with a placard.

It said, *SS Lapland to bring survivors of Titanic home…*

'Sorry,' she said, shoving the boxes at Angelo. She ran over, paid the boy for a paper and picked it up. 'Look!' she said.

The article read; *SS Lapland to dock at Plymouth tomorrow bringing home saved souls from tragic RMS Titanic.*

'Oh, my goodness, people are coming home!' Susan cried.

Angelo put down his boxes and looked over her shoulder. Sure enough, article after article dominated the newspaper, talking of how the American Inquiry was now over and the passengers and crew survivors from *Titanic* would be steaming into Plymouth Harbour the following day on April 28th.

Susan suddenly felt a feeling she had not known in days. Hope. Yes, her brothers' names had not been on the list of survivors. But they had not been on the list of the dead, either.

'I know now ... there's a chance Jack and Ernest could be on that boat,' she says. 'There's still a chance, isn't there?'

'There's always a chance,' Angelo smiled.

They picked their boxes up and walked on. They reached the first address, a thin, smog-covered sliver of a house with only one window at the front. A child's hoop lay discarded outside.

Angelo knocked on the door. A few moments later, a haggard looking woman answered. When she asked who they were, Susan saw she had no teeth.

'We're from the Salvation Army. We have a nourishing food parcel,' Susan said, handing it over.

The woman grabbed it quick as a flash. She took it in and placed it on the floor. She waited.

'Well, that's that,' Susan said.

'What about next week?' the woman asked.

'Next week?' Susan said.

'My husband and three sons drowned on *Titanic*,' the woman said, her eyes dry but her voice harsh with days of crying. 'I can't survive. This box will do now but what about next week? My rent is due.'

Susan looked at Angelo. 'Next week we will come back,' he said.

They backed away and the woman slammed the door.

'I hadn't thought about all this,' Susan said.

'All this?'

'Yes. My mother relies on my father and brothers but she has me. I earn and bring money into the house. We're poor but we won't starve. But for women like that ...' she gestured back at the filthy house. 'How will she survive?'

Angelo took a deep breath. 'We can't save everyone,' he said. 'But we can try.'

The pair walked on, dishing out food parcels to anyone who needed it. In the course of one morning, Susan saw horrors she knew of but could now not unsee. She saw pregnant mothers so bony their ribs showed. She saw toothless crones who were mothers of drowned sons, unable to get out of bed with grief. She saw children lying in bed feverish with diphtheria, too ill to be told their father had drowned on *Titanic*, the ship of dreams. Their mothers hovered over them, knowing in days they'd be gone too.

By the time the last parcel had been delivered Susan was exhausted physically and emotionally.

'Come,' Angelo said.

'Come where?' she said.

He guided her along the street to a familiar location. Rizzi Ices.

'Come in. I'll make you an ice cream. You need something sweet.'

Susan's mouth began to water. She hadn't had an ice cream since Empire Day three years ago. Her earnings didn't stretch to regular treats.

'I can't,' she protested.

'Come on, I mean it,' he said. He pushed open the front door and Susan was met with a dark-haired older woman behind the counter.

'Mamma, voglio presentare una persona,' Angelo began.

What followed was a blur of beautiful Latin sounding words and the only word Susan understood was her own name.

The dark-haired lady came out from behind the counter. She was short, round but with piercing intelligent eyes.

'Susan, piacere,' she said.

Angelo nodded.

'Er, piacere,' Susan replied.

Angelo introduced his mother as Sylvia. As if sensing she was in the way, Sylvia then took off her pinafore apron and vanished into the back of the shop.

'So, you would like vanilla or crema?' Angelo said.

'Vanilla, please,' Susan said.

She watched as he opened a metal vat and scooped out something gooey and cold from inside. He placed it into a small white dish and handed it to Susan along with a thin spoon. He made one for himself and then joined her at a table.

Susan dug her spoon into the ice and scooped some out. As she placed some on her tongue, she felt it fizz and the sweet sensation of sugar and vanilla erupt onto her tastebuds. 'Mmmm, that is so wonderful,' she said.

Angelo ate his and smiled. 'Yes, it is. Our recipe,' he said.

Susan fell into silence as she scooped more and more of the delicious ice cream. When it was finished, she patted her lips with a serviette. 'Delicious,' she said.

'You deserved it,' he replied.

'Me?' Susan said. Her thoughts trailed away to poor Lucy … She remembered how she'd collapsed when she'd read Joseph's name on the letter from the White Star Line. She had not heard from her since. She'd banged on the door several times. The curtains remained drawn and Lucy never answered.

'I don't deserve it,' she said, sadly.

Angelo frowned. 'You are a wonderful woman,' he said suddenly.

'Pardon?' Susan frowned.

'I mean it. You are clever. You are kind. You are beautiful …'

Susan looked into Angelo's eyes. They were so dark they were almost ebony. She had felt nothing but pain and loss and hardship for days since *Titanic* sank. But now, with the taste of sweet ice cream on her tongue and Angelo's kind face in front of her, she felt her age once again. She felt like a young woman.

'Susan, may I see you again?' Angelo asked.

Susan wanted to retort with one of her suffragette sayings. That men were the oppressors. That marriage was shackles. That women did not need a man.

So why, oh why, did she hear her own voice reply, 'That would be wonderful'?

# Chapter Eighteen

**Catherine**

Catherine was now so used to the skeletal fingers buried deep into her arm flesh that she almost missed the feeling when it was not happening. Percy's mother Kezia squeezed Catherine's arm even tighter as the steam from the train became visible on the track.

'Oh, they're here. They're here!' she squealed.

The crowd was the biggest Catherine had ever seen. It was evening on the 29th April. It was pitch dark and nine in the evening but the city had never been so busy. Reporters from the local and even national press pushed their way to the front as the train steamed into Southampton Central Railway Station.

This train was bringing home the survivors of *Titanic*.

As the train stopped, the crowd surged forward. Catherine looked the other side of Kezia and saw Percy's father already snivelling into a handkerchief.

Catherine looked around her. People of all ages were here, surging forward, desperation on their faces. Many had already had news their loved one was alive and was coming home on this train from Plymouth where the SS *Lapland* had docked. But many came even without that knowledge. Some, Catherine saw, stood bewildered, craning their necks to see over others. They were clinging to hope. They had had no letter confirming their loved one was alive. But they came anyway.

Just then Catherine saw Susan. 'Over here!' she waved. It was so noisy, but Susan saw her and waved back, unsmiling. She was with her mother.

Catherine noted how terrified Susan looked. She knew her friend had only had word her father had died. She had no idea if her brothers would be on this train. Like so many others, Susan had clung to optimism. While there was no news, there was still hope. The gates from the station opened and suddenly people surged forwards again as passengers poured out. The bony fingers dug in with a greater vigour into Catherine's arm, so deeply that she even cried out in pain.

'He will be here. He will be here,' Kezia was repeating. Catherine scoured the crowd of men coming out of the train station. She knew who the stokers were – the hard-looking ones, carrying a kit bag over their shoulder, a tiny sliver of cigarette hanging ubiquitously from every mouth.

Then came the stewards, less aggressive-looking than the stokers. Heads bowed. Kezia's eyes were darting through the crowds.

Then Catherine saw him. But although it looked like Percy, he moved differently. The Percy she had known moved quickly, rather like a squirrel or a small rodent. He was always sharp, alert, like prey that could be predated at any time. This man looked had a completely different gait. He walked slowly through the crowds. He carried a sack over one shoulder. His eyes no longer had that brightness, that eagerness to please they'd once had. His eyes looked dead.

Catherine nudged Kezia in the side. 'Look,' she said, pointing to Percy. Kezia looked over and cried out.

'Oh, Percy! Percy! My son!' she ran over to him, finally letting go of Catherine's arm. Percy's father followed, sobbing loudly. The pair of them wrapped Percy in an embrace so tight his head poked out the top just to seek air.

'Percy, oh, my love, oh, my son, my boy ...' Kezia cried, squeezing him.

His father, now sobbing so much he had to bend down

and grab his own knees, was gasping for breath and shaking his head, occasionally saying 'Thank you, God ...Thank you ...'

Catherine stepped nearer. She waited for Percy to be freed from his embrace, for him to come nearer and surely demand a kiss. She was prepared to do that. He had been through so much. She knew, even at her most calculated and cynical, she owed him that much. When he was freed from his mother's bony expressions of love, she dragged him over to Catherine.

'Here,' Kezia said, her eyes brimming with happy tears. 'Here's your Catherine. Oh, she's been a tower of strength to me. Always there. She's here now for you, my love. Oh, my love, your fiancée truly loves you ...'

Catherine smiled at Percy.

He did not smile back.

She stepped nearer. She cleared her throat. 'Thank God you are all right,' Catherine said.

He nodded, like a toy or a puppet. He wouldn't meet her gaze.

She reached out a gloved hand to him, but he didn't respond. Instead, he stood there, numb-looking, mute, gripping his kit bag.

'You'll be tired,' Kezia said, grabbing his arm with her fingers. 'Come on, we'll get you home. I've made your favourite. Kidney pudding. Catherine will come as well, won't you, my love?'

Catherine nodded. But she was frowning at Percy, puzzled. The man who had left her was full of ardour, of excitement, of wanting to please. This man looked like Percy but was nothing like him. He was like Percy's shell. As if someone had scooped the real Percy out and replaced him.

As they began to leave the crowd, Catherine looked over at Susan. She was holding her mother up as they strained their necks to see over the crowd.

'Excuse me, Kezia, might I go and see my friends, just for a moment?' Catherine said.

Kezia nodded, too joyful to care. She waited at one side with Percy and her sobbing husband as Catherine made her way through the crowd of hundreds and over to Susan.

'Seen anything?' Catherine asked.

Susan shook her head.

The people coming off began to straggle now. A huge pouring of people became a handful. Susan's mother was shaking her head, cursing under her breath.

'No point coming here at all …' she was saying. 'Just false hope and lies …'

It was then that Susan gasped. She stood more upright and opened her mouth. Catherine watched as Susan tried to shout but no sound came out. Catherine followed Susan's gaze to where a man was walking slowly out of the train station. Catherine knew that face, that expression, that hair. She'd played hoops with him too many times as a girl. While Susan tried to shout but couldn't, Catherine stepped in for her.

'Ernest! Oi, Ernest!' she yelled over the din.

Susan's mother raised her head slowly. She looked at Catherine, then she looked at Susan, still trying to shout but unable. Then she stared straight ahead as a young man made his way towards them. On his back he carried a kit bag. Between the finger and thumb of his right hand he held the remnants of a cigarette. He flicked it at the floor now and a smile passed across his face. He came nearer and Catherine reached out a hand to steady Susan, for she was wobbling where she stood.

'Ernest?' Susan gasped finally.

He nodded, a tear rolling down his face.

'Ernest!' his mother cried out. She stepped nearer and grabbed him round his waist. 'Oh Ernest …'

The tiny sherry-drinking woman held her son around his middle. It would have been comical had it not been for the young man's expression. Other survivors were gleeful, drinking from bottles, singing, shouting greetings to old friends. Reporters were stopping people to ask questions. Catherine heard one journalist asking a stoker what had happened and was frantically taking notes. She listened as he spoke. 'Well, the watertight compartments had closed and every man stood at his post,' he was saying. 'Chief Engineer

Mr Bell ordered us firemen to draw the fires, presumably to prevent an explosion, and we continued to do this until we were up to our waists in water. The firemen stayed at their posts until they couldn't any longer and then our superiors told us to go aboard. We'd just got into our stokehold gear which, as you know, consists of only trousers, flannel shirt and boots. That was all we had to take our plunge into the water …'

Catherine gritted her teeth at the man's terrifying account. She walked over to Susan and her mother. Ernest stood in his mother's awkward embrace as another tear fell silently onto his coat lapel.

'Where did you get this coat?' his mother asked, pulling at it.

'Donated. In New York,' he replied. His voice was deeper. Raspier. Catherine stood and watched as Susan now stepped forward to hug her brother.

'You know that Father …' Susan's voice trailed off.

Ernest nodded.

Suddenly Susan's mother seemed to remember something very important and her head shot up again.

'And Jack? Where's your brother?' she said, looking behind him.

It was then that the tall, burly stoker dropped his kit bag and let all the tears that he had kept inside him since New York flow. He put his hands to his unkempt hair and dragged his fingers through it. 'Mother I am so very sorry …' he rasped. 'I am sorry …I couldn't find him. I swam and swam and I couldn't find him Mother …'

Susan's mother's face fell. She suddenly looked like she was made of stone again.

'Our Jack? Our youngest?' she said.

Susan reached out a hand to steady Ernest. Catherine stepped forward now too, fearing he might fall.

'But where is Jack?' the mother asked again.

Ernest began rocking on his heels. 'We was on the same shift. We'd just finished. We was coming up the stairs when she hit the iceberg. The sound Mother …the sound was so terrible. I can still hear it …'

'Go on,' his mother said, irritated now rather than emotional.

'We tried to get to the top. To our deck. I was dragged by an officer and told to man a lifeboat. We had to get passengers in it. But I refused. I didn't want to leave Jack …'

The women, including Catherine, listened as Ernest told his story. Crowds passed by, people chanted happily. There they stood, the only ones left, listening.

'We ran to try and get in a boat together. He was my …my baby brother I had to look after him you know?' He searched their faces. The women nodded.

'We got to a deck. Then there was a sound. A hideous, bloody, screeching, hellish sound. Next thing I knew, we was in the water. Well, I was. It was so cold, Mother. So cold. Like ice and death. I swam. There was debris everywhere. Chairs, cutlery, plates. I swam. I was calling 'Jacky! Jacky' like I did when we was kids. I never found him Mother. I swam and swam. I tried …I tried so hard …'

The man burst now into hideous, racking sobs and Susan stepped forward to hold him. His mother stood there, bereft, lost, unable to touch him.

Catherine backed away, now, stunned into feeling emotion for the first time in living memory. She wandered over to Kezia, Percy and his father. All hugging.

She went to Kezia, took her arm and said, 'Let's go home now.'

# Chapter Nineteen

**Lucy**

Lucy lay back in bed and stared at the ceiling. She pulled her blanket up over her for modesty. 'But I can't be. I just can't be,' she said.

The red-faced woman rolled her sleeves down and stood up. 'You been to bed with yer husband 'fore he went away on *Titanic*?' Mrs Stoat asked with no shame whatsoever.

Lucy blushed by way of reply.

'Then there's no two ways about it. You're expecting,' she said.

She lay there, unable to reply. She'd asked the local midwife to come by after yet another fainting episode, this time outside a shop. A woman had helped her up and gently whispered, 'Mrs Stoat, number 85.'

Lucy had heard of Mrs Stoat. People joked that her name should be 'Stout' rather than Stoat because of her rotund body shape. She had a permanently red face, red hands, a red nose. It was she women went to if they'd been doing something they shouldn't, or if they'd had enough children and couldn't cope with just one more.

Now Mrs Stoat stood over Lucy in her bed, red hands on her hips. 'You want to keep it or not?' she said bluntly.

Lucy suddenly gaped. 'Keep it!' she cried.

'Then you'll need feeding up. There's nothing of you,'

she said, prodding her ribs. 'Milk's what you need. Milk and butter. Eggs,' she said. 'Do you have family, my girl?

Lucy thought of her parents' graves, in a country churchyard in the village of Eling where she had grown up. There would be ivy covering those wooden crosses now. She shook her head.

'Well, try then to get a woman in. Some home help. There are plenty of charities helping *Titanic* widows now. Some say you lot'll be richer than before.'

She thought of the Salvation Army parcels that had come. She was thankful for them. Susan had dropped them off herself with her new friend. The food was gratefully received. But it wouldn't pay her rent or buy her coal and it certainly wouldn't stretch to a second child.

'I'll take my leave, then,' Mrs Stoat said. 'Remember, if you change your mind, I'm at number 85. But be quick about it. The longer you leave it, the bigger the mess and the bigger my fee.'

Then she made her way out of her bedroom and Lucy heard her feet hurriedly banging down the wooden stairs. Clearly, she had other women to see that day.

With Mrs Stoat gone, Lucy pulled her stockings back up and eased her dress back down. She shook her head. Thank goodness Florence was sleeping. She could not have coped with her crying now. Heaving herself off the bed, she walked to the bedroom window. The glass was thick with black mould spots and dust. She breathed on the glass and wiped a round hole in the steam her breath made. Outside, the Muffin Man was trundling his cart down the street. She realised that in all the time she'd lived in the city she had never tasted a muffin. She touched her stomach. It was still so flat.

'How?' she asked aloud. She pressed harder against her stomach, her fingers trying to find this source of life that she had had no idea was growing. And there it was. The tiny swell that said, *I'm here*. She felt her fingers course over the smallest bump. No one would ever guess she was pregnant. It was only her fainting and the stopping of her courses that had made her seek Mrs Stoat's opinion. She'd never dreamt it could be this. She thought perhaps she was dying of a broken heart. Now Mrs Stoat had soon put her right and explained that her condition was the opposite of death; it was new life. She was three months' gone.

She cast her mind back. Three months. Then, yes, it was possible. She remembered one morning. A misty morning. The ships' horns had been blaring as the coal strike had ended and life seemed hopeful again. Joseph had kissed her neck, her back, and her shoulders. She touched her tummy again and whispered, 'And that's when we made you, little one.'

She wanted to feel joyful. She knew that would come in time. But now she could not. In the wardrobe, a shirt of Joseph's still hung. His best trousers were still hanging folded over the single wooden chair at the side of the bed.

She couldn't get rid of them. She knew locals needed clothes. She should do her bit and donate. But she couldn't. Not yet.

Florence's cries interrupted her. She went to the baby's crib and lifted her. She was heavy now and her hair was growing. Her eyes, that had started off blue, had changed to a hazel colour, almost the brown of her father's.

'There, there,' she said, cuddling the girl. Florence didn't cry so much now. She had stopped. She cried when she was hungry, yes, but not for anything else. It was as if the girl knew this had to change now, that she had to help her mother.

And she did, without knowing it. When Lucy had first read the letter informing her of Joseph's death her initial thought was so very simple; Then I will join him. She wanted nothing more than to die.

But Florence had saved her. Her bright eyes, her soft cheeks, the way she held her soft little arms out for her mother, had all conspired to turn a hatred of life into a tolerance, and then, bit by bit, into an acceptance. She could never leave this little girl. She needed her. They needed each other.

And what would Joseph have said?

'Leave our little one? Are you mad?' he'd have said.

And she knew then that it was her duty and her life's work to raise the little girl, to tell her all about her father as she got older, to tell her about all the wonderful plans he had. Lucy had even kept the newspaper article about the charabanc. She'd folded it out neatly and placed it behind a candle on a dresser. She ran her fingers over the picture every day. She couldn't dwell on the fact that it would never happen now. She just kept it as a reminder of how life could have been, of the vivacity and zest for life Joseph always had. The charabanc was just a vehicle before. Now, the image of it represented the escape they had planned but would never come. She would never throw the article away. Never.

She dressed Florence and took her out in the pram. The month of May had come and the weather was fine. As she walked past the butchers that she could no longer afford to visit, and past the baker she could no longer afford to frequent, she overheard some women talking.

'Relief Fund, it's going to be called, so I heard,' one of them said.

'Yes, there's lots of donations. Them widows will be rich …' muttered the other, looking disapproving rather than sympathetic.

'Lucky them,' replied the other.

So far, Lucy had survived on money left in various hidden spots in the house. Joseph, never a drinker and always a saver, had stashed a selection of coins and notes around their dwelling. She kept finding new ones. It meant that although she was not well off and had to scrimp, she could afford to eat and feed Florence.

But now talk of this 'relief fund' aroused her interest. And hope. Maybe they would be all right. Maybe this was Joseph's way of looking after her.

# Chapter Twenty

**Susan**

For days, Susan had only seen her brother's back and shoulders. She'd forgotten what his face looked like. She'd go up, every few hours, poke her head around his door and offer him some tea, or take him a tray of food. But he would never turn to face her. He just stared at the wall, lying on one side in bed.

'He's feeling to blame,' Susan told her mother one evening.

Her mother scoffed. 'So he should,' she said, taking a swig of drink from a glass.

Susan couldn't believe her ears. 'How can you say that?' she asked. 'How can you, Mother?'

'How can I say that?' her mother hissed. 'Because he was s'posed to look after Jack, that's why. He promised as much. So why did he get home all right and Jack didn't?'

Susan shrugged. Truth was, she didn't know. Why did Jack and her father die? Why had Ernest lived? Why had Joseph died when many men had come home? Yet there was one searing piece of truth that was undeniable. No one should have died. No one.

The American Inquiry had been published in dribs and drabs in the British press. Susan's mother refused to read it, but she had devoured every article. The general consensus was that there had been insufficient lifeboats aboard *Titanic* to save every life. The British Inquiry had now taken place that May and had said the same thing; if there had been enough lifeboats, the outcome would have been different.

Susan heard her mother muttering, re-pouring liquid into her glass.

'Captain Smith went down with it. He was a man,' she was saying. 'Why did Ernest come home?'

'Mother, I thought you'd be pleased!' Susan yelled. 'He came home! Can't we just be grateful for that?'

'Yes, but how am I supposed to look Mrs Humby in the eyes, eh?'

Susan blinked and shook her head. 'What about Mrs Humby?'

'Oh, you didn't hear? She lost her Fred on there. He signed on as a plate steward. Sixteen he was! He went down like a man! Your brother up there, loungin' in bed, is 20. Why did he come home? How do I face 'em and tell 'em all that?' She slammed her glass down on the sideboard and put a hand to her head.

Susan couldn't speak. It was absurd. Mothers whose sons had come home were all feeling this way – guilty that their boy had not died 'like a man'. Yet, Susan knew, if Ernest had died along with their father and Jack, she would have grieved for him too. The poor boy could not win.

Susan stood up and pushed herself away from the table. 'Truth is, Mother, no man should have died on *Titanic*. And no child. And no woman. And no baby. But they did, Mother! And you can't go blaming Ernest that he's alive and Jack isn't!' She took her coat from the peg and made for the front door.

'And where are you going?' her mother asked.

'Never you mind,' Susan replied. She slammed the door and walked down the street. Children had started playing once again and the May evenings meant they had more light to stay out later. She walked past them and smiled. She knew them by name and knew each and every one of them had lost a father on *Titanic*.

Reaching in her pocket, she pulled out the leaflet she'd

been hiding until today. She read the address and followed the directions. She arrived at an unassuming-looking house and knocked on the door three times. She heard the voices inside that had been so animated suddenly stop. The door opened just a crack and a pair of eyes peered around.

'Name?'

'Susan Jarvis,' she replied.

The door opened and Susan was led inside. She followed the woman down a narrow corridor and into a back room. There, in a space no bigger than her own mother's kitchen, sat around twenty women. Susan felt all eyes on and sat in a spot in the corner on the wooden floor. She folded her skirts underneath her and looked at the woman next to her. She smiled and the woman – in her forties – smiled back.

'… the rally will be in Trafalgar Square in ten days' time,' the woman was saying. 'I suggest we muster at the station and but only in groups of three so as not to arouse suspicion …'

Susan was listening avidly. With the deaths of her father and brother, suffrage had slipped from her mind of late. But now, as she heard talk of emancipation, of freedom and choice, she felt that old fire she had had resurface. And were the two so different? Were the rights of women really so different from the rights of the working class as a whole? The two combined in her to form an anger at injustice so great she could barely swallow at times. Women were oppressed, so was the working man. Her father and brother had died in aristocrats' places because their lives were worth less. It was as simple as that.

'So who is for the rally in London?' the voice came.

All hand shot up. Susan raised hers too.

Next morning, Susan faced her pupils at school. She had not wanted to discuss *Titanic* at first. For days, no children had come in. Then for days afterwards, some had been unable because their mothers had had to pawn their school boots when they lost their man's earnings. Some had fallen ill, or their mothers had simply stopped telling them to come in. Now Susan had a relatively full class. She looked at the faces. She decided it was time to ask.

'Who here had a family member on *Titanic*?' she asked. She watched as two hands raised up, then five, then ten, then, as Susan counted, she stopped. The entire class put their hands up. Every single one of them had a man on *Titanic* in their family.

Susan cleared her throat.

'And children, who here lost a family member on *Titanic*?'

She waited, thinking perhaps half would lower their hands. But only two did. Only two of the twenty children in her class that day. That was eighteen children in her class who no longer had a father or elder brother. Eighteen children who had lost a breadwinner. Eighteen children …

At lunch, Susan met with the other teachers. 'How many were lost on *Titanic* in your class?' Susan asked a friend.

'All of them lost a father,' the teacher replied.

The other one nodded. 'All but four of mine lost fathers and brothers,' came the other answer.

Susan watched through the school window as the children played with their hoops and at hopscotch. Some seemed oblivious to the suffering. But was she imagining it or did they hop a little less gaily? Did they roll their hoops with a little less vigour than before?

# Chapter Twenty-One

**Catherine**

As proposals went, it was not what Catherine had expected or dreamed of as a little girl. She sat in a damp armchair in Kezia's house, Percy on one side standing up and Kezia the other. Catherine had read magazines where the man got down on one knee and presented the woman with a ring. Violins would play, the woman would say yes and they would embrace …

Not now.

Now it was Kezia, not Percy, who presented Catherine with a ring. It was not in a box, just in the palm of Kezia's hand. It was a simple gold wedding band.

'This will be yours. It was my mother's,' Kezia said. 'Percy wanted to show you now, didn't you, Percy?'

Percy stood up, silently nodding. He didn't look at Catherine. He didn't even speak.

'I want you to know that our Percy stands by his vow to marry you, Catherine,' Kezia said, smiling. 'He loves you so very much, don't you Percy?'

Percy nodded again, meeting no one's gaze.

Kezia took the ring away again and wrapped it in a bit of gauze. She placed it in a slim wooden drawer in the dresser.

The truth was, since Percy had come home Catherine had been trying to think of how to break it to him that she no longer wanted to marry him. If he'd been a shadow of a man before, now he was invisible. He barely spoke, just nodded or grunted. He went to work in his father's cobbler's but often had to walk out half way through the day to 'clear his thoughts'. Sometimes he shook without realising.

Catherine had asked Percy about his earnings one evening when Kezia had been serving up dinner. 'Did you make tips?' she'd asked, trying to not sound interested.

'All lost,' Percy had simply replied.

It was his mother who elaborated that everything on his person had been lost at sea, including some generous tips from the people he had served in first class.

Catherine could not help laugh at herself and the sheer irony. It was she who had pushed him to this, she who had inspired him in the need to get tips for them to forge their lives together. Now he had come home with nothing, not even a smile anymore. She had to end this.

'I need some air,' she said suddenly, and got up, pushed out of the house and out into the street. It was a Wednesday. Her day off. Normally she might have visited Susan or Lucy. But the thought of seeing Lucy now was just too impossible. Susan had told her about Lucy's pregnancy. She didn't know what to say. Should she be joyful and buoyant or was that disrespectful? Her very being seemed to irritate Lucy because Percy – unloved and unwanted by her – had come home while her Joseph had not. And now, to her, Percy was useless. He had no tips. He would clearly never go to sea again. And now he was of no use even in his father's cobbler's, needing breaks to think and walk.

'What have I done?' Catherine muttered.

She stopped at a shop selling leather gloves and stared through the window. She was gazing at a particularly lovely blue pair when she felt someone touch her arm. 'Susan,' she said.

'Buying some gloves?' Susan asked.

'Hardly!' Catherine replied.

The pair walked on together, linking arms. Children had come home from school and were running in the street, dodging lumps of manure and dirt.

'Remember us doing that?' Catherine asked.

Susan cast her mind back and remembered a life of dirty, cut knees, running breathlessly, being scolded for running through their mothers' hanging laundry, watching better off people buy from the Muffin Man as their mouths watered …

'Yes,' she replied. 'I do.'

'Easier then, wasn't it?' Catherine mused, staring at a girl with a hoop.

Susan thought of her mother at home drinking herself slowly to her grave, her brother lying on his side in his room day and night.

'It was,' she said.

'How is Lucy, have you seen her?' Catherine asked.

'Yes, matter of fact,' Susan said. 'She seems well enough. She saw Mrs Stoat.'

Catherine burst out laughing. 'Lucky she's still expecting then!' she erupted.

Susan laughed too. 'Don't. Mrs Stoat's not so bad.'

'Hope I never have to use her,' Catherine said.

'And why would you?' Susan asked. 'Aren't you marrying Percy now he's home?'

Catherine walked on ahead. 'Don't know.'

'Don't know?'

'Yes, you heard. I don't know.'

Susan grabbed Catherine's elbow and spun her to look at her. 'If you don't want to do this, you need to tell him,' Susan said.

'This? Coming from you, the suffragette?' Catherine spat. 'What do you care about men's feelings?'

'I care about a survivor from *Titanic*,' Susan said. 'He needs you. Don't lead him up the garden path. If you don't love him, break it off now.'

Catherine threw her head back and sighed. 'And how can I?' she said. 'His mother loves me. She gave me her mother's ring! She needs me more than Percy, I swear it. And as for him …'

'What about him?' Susan asked.

Catherine remembered the thin shell of a man. Mute. Black rings around his eyes.

'Well, how can I stay married to that?' Catherine wailed, a red rash of anger snaking its way up her neck. 'He was pathetic before. A worm! Now he's even less! He can't speak. He can't look at me! He lost all his tips in the sea and now I have to wed him?! And this coming from you, the voice of women's freedom!'

Susan looked away. The irony was not lost on her. 'You know if I had my way no woman would ever have to marry any man. But you made a promise to Percy and now he's…well…' her voice trailed off as she thought of her own brother, lying in his room facing the wall. 'Men suffered on *Titanic*,' Susan said.

Catherine rolled her eyes.

'No, you listen,' Susan said, 'they did! We think they're hard. They work. They come home. They drink. They fight. But I see my brother day in, day out. He can't talk of it. He lies in that room day and night, unable to speak. They're still in shock, Catherine. We have to be the strong ones now.'

Catherine pulled her arm free from Susan's grip.

'So what do you suggest I do, Mrs Pankhurst?' she said, her eyes flashing anger.

Susan took a deep breath. 'You have to marry him. Or tell him it's off. But one way or another, you have to be honest with him.'

# Chapter Twenty-Two

**Lucy**

The temperature in the courtroom was so high that Lucy saw several ladies undo their top collar buttons and run a finger between their neck and their clothing. Lucy, now five months pregnant, felt permanently hot and so had cleverly worn her lightest dress today with a lower collar than usual. Catherine's mother had Florence for her, and she was alone for the first time in months. Alone, except for the dozens of other women sitting around her, all waiting for one man to enter Southampton County Court.

Suddenly a door opened and in the judge walked. He was not wearing his usual wig and gown. The heat had made usual laws of comportment go out of the window. Judge John Gye sat at his bench and stacked his papers.

Lucy had never been in a courtroom before. She imagined judges to be terrifying men wearing long robes and wigs or donning a black hat when sending someone to be hanged. This man looked like an ordinary man. Yet he carried with him an air of importance.

'Bring the first case,' he uttered.

Lucy watched as a woman, slightly older than her, was shown to the witness box.

'Name?' came the question.

The woman tried to answer but her voice was too quiet.

'Name?' came the question once again.

'Vera Bristow,' she said at last.

Lucy watched as the woman gripped the witness box with one hand. Around the court room, all eyes were on her. This was a momentous occasion. The *Titanic* crew widows were seeking compensation from the White Star Line under the Workmen's Compensation Act. Lucy had heard that the White Star had already decided what the awards would be; a maximum of £300 per dependant on a strict criteria of £294 15s per leading fireman, the same per greaser, £237 12s for each ordinary fireman and £223 15s per trimmer.

Joseph had earned £6 a month as a fireman. Lucy could not imagine what she would do with over £200. The truth was, she didn't care anymore. It would not bring her husband back. She looked around at the other women, all wearing black as she was, all still in mourning. Some held handkerchiefs to their eyes. Others sobbed openly.

She sat there, silent, watching how Vera Bristow answered the questions fired at her.

'... and when did you marry your husband?'

'March 1905,' she replied.

'And you have dependants?'

'Four, sir,' she replied.

'Their names?'

She reeled off the names of her children. But her sense of agitation was beginning to show.

'Ages of each?' the voice asked.

Women shifted in their seats next to her. This felt more like an interrogation than a simple questioning.

'Husband's position on the vessel?' came the voice.

'Greaser, sir,' she said.

Lucy remembered the greasers Joseph knew. They worked alongside each other. While the stokers toiled lifting the coal into the furnaces, the greasers kept the engines lubricated, hence their title.

When the woman had finished, she stepped down,

shaking a little. Another woman now stepped up, and older lady. It transpired her son had been a stoker on Titanic.

'I relied on his earnings,' she told the court.

But an official at the front read some papers and then interjected. 'This lady has not received any money from her son for eight years, my Lord, and therefore cannot be described as a dependant.'

The mother's face fell. 'But … But I lost my son …' she stammered.

Her case was dismissed. She was not awarded her compensation for her son's death because he had not supported her for eight years.

She emerged from the witness box, trembling. She was crying. 'But how will I manage? How will I manage?'

There was no answer to her question.

Lucy sat through tens of other claims. Women who were pregnant, women who had only just married and lost their new grooms to the sea, mothers who had lost three sons in one go, mothers who had lost only sons, their only child.

At various points, Judge John Gye stopped proceedings.

Exasperated, he said, 'There are a great many ideas abroad which are wholly fallacious.'

A solicitor at the front called Mr Emmanuel said, 'Just the same as they all think they are entitled to £300 when they are not,' he replied wryly.

Lucy watched as another young woman fainted under oath. She fell from the witness box.

'Can someone help this lady?' a voice said.

The St John's Ambulance workers ran in and lifted her over their shoulders. As she was dragged, faint, from the witness box, finally she heard her name.

'Lucy Williams?'

Touching her growing bump, Lucy stood up. She walked forward and climbed into the witness box. She stood up, lifted her head and suddenly blushed furiously at all the eyes on her.

'Is your name Lucy Williams?'

'It is,' she replied.

'And you are the wife of one Joseph Williams, Stoker, of Northam, Southampton?'

She swallowed hard at hearing his name said by someone else. 'I am,' she said.

'And you have one daughter, Florence, and were completely dependent on your husband's income of six pounds a month?'

She nodded, touching her stomach.

A croak erupted from her lips and the interrogator said, 'Pardon?'

Lucy's lips felt so dry. Her throat was parched. 'I meant to say … I am also pregnant now. With my husband's second child.'

Lucy looked as women turned, leaning into each other to whisper. She knew what they were thinking. She'd heard of other women getting pregnant by a lover and claiming it was her dead husband's from *Titanic* to seek compensation. She knew this was what they were now whispering about her.

'And you were how far along in your pregnancy when your husband died at sea?' came the voice.

'Three months, sir,' she replied.

There was a murmuring between solicitors at the front of the room. Lucy felt her pulse racing.

Time seemed to stand still. Men in suits discussed her case in murmurs and whispers. Finally, a resolution came.

'Awarded,' came a voice.

'Next!'

Lucy stepped down from the witness box. Her legs were shaking. Her face was red. She went back to sit down, not daring to believe it. She'd been awarded some money. Over £200. She bit back tears as she touched her stomach. She thought of the morsels and scraps she'd been eating, and the tiny bowls she had feeding Florence. She thought of how every night she had gone to bed without any tea or supper since *Titanic* sank, saving anything for her daughter. At first she had been unable to sleep; the pain of the hunger was so bad. Then she'd got used to it. At last, now, that could change.

But then she listened as it was described to the widows

how the money would be paid.

'Each dependant will receive their compensation in rounds of £4 per month. If children are older, half the sum will be awarded to the children, half to the dependent wife …'

A female voice from the court piped up, 'And what if your husband had debts?'

Everyone turned to face this woman. She had a proud look on her face but was trembling.

Judge Gye sighed. 'Compensation will be received by the dependants and should be free of the debts of the deceased,' he confirmed.

A collective sigh of relief was audible in court.

When all the cases had been heard, the Judge stood up and addressed the widows.

'Beware of vultures,' he said. 'There are many around who see a poor widow with a good round sum and immediately take steps to get some of it. You widows need careful protection.'

Lucy stood up as the court was dismissed. She filed out with the other widows. Some were still sobbing. Some filed out in stunned silence. Others were talking excitedly.

'Well, I'm starting a business,' one said.

'I'm emigrating,' another said. 'America, I think. God knows I can't stay around here …'

'I knew Bob would look after me, this is from him,' a weeping widow was saying.

Lucy said nothing to anyone. She stepped out into the early summer sunlight, down the courthouse steps and onto the street.

Nothing would ever bring Joseph back. No money would ever compensate for the aching, black hole in her heart. But she was a mother. A mother soon of two children. She couldn't dwell on her heartache any longer. She had to take the money owed to her with both hands and fight.

For her children.

# Chapter Twenty-Three

**Susan**

It was a first step but an important one. It had now been four months since *Titanic* had foundered and at last Ernest had left his room and was sitting at the kitchen table. It was a Saturday afternoon and both Catherine and Susan had the day off. They sat watching Ernest sip some soup, sitting on a chair for the first time in weeks.

'Well, he looks all right to me,' Catherine said, taking a sip of tea.

'Shh, don't talk about him like he's not there,' Susan said.

'Well, he's not there is he?' Catherine said, staring at him. Before sighing and adding, 'None of 'em are.'

'How is Percy?' Susan asked, helping Ernest's hand as it shook holding his soup spoon.

'The same as this one,' she replied, nodding towards Ernest. 'Bloomin' useless.'

Susan slapped her hand. 'For God's sake Catherine,' she hissed.

'What? He can't hear us, can't you tell?' Catherine said, pointing at Ernest and waving a hand in front of his eyes.

Ernest didn't even look up.

'Percy's the same. It's like they left their brains in the Atlantic,' Catherine sighed.

Susan looked at Ernest. Catherine was as blunt as an axe and mostly spouted rubbish. But now as she looked at her brother, she realised how astute Catherine was. Her brother was empty. He wasn't 'there'. She wondered how many other survivors of the *Titanic* were the same. She'd seen the men staggering about after they'd come home. Some looked cocky and happy to be alive. But most of them were gaunt shadows of themselves. That and the shame they displayed whenever they walked past another home with the curtains drawn. The unsaid question on everyone's lips was: Why did he survive when others did not?

Ernest finished his soup and Susan cleared his bowl and spoon away.

'And where's dear mother today?' Catherine asked, noting the empty kitchen.

'On errands,' Susan replied.

Catherine joined her in the kitchen area. Susan said, quieter now, 'She blames Ernest for Jack's death.'

Catherine looked over at Ernest, sitting with his two fists on the table. 'Well, it isn't his fault, is it?' she said.

'Mother thinks it is. She says he should have stayed with him. She also feels ashamed that her son came back when women and children died …'

Catherine threw her head back and laughed. 'What a load of old codswallop!' she said.

'Shh! For goodness' sake!' Susan hissed.

'What? It's tiptoeing around them that makes this worse,' Catherine said, suddenly storming across to where Ernest was sitting.

She pulled up a chair, sat right next to him and turned his face to her. 'Ernest, what are we doing about work?' she asked.

Ernest looked at her beautiful face. He'd always had a soft spot for Catherine. Every lad did.

He shrugged.

'What would your father do?' Catherine said.

Ernest blinked furiously. He was trying to hold back tears. He turned his face away from Catherine, but Susan watched, stunned, as Catherine turned his face more gently back towards her.

'Come on then, let's have them tears,' she said.

Susan put a hand to her mouth and watched as her brother's bottom lip wobbled.

'That's it. Let it out now. Can't keep it bottled up,' Catherine was saying.

Susan stared, silent, as Ernest laid his head on Catherine's bosom and began talking. Talking and weeping for the first time since the disaster.

'I ... I ...'

'Yes, yes, come on Ernest, I'm all ears,' Catherine was saying bluntly. There was no softness to her voice. No sympathy. Just a matter of fact, hard woman giving orders. But Ernest seemed to thrive on this. He began talking all at once.

'It was so cold ... and so dark ... but the stars were everywhere,' he said. 'It was like a beautiful dream ... I heard the ship hit. It was a terrible, horrible sound of screeching and crunching. Then it fell silent. Me and Jack were about to start the 12 'til 4 watch. But it struck the iceberg before we went down ...'

Catherine was patting his head against her chest. 'Go on, Ernest,' she said.

Susan watched as he carried on. 'I was with Jack. We ran up to deck. Officers were there lowering lifeboats. One grabbed me by my collar and shouted 'Get in and row!'
I turned back and Jack had gone ...He'd gone ...'

Susan carefully walked over to the table. She pulled a chair up next to Ernest and listened.

'I pushed the officer off me. I told him to go to hell, that I was finding my brother,' he said. 'I ran where I last saw Jack, but he was gone. I bumped into three men from my shift – Will, Walter and Tom. I asked if they'd seen him. Tom said he'd run in one direction. Will said another. I ran all over that ship. But it was listing. Then suddenly there was an almighty noise and the ship was raising up one side. Everyone fell like dolls to the bottom as the ship rose up, hitting their heads, knocking themselves out. I saw a baby fall from its mother's arms. It hit its head and died instantly.'

Susan put a hand over her mouth again.

'Go on,' Catherine said, softer now. Kinder.

'I ran all over. But the ship was going down. Then, it was so fast … but suddenly we were going down … down, and the suction from the water was so huge it was like being eaten alive. I tried to cling on, but I was ripped from a doorway and thrown downwards. Next thing I knew it was black and cold. So cold …

'I kicked my legs. They'd barely move. It was so cold,' he suddenly looked at Catherine now, then at Susan. 'Not the cold we know. Not the cold of January or February. The kind of cold that makes you gasp then be too afraid to gasp again. My limbs were frozen, I couldn't kick or swim. But I tried. I kept trying. I was moving my belly like an eel trying to move. I came to the surface and gasped. I looked around me and there were people everywhere. Some screaming. Some were begging for help. But then it went quiet. Next thing I knew it went black.'

Ernest suddenly turned to Susan. He reached for her hand. He held it for the first time since he'd come home.

'You have to believe me I tried to find Jack,' he said, tears welling in his blue eyes. 'I'd have swam to America to find him. I swear it. I couldn't move. I couldn't even think. I swear if I could go back, I'd yell at God to take me! I swear it!'

Susan wrapped her arms around her brother.

'Oh, God, oh, God, take me …' Ernest was sobbing now, his huge frame racked with aching gasps. Catherine moved away as Susan held her brother and saw a woman standing in the doorway. She looked like she'd been there for some time.

Susan looked up now and saw her mother. She had tears in her eyes. She'd lost that hard, hateful look she reserved for Ernest these days and walked over.

Ernest saw and said, 'Oh Mother, I am so sorry … I want to die too …'

And the mother pushed Susan aside as she wrapped her son against her body in an embrace, an embrace that should have happened so many weeks earlier. She held him to her chest and let him cry now.

'You cry, son, that's it,' Susan's mother said. 'You let it out …'

Susan went to Catherine and reached for her hand.

'What you did…' Susan whispered. 'What you did waskind . Thank you.'

Catherine shrugged. 'It was nothing. Just told him straight.'

Susan watched now as her mother kissed Ernest's head and told him she was sorry, so sorry. She watched as she forgave him for her brother's death and how she held him to her like a boy again. And the Ernest she knew and loved came back that day at the kitchen table.

Susan looked at Catherine.

'If you can do this for Ernest, you know who you have to help now?' Susan said.

Catherine looked puzzled. 'Who?'

'Percy,' Susan replied.

# Chapter Twenty-Four

**Catherine**

Next day, Catherine was sweeping out the soot in the drawing room at the big house when she heard the conversation.

'Of course, four hundred and twelve thousand pounds is a great deal of money,' the vicar's wife was saying. 'I hear it's been donated from all over the world. A great many churches have contributed, including our own.'

'The Mayor of Southampton really is a wonderful man starting all this,' Catherine's mistress of the house replied. 'We really are lucky.'

'Yes, came another lady's voice. But how on earth will they distribute this 'relief fund for widows'? I mean, one can hardly dish out thousands of pounds to those wives in one fell swoop!'

'Exactly,' the vicar's wife added. 'They need guidance. They would spend it all in one go on drink otherwise.'

Catherine stopped sweeping and moved nearer on her knees to the doorway. From her place on the floor, she could see through a crack in the door the three women taking tea.

'It will be called The *Titanic* Relief Fund,' her mistress said, looking smug at her insider knowledge. 'It might just drag some of them out of their hovels and make them look respectable. Might even get them to send their offspring to school.'

Catherine breathed in hard through her nose. She gripped her scrubbing brush. Oh, to throw it right between that cow's eyes. She thought of the women she knew. Decent folk who had nothing since their husbands had drowned. If only they knew how the rich sneered down at them even in their greatest hour of need.

When she'd finished for the day, Catherine left by the back door as usual and set off home. On her way, she saw Ernest, walking out in the street for the first time.

'You all right Ernest?' she said, stepping nearer to him.

He smiled. 'I am, thank you,' he said, looking at his feet. 'I've you to thank for that.'

She smacked his shoulder. 'Don't talk daft,' she said. 'You just needed to get it all out. No point bottling things up, is there?'

He smiled sadly and shook his head.

'So where you off to then?'

They both dodged a horse and cart with manure heaped in the back and Catherine screwed her nose up.

'Off to sign on again,' he said.

Catherine raised her eyebrows. 'You're going back to sea?'

He shrugged. 'What else is there to do? It's what father and Jack would have done. I'm signing on to the Union Castle Line. I won't work for White Star again.'

Catherine nodded, her face serious. 'You couldn't get anything from them then?' she asked. 'No charity money or anything?'

He shook his head. 'Mother got some money for Father and Jack,' he replied. 'We survivors … well,' he added, trying to look brighter. 'We're here, aren't we? The sea is all I know. So I'll be going back.'

Catherine wiped an imaginary piece of dust from his shoulder. 'Well, you be careful,' she smiled.

He smiled and made to walk past her, on his way to the docks. Before they parted, he reached for her hand.

'You're a lovely lady, Catherine,' he said.

She laughed sardonically. 'Yes, I am,' she replied.

On her way home, she passed Percy's cobbler's. She saw Kezia talking animatedly to a lady outside. She tried to skulk past unnoticed, but Kezia saw her.

'Catherine! Come over here, my love!' she called.

Catherine smiled tersely and walked across the street.

'Have you heard?' she asked .

'Heard what?' Catherine asked.

'About this new *Titanic* Relief Fund?'

Catherine nodded. 'Yes, I have,' she said. 'That cow and her hoighty-toighty friends were talking about it at the big house today.'

'Well, I wouldn't change places with them now I have my Percy back, but isn't it good news for the widows? Your friend Lucy will benefit no doubt?'

Catherine smiled and nodded. Truth was, she hadn't seen Lucy in an age. She couldn't face her. She could feel Lucy's seething inner anger even through her smile. It was a look that said, 'Why did your Percy come back – a man you don't even love. Why did my true love die?'

'I'm sure she will,' Catherine said. Changing the subject, she said, 'May I see Percy?'

'He's out the back, ducky,' Kezia said.

Catherine pushed the door open and heard the ding-a-ling of the bell. Percy popped up from behind the counter.

'Catherine,' he said, forcing a smile.

'Percy,' she replied.

He came nearer. He still shook when he spoke but had been helping out in the shop for some weeks now. He reached for her hand. 'I want you to know now that even though I can't quite be happy yet … I want you to know that without you I could not go on,' Percy was saying.

She looked at his hand, gripping hers for dear life. She would keep her promise to Susan. She would help him, as she had helped Ernest. But then she would tell the truth and break this off. She didn't love him. She knew that much. 'I think we should take a walk on our next day off,' Catherine said.

Percy's eyes lit up for the first time in as long as she could remember. 'Yes, yes,' he said. 'I should like that.'

Catherine nodded and smiled, pulling her hand away from his.

'I want you to know that it makes me the proudest man ... the happiest man that you will be my wife,' Percy said. 'I know I am not myself yet,' he added, trying to steady his hands, 'but I will be.'

She smiled and left the shop. 'I believe you, Percy,' she replied. She set off home. She reached the front door, pushed it open and walked inside. At the table her father was clean and sober. Her mother was standing over him.

'What's wrong with him?' Catherine asked.

'He's signing on again,' she replied.

'Is it safe?' Catherine asked.

Her father pursed his lips and nodded reverently. 'I lost so many crewmates on *Titanic*,' he said. 'I can't stay around here no more, seeing women crying and men lost. I'm signing on to *Olympic*.'

'Mother!' Catherine said.

Her mother folded her arms. 'I am in favour,' her mother replied. 'It's a man's duty to go back.'

'But a White Star ship? A death trap?' Catherine said.

'There's enough life boats now, the Inquiry saw to that,' her father said. 'Laws are changing now, Cath. I'm going back.' Her father had changed since the tragedy. True, he had not been on the ship. But so many of his friends and drinking partners had. Instead of sneaking off to the King's Arms like a naughty schoolboy, he now sat at the table, staring into space. It didn't matter if you hadn't even been on *Titanic*. The tragedy, it seemed, seeped into everyone's bones in Southampton.

'Well, I don't know how you can toil for them,' Catherine said, slumping onto a chair with a sunken middle.

'Listen here, missy,' her mother spat. 'Work's work. They've said they're sorry. They've put more lifeboats and that's that. We can't go on mourning everyone forever! Just because your idiot of a man can't get over it, don't mean we all have to sulk and skulk about! Some have to put food on the table!'

Catherine let her mother's words sink in and felt the strangest feeling. It hit somewhere in her stomach and then snaked its way up to her heart. It hurt. She thought perhaps at first she had indigestion. But then she realised what it was. It was what her mother had said, '… just because your idiot of a man can't get over it …'

And Catherine suddenly understood what she was feeling. It was pain. Pain and hurt at what her mother had said about Percy. It made her stomach ache. She was feeling … *protective* … She didn't reply. She walked off up the stairs and to her bedroom. She lay back on her bed and looked at the stained ceiling. What on earth was happening?

'I can't … I just can't …' she whispered to herself. But she thought of Percy's face, his eyes that were getting brighter, his keen, innocent love for her. She felt a sense of warmth and affection for him growing inside her.

She shook her head.

'Oh my goodness, no' she cried out.

# Chapter Twenty-Five

**Lucy**

The floor was swept, the hearth was dusted, the baby's blankets and clothes had been folded and the place smelt of carbolic soap. Lucy ran her chapped hands down over her dress. It was getting so much tighter now. Did the house look clean enough? She hurried to the window and spat on a cloth to wipe it a bit. Then there was a knock at the door.

'Oh, gosh,' Lucy said. 'She's here ...'

She ran to the front door and pulled it open. A woman was standing on the front step. Lucy could just make out the handlebars of a pushbike leaning against her wall.

'Miss Stevens,' the woman said, holding out her hand. 'May I?'

Lucy stepped backwards and invited her in. She'd known this woman was coming for days now. And for days, she'd been dusting, cleaning, sweeping and generally tidying, terrified of a tiny portion of the house looking untidy.

'I'm the Lady Visitor,' the woman said said.

Lucy smiled. 'Yes,' she said.

The Lady Visitor – called Edna Stevens – had been appointed by the *Titanic* Relief Fund. The charity fund had amassed over £400,000 in donations from all over the world, from the rich, to the poor, from the famous down to the working man.

The Lady Visitor's role was to visit the *Titanic* widows and mothers of crew who had died and ensure they were deserving of their charitable hand-outs.

'And where is your little one?' the Lady Visitor asked.

'Oh, yes,' Lucy said, flustered.

She ran up the stairs and brought Florence down on one hip.

'Ah, how lovely,' the Lady Visitor said. She looked at Lucy's middle. 'And my notes tell me you are expecting again?' she asked.

Lucy nodded, instinctively touching her bump. 'I am.' Was Lucy imagining it or did the lady look at her and linger slightly longer than expected? She'd seen that look before from others. It was a look which said, *Is that baby really your husband's?* Lucy walked to a corner and set the baby down on a blanket.

'And how have we been?' the Lady Visitor said, casting an eye around the house.

'I've been as well as can be expected,' Lucy replied.

'You have help?' the lady asked.

'I have two good friends who come,' she said, thinking of how she had not seen Catherine for weeks. Still, at least she had Susan.

'And you are managing financially?' she asked.

Lucy glanced involuntarily at the kitchen cupboards. Behind the doors there was nothing at the moment.

'Well, sometimes,' she said.

'We can award special grants when needed,' the Lady Visitor said. 'Just let us know and we can arrange one if you require it?'

'Thank you,' Lucy said.

The woman went over to the baby. She lifted her up and held her. 'A good weight,' she said, smiling.

Florence gurgled and reached out for the woman's hair before the Lady Visitor put her back down on the floor.

Lucy watched as the woman's eyes flitted around the

house, from peg to cupboard, from seat to table. She knew what she was doing. She'd heard as much from other *Titanic* widows. The Lady Visitor's visits weren't just to ensure *Titanic's* widows were surviving and that their children were being cared for. Her visits were also to ensure that a widow had not found another man or remarried. If she did so, she would be struck off the Relief Fund, losing her allowance.

As Lucy watched Miss Stevens's eyes darting around her small house, she knew what she was searching for; a pipe here, a pair of shoes there, a cap here, a coat there. Lucy suddenly felt incensed.

'There is no one else,' she blurted out.

The Lady Visitor suddenly met her gaze. 'Beg your pardon?' she said, smiling politely.

'I said there is no one else,' she said. 'I've heard about what you're looking for – another man, another husband, someone else. I know some wives might do that just months after their husband died but not me. I loved Joseph. I won't ever find another man. I'll never ... I'll ...' her voice trailed off now and hot tears sprang to her eyes. She shook her head. Pregnancy made her feel on the verge of tears all the time. It didn't help. But nor did a woman coming to 'check' her for her way of life. She didn't care about being checked for cleanliness, or to ensure her child wasn't being neglected, or that she wasn't malnourished. But this idea that a woman could just move on so quickly after her husband's death and that needed to be checked by the Relief Fund ... that was offensive. Deeply so.

'I quite understand, Mrs Williams,' the Lady Visitor said. She stood up, her visit complete. 'I'll see about a nourishing parcel of food for you, Mrs Williams,' she said, looking at Lucy's thin face.

Lucy nodded.

'Oh, and one more thing. We are sending select widows off to a place of respite should they need it,' she said. 'It's called the Dolling Home and it is in Worthing.'

'Worthing?' Lucy said. 'Where's that?'

'Sussex,' the Lady Visitor replied. 'It is all paid for by the Fund. You'd get to take your daughter and stay there. There are clean rooms and your food is provided. You can take the sea air and, well, have a rest.'

Lucy took it all in. She looked at Florence. She'd never been away from their streets, let alone another town. 'All right, then' she said.

'I'll see about organising it,' the Visitor replied. 'Keep well, Mrs Williams.' Then she opened the door, stepped outside, got back onto her push bike and rode away.

Lucy slammed the door, furious. She went over to the table and deliberately moved the things she had placed so tidily on top. She pushed some papers to one side, threw a blanket that was folded there onto the ground.

Florence blinked up at her, holding a wooden rattle.

'Make a mess, my love!' Lucy was almost shrieking, tears beginning to fall down her face. 'Make a mess! She's gone now and can't judge us now.' She slumped to the table and rested her head in her hands. She pulled her hair down from its twist and let it fall about her shoulders. When it touched her skin, she thought of Joseph. He loved her with her hair down. She'd sometimes take it down before he got home from another trip, so she could greet him at the door that way. She ran a hand shakily through her hair. It used to be so thick and shiny. Now it was brittle and thin. She barely ate some days, giving what she had to Florence. All the promises people had made to the *Titanic* widows made her laugh. Compensation? Yes, but handed out in meagre monthly portions of £4 a month – less than Joseph had earned. The *Titanic* Relief Fund? Even that was done in class order.

Just as there had been a hierarchy on the ship, so it was in the charity hand-outs. There were seven classes of award, from A down to G. Wives of officers were in class A and they received £2 a week. Class B was for the saloon stewards and bedroom stewards – their wives would receive £1 12s a week. So it went down through class C, for lower class stewards, all the way down to class G for scullions, stewards and firemen.

That was Lucy. The lowest class of award. For the lowest member of staff on *Titanic*, the stokers. She received twelve and six a week. She wiped her hands over her face and thought of the empty cupboards and empty bed upstairs. If it had not been for Florence and her unborn baby … she didn't want to think about it. She got up, walked over to Florence and saw the baby beam at her. She bent down and scooped the child up and covered her with kisses. Florence no longer wailed or cried. It was as if the girl had a sixth sense that her father was not coming home. Instead, she sat quietly as her mother cradled her, enjoying her warmth and soft skin. 'There'll never be another man in place of your father,' Lucy said now, kissing Florence's soft head.

She rocked her to and fro on her lap. Other wives might have been hiding a new man under the stairs and claiming their money but not her. Joseph had been the love of her life. He always would be.

# Chapter Twenty-Six

**Susan**

Susan had noticed something strange about her route to school of late. Usually she took the quickest route, out of her house, down the street, past the bakery. But now her trip took longer. It took a while for her to understand why. Then she faced it.

She was deliberately walking past Rizzi's Ices shop.

She had not seen Angelo for a while. All her energies had been on helping the bewildered orphans at school and helping Ernest get back on his feet again. Now that her brother was much better, and their mother had forgiven him, she was able to think about other things.

The first of those things had a name; Angelo.

On this morning as she walked past, she saw movement in the shop window. She stopped, picking something imaginary off her boot, when she saw him. He opened the door and waved to her. She smiled brightly and waved back.

'Come over here,' he mouthed, beckoning her.

Checking the road for carts, she hurried across. When she reached him, she felt her heart quicken and her cheeks blush.

'Are you all right, Susan?' he asked.

'Er, yes, thank you,' she replied.

'You look flushed.'

She flushed even more. 'Just these warm summer mornings,' she said.

He grinned.

'And how are you?' she asked him.

'Oh, you know,' he replied. 'Getting busier now the English sun is coming. Is that what you call it?' he said, peering through the smog at a tiny yellow dot in the sky. 'The sun?'

She laughed and looked into his eyes. 'Er, anyway. I must get to school before the bell,' she said.

'Would you take a walk with me one day?' Angelo asked suddenly.

'A walk?'

'Yes, through the gardens perhaps?'

'I'd like that very much indeed,' Susan replied.

She walked away, feeling her heart hammering and her stomach churn. She didn't know if it was the sickly-sweet smell of the ices shop, but she felt ever so slightly queasy. She cast her mind back to the recent suffragette meetings. Phrases and lines whirled in her head.

*Men are the oppressors*
*Down with the patriarchy*
*Marriage is shackles*
*A vote for women is a vote for all mankind*

She believed in every word. She repeated them like a mantra. So, why, when she looked at Angelo, did none of these phrases matter? She'd felt sure she'd be a spinster for life. Marriage had always appalled her. But when she was met with his dark eyes, his smile, his kind demeanour and, best of all, his respect for her ... well ... none of that seemed to mean anything anymore,

At the school, she taught the children mathematics. At lunchtime, she saw another teacher writing in the school log book. She peered over her shoulder.

*'Twenty-four meals given today...'*

'What's this?' Susan asked.

'Free dinners for the children,' the teacher replied. 'The families can't afford to feed them or send them with money for food. We're giving meals for free to the *Titanic* orphaned children.'

Susan felt suddenly very tired. She had lost a brother and a father on *Titanic*. She ached every day with grief. She ached even more with worry about her brother and the guilt he carried. But now she saw this was nothing compared to the losses of some families, of children who had lost a father so young, of others whose mothers had also died so they were now orphaned completely.

She knew with a sudden horror *Titanic* would never truly be out of any of their minds. Not this generation and not the next.

It was two days later, on her day off, that Angelo met her for a walk in the city gardens. As they walked through summer flowers, the smell of cut grass was everywhere. Susan stopped at a spot where grass had been cleared.

'They're to erect a statue here to the *Titanic* losses,' she said thoughtfully.

Angelo stood next to her in silence. 'As they should,' he said. 'They were heroes.'

'Were they?' Susan said.

'Oh yes, I heard stokers who came back talking of nothing else. How the stokers and engineers kept the furnaces going even as they sank, to keep the lights on for the passengers. Your father and brother helped do that. They saved lives …'

Susan suddenly felt her face wet with tears that she had struggled for so long to contain. She wiped her cheeks but the tears kept coming. 'Truth is, we don't know where any of them were,' she wept. 'Ernest said he hadn't seen Father and Jack got lost. We'll never know what they did. Whether they were "heroes" or not … what does it matter?' She wept now, her back heaving with loss. She felt an arm wrap around her and then turn her inwards to him. She fell against his chest and felt the hardness of it. She let her head fall against his neck and she cried at last. A proper cry after all these months.

'They were all heroes,' Angelo whispered into her ear. 'That's how we must all think of them, Susan.'

She nodded and sniffed, wiping her eyes. She looked at

his collar, wet with tears. 'I'm sorry, look,' she said, wiping her tears off his clothes.

He shook his head. 'No matter,' he said. He stared into her eyes. She looked into his eyes, dark as night and rich as chocolate. She felt her tears stop then, and a feeling of the desperation to live, to feel, to be happy in the place of her dead family overcame her. What was life without that? What was life without … well, love?

She turned her face upwards to him and he kissed her. She felt his lips cover hers and a sweet, painful feeling rushed through her. When he finally pulled away, she gasped and he moved away from her.

'I am sorry,' he said. He stepped away. He looked at the floor. 'I don't know what I was thinking.'

Susan looked around her. There were no prying eyes in the park. No damage done to her reputation. 'No, Angelo, I wanted to kiss you too,' she said, stepping forward and reaching for his hand.

Angelo looked relieved and joyful all at once. 'My suffragette, she wanted to kiss me,' he grinned.

She shook her head. She could hardly believe it herself. 'You're not like other men,' she said, shaking her head in disbelief at it all. And she couldn't believe it, couldn't even believe she was saying this. Weeks earlier, she'd been a different woman. The thought of marriage and all it represented sickened her. She wanted a future for women where they had a say in what went on, in what laws were made. For heaven's sake, she wanted a world where a woman could choose what to do with her own money, instead of relying on men who were so often drunk or unreliable to survive. But that was before *Titanic*.

She thought of the big ship she'd seen days before it sailed, gleaming, shiny and new in the April sunlight. It had represented all that was powerful, big, modern and … masculine. It was patriarchy and maleness all represented in one huge hulk of steel and smoke. Boats were known as 'she', she thought, almost laughing aloud at the thought. But these liners were male through and through – thinking they were all powerful, ruling the seas, stronger than God …

Look where that had got Titanic, and her father and brother. Look where that had got Joseph, and countless other men like him. Her feelings about women's rights had not changed. *Titanic* had only strengthened them. She saw how women relied on their men. Now that they were gone, they had nothing. Something had to change so women never went through that again.

But, she realised, she could still be that angry woman, fighting for women's rights *and* feel love and hope for her own future. The one did not preclude the other. As she squeezed Angelo's hand she knew that now.

'So, you'll be my sweetheart?' he asked.

She found herself nodding and her face erupting into a grin that made her cheeks hurt.

'Come on,' Angelo said, squeezing her hand back.

'Come on, where?' Susan asked.

Angelo shrugged. 'I'm Italian,' he said, simply. 'So, you know who you've got meet properly, properly now?'

Susan frowned.

'Mamma,' he smiled.

# Chapter Twenty-Seven

**Lucy**

The wrought iron gates were closed and for a moment Lucy thought about turning around and going back to the railway station. She'd boarded the train in Southampton early that morning and had arrived in Worthing exhausted and hot. It was May but for some reason it was warmer than usual today. She put her bag on the floor and heaved Florence higher on her hip. She recalled the letter the Lady Visitor had given her just two days earlier:

'Inmates at the Dolling Home should bring their own change of linen, a brush, comb, towel and slippers. Alcohol is strictly forbidden. Church will be attended on Sundays.'

Lucy flinched slightly at the word 'inmates.' The gates were high and certainly looked like they could belong to a prison. But as she peered through them, she saw the house seemed nice enough. It was huge and one portion of it was covered in ivy, growing up the wall and only stopping for two windows to peep out.

Finally, a woman emerged and walked towards the gates. 'Mrs Williams?' she smiled. She carried a large bunch of keys.

'That's right,' Lucy nodded.

'Come in,' she said. She unlocked the gates and opened them. They made a piercing, screeching sound as they parted. Lucy stepped through, carrying her heavy bag in one hand and Florence in the other. The lady did not seem to notice.

Lucy followed the woman up the steps and into a large hallway. The floor had clean black and white tiles. Lucy dropped her bag to the floor and could have wept with gratitude.

'Come through, your room is on the first floor,' the woman said.

Lucy followed up the stairs. The house was bright with windows letting the May sunlight in.

'I am Mrs Acreman,' she said. 'I'm housekeeper here. This is your room.'

She opened a large white painted door and Lucy stepped over the threshold into a room that was bigger than her entire house. A large bed was against the wall and was covered with a pale pink embroidered bedspread. A huge window let even more light in. She had a wash basin and a chest of drawers. Even a mirror.

'We've arranged for a cot for young …?' She looked at Florence and raised her eyebrows in question.

'Florence,' Lucy said.

'Florence,' Mrs Acreman smiled.

'So, I shall leave you to unpack your bag. Tea will be served at four.' Then she closed the door behind her.

Lucy carried Florence over to the cot. It was much bigger than the one she had at home. She cast a glance around the wood. It was pure white painted. Unlike the one at home that Florence slept in, this one had no mould patches, no dirt. She lowered Florence into it and handed her her dolly.

'That's your bed,' Lucy smiled. She then went over to her bed. She sat down and sank into a bouncy, springy mattress. A carpet covered the majority of the floor so she took her boots off and let her feet touch the softness underfoot. It felt so different to wood and dust and damp. She let herself lay back on the soft bed. The bedspread smelt of roses. Her pillow was soft and plump and full of down. 'Oh, this is the life,' she sighed, closing her eyes.

At four, Lucy summoned the courage to leave her room and go down for tea as arranged. Florence was sleeping so she left her and tentatively stepped down the stairs. When she reached the hallway, she had no idea where to turn. There were so many doors and rooms. Then she heard voices. She followed the noise and heard teacups clattering. A peek around a door confirmed it. Lucy stepped into another beautifully decorated room.

'Ah, Mrs Williams,' Mrs Acreman said, 'come in.'

Lucy stepped inside and smoothed her dress down. Mrs Acreman showed her to a seat. It was padded and soft and felt almost as comfortable as her bed.

Lucy eyed the other women in the room. There were six of them including her. Three were elderly and sick-looking. Mothers of *Titanic* victims, Lucy reasoned. Two were her age. She made eye contact with them and one of them looked away. The other smiled faintly.

'All these ladies like you lost a man on the *Titanic*,' Mrs Acreman said. 'This is your place of refuge to rest, to talk and to grieve.'

She handed Lucy a cup of tea. It was on a saucer. Lucy didn't even own saucers. She held it under her cup and watched it wobble. The girl who'd smiled at her stifled a friendly giggle and Lucy smiled back. After tea, Lucy moved nearer to the girl who'd seemed friendliest.

'I'm Ada,' she said.

'Lucy,' she replied.

'Who did you lose?' Ada asked.

'My husband, Joseph,' she said. 'He was a stoker.'

Ada nodded. 'Mine was my husband, Harry,' she said. 'He was a steward.'

They talked and Lucy learned that although Ada too hailed from Southampton, their paths would never meet. Ada lived in an area called Freemantle, a suburb of the city. When Lucy explained where she lived, Ada bit her lip.

'Where the streets always flood, by the margarine factory?' she asked.

Lucy nodded.

'Must be hard now,' Ada said.

Lucy shrugged.

'I've got my mother, and Harry's mother,' Ada said. 'Thankfully we had no children. Although on occasion I wish we had. It might have been something to remember him by.'

Lucy thought of Florence upstairs. 'I have a daughter, Florence, and one on the way,' she said, touching her stomach.

Ada's eyes widened. 'I wish you well' she said. There was no malice there. She meant it.

Lucy's stay at the house was one week. Over the days that passed, she stuck with Ada. The two of them promenaded along Worthing's seafront. Lucy was shocked at how sea air could smell and taste so fresh.

'I thought Southampton was a sea town,' she said. 'But now I know why some people say the sea is good for you. This actually smells nice!'

Ada smiled, breathing in the salty air as the sea wind whipped her face. 'Well, it is supposed to be health-giving,' she said. 'Even the Royals come here!'

They walked on, feeling the sun on their faces and talking. Lucy told Ada all about how she'd met Joseph, how they'd taken a gamble and swapped the farming life that had no future for a seafaring one.

Ada told how her husband had only gone to sea because his two brothers had gone before him.

'But they came home,' Ada said.

Back at the Dolling Home that evening, the women ate a hearty meal of kidney pie and fluffy potatoes. Dessert was a fruit pudding. Lucy ate every morsel and looked at her empty plate. She could eat it all over again.

'We may be inmates,' Ada whispered, leaning in towards her. 'But the food is good!'

When the week was over, Lucy packed her bag. She didn't want to leave. The bedroom that had become hers was filled with light and promise. The bed didn't creak or hurt her back. The mattress and eiderdown had cocooned her like a matronly kind woman giving her a hug each night. Even

Florence had taken to the seaside, enjoying the sea air and watching the birds and seagulls.

'Shame it has to end,' Ada said, meeting her in the hallway.

They took the train home together. At Southampton Central Station, they lingered a while.

'I probably won't see you again,' Ada said, 'Freemantle's quite a way from Northam. And I have no reason to go there.'

'I know,' Lucy said.

'But here's my address, in case you ever need it,' Ada said, passing her a scribbled piece of paper.

'I'll write,' Lucy promised.

'Good luck to you,' Ada said, giving her a peck on her cheek.

'And to you,' Lucy replied.

And then Ada turned and walked away.

When Lucy turned the key in her lock in Northam, her heart sank. She stepped through the doorway and was met with a dark, dank hovel. The stench of mould and damp hit her first. When she was home, she never noticed it. Now, after sleeping in a clean, warm room, this place smelt to high heaven.

She walked in and placed Florence in her pram which she'd left by the front door. She hadn't taken it on the train. She wandered into her kitchen and looked at the mould on the ceiling and the dirty floor. The 'rest' was over.

Now it was back to reality.

# Chapter Twenty-Eight

**Catherine**

Sometimes his hands shook, sometimes they didn't. Sometimes he'd stare into space, other times he would be 'with it' but then lose interest and look 'through' you rather than at you. Catherine stood on one side of the cobbler's counter now and Percy stood on the other, his apron on ready to serve.

Catherine drummed her fingers on the wooden desk and cleared her throat. 'You know, I talked to Ernest a few days back?' she began. 'Susan's brother.'

Percy was hunched over the hobbing foot mending a shoe. He had the contraption between his legs, a bradawl for boring holes lying next to him and a hammer and nails next to that. 'Oh?' he said, working harder on the shoe.

'Yes. And he said what he saw gave him the horrors. On *Titanic*, I mean,' she said.

Percy nodded, turning the shoe over, checking its soles.

She leaned in and reached for his hand. She stopped it, held it fast. He gripped the shoe tighter. 'You see, I would like it if you could tell me about what happened on that night,' Catherine said. 'I reckon if you did, you and me would feel much better.'

Percy's hand stiffened under hers. He tried to move but she gripped harder; she'd learnt that from the best – his mother.

'We can wed, Percy, but not with you like this,' she said. 'Tell me what happened on the ship.'

Percy put the hobbing foot down. His father was sleeping upstairs. His mother had gone to the weekly market. He stepped out from behind the counter and walked to the shop door. Catherine watched as he turned the paper sign in the window from 'open' to 'closed.' He came back and sat on a bench, the bench where ladies usually sat to try boots on. He rested his fists on his knees.

'At first, I couldn't believe my luck,' Percy began.

Catherine sat next to him now, pulling her skirts from under her to get comfortable. She listened.

'I was so proud … so proud of everything. My uniform. My shoes. My shiny buttons. Proud I had a sweetheart back home,' he added, turning to her. He bit his lip and looked at his hands.

'I was shown to the quarters I'd be working in. First class bedroom steward was my job. I had a family to look after – a wife, her husband and one daughter. They had a suite. Beautiful it was. Like something out of dream. I couldn't believe I was even in that suite,' he said. 'I'd turn the bedding down, turn it back again, clear up their tea cups and make sure the temperature was just right. I'd clean the glass in an adjoining door in the suite. I …' he shook his head again and smiled. 'I was walking on air, Catherine, truly I was.' He took a deep breath.

'The lady was a cold one. But her daughter was a lovely thing. So well turned out. Always looking nice. The gentleman was kind. Every time he saw me of a morning, he'd hand me a tip. Same every evening. I'd made twelve shillings in my first half day!'

Catherine's eyes widened. Susan had told her how Lucy was living off twelve shillings a week from the Relief Fund. 'Go on,' she said, quietly.

'As I say … they were good. I believe we're taught to hate 'em, Catherine, but they were good. Nice decent people.

As the ship sailed, I got used to the movement. I didn't like it at first. Two other stewards on my deck were sick at night! I wasn't. I was feeling proud of myself and wondered what my mother would have said. Little Percy getting his sea legs! When my shift ended, I'd go to my quarters. I shared with three other stewards, all from round here. I recognised one in the bunk across from me and realised it was John Steel. We'd been at school together! So we had a good old catch up ...'

Percy was smiling at the thought of it. Then his face suddenly darkened. 'On the night it happened ... on that night, well the boat was gliding. She was just gliding because the sea was so calm, you see? There was barely a wave. And I was polishing a window and looked out and all the stars were out. So many of 'em. I'd never seen so many before. There were thousands. So bright and shiny, like God had tossed a load of diamonds up in the air and seen where they fell. I was on my shift, waiting at the suite for the family to come back from their dinner. The gentleman liked to stay late. He had a thing for brandy. The lady and the little girl would wait with the other women, then he'd come back with them all together. Well, they were just coming back down the corridor when there was the most ungodly noise and movement. It made the lady fall against one side of the corridor. Then I saw on this night the gent was with her. He had to steady her from falling when the ship moved. The little girl was giggling ...'

Catherine nodded, urging him on.

'I opened their suite door for them and let them in. The gentleman slipped me a few coins, as usual, and I thanked him. They closed their door. I waited there a little. I had to be relieved, you see, by the next shift. But no one came. Then, next thing I saw, was some officer type in uniform running down the corridor. He was holding life vests. He pushed me aside and banged on the family's door ...'

Percy frowned, flexing his fingers before forming them into tight fists once again. 'Next thing, things seemed to speed up. The family ran out, the lady and the girl in their life vests. The gentleman followed them up, carrying his. They were being urged to get onto the deck. The girl wanted to get her dolls, but she was told not to and she started to cry then. Her mother just said she was tired, but I could see it wasn't that. They were scared. No one knew what was going on. Other families from my deck came past, all in life vests. Some were in their nightclothes where they'd been asleep. Some had night dresses on with top coats over the top. It felt like a strange dream. I'd seen this people in their finery. Now I was seeing them in their night clothing. Everyone was ushered up off our level. Next thing, someone's shoving a life vest at me and telling me to get up to the deck.

'I honestly thought at that point it was a drill. I reckoned this was a test, because the boat was new, you know, and it had to be realistic. But then I thought, No, that can't be. They wouldn't do that to these rich folk, would they?'

Percy noticed a pair of shoes that were not symmetrical in the window. He got up and adjusted them. Then he came back and sat down.

'Go on,' Catherine said.

He breathed in sharply. She could see his pulse twitching in his neck. 'Up top, it was so cold. You could see your breath coming out like smoke. It was chaos up there, people running, people crying, some people standing still not believing a word of it. Someone was saying her engine had failed but then I heard two officers talking about a leak. I knew then we were in trouble.' Percy closed his eyes. 'Do you know, amidst all that, there was the softest, most beautiful music playing?' Percy said, keeping his eyelids shut. 'I could see a violinist and some others playing a hymn. It was so soft. It seemed they were lost in their own world. All around people were running and crying but these musicians just carried on playing their tune. It made me stop and take a bit of comfort, I think.' Percy opened his eyes. Catherine could see tears forming, welling in them.

He swallowed hard. 'What happened next is the hard bit,' Percy said, his voice husky. 'I saw my gentleman again. He was pushing his wife and the girl to a boat. He noticed me and told me to get them in. They weren't listening. So, I grabbed the lady as nice as I could and I said, "Get in the lifeboat, Madam, you must." The girl was sobbing and reaching for her father. He was pushing her away, almost violent, like. He told her women and children had to get in that boat and that he would get in another one. The child was still crying but the mother was dry-eyed. I think she knew he was lying. They got in a boat and it was lowered down. He stood at the top looking down at the, and waving. When they could no longer be seen, he turned to me and said, "That's it for us then." Then he walked away, his hands behind his back. I didn't know what to do. We were being told to get people into lifeboats and not get in ourselves. I felt ashamed because I just wanted to get in one, to get back to you, to Mother …'

A tear fell down his cheek now. 'But there were women and children everywhere and I knew they had to go first. So I stood back. It was a while later that someone in a boat called to me, another steward. He was sitting in it. I didn't understand why. He yelled over, "Get in! There's a space here!" Well, first I looked around me 'cos I knew that if a woman or child was there, I had to let them first. But my part of the deck was empty. I stood there. It must have been seconds. I knew, I promise you, if a woman came I'd have pushed her in it. I swear it. But no one came. So I made a choice. I chose to live. I climbed over the side and got in the boat. I was the last one in. Then it was lowered.'

Catherine watched as Percy put his head in his hands. 'It was only when we were in the water, when we were rowing away, that I saw it. There were women and children in the water. I thought they had all got in boats, that's why I got in. I swear it!' he gasped, weeping.

Catherine nodded.

'You must believe me,' he said. 'I had no idea there were some women left. But there more than some, there were dozens, some with children, some without, some crying, some screaming, some begging for help. One woman was crying "Oh, it's so cold, so cold …"

She went quiet soon after and just bobbed there in the water. We never went back for them because our boat was full. Then, I don't know when this happened, because I was so cold my head ached and my eyes were stiff with the cold. But I saw *Titanic* suddenly get pulled down by the water, as if some great big hand was pulling it down just like a toy. Then it was gone and the water was black again. All the lights went. It was pitch dark, except for the stars.'

Percy's hands were trembling again. He was weeping now and sobbing. His face covered in tears. 'I swear, I swear, I swear, Catherine, I would never have taken the boat if there'd been a woman on my deck,' he was saying. 'But I can't get their screams out of my head. I can see them, holding their babies up, begging someone to take them … then the silence. That was worst of all …'

Catherine stared at Percy. She reached out her hand and placed it in his. He gripped it. 'I believe you, Percy,' she said.

He looked up at her now, with a flicker of hope and that look of earnest in his eyes. The look he'd had before setting sail. 'Do you?' he ventured.

She nodded.

'And you'll marry me? You'll marry a coward?' he asked.

Catherine held him to her. She said something that she meant with every fibre of her being. 'You're no coward, Percy. You helped women to safety. You waited until you believed there was no women left. You did everything right,' she said.

He sat a little straighter then. He sniffed, wiping his nose with the back of his hand. 'I only went to get tips for you,' he said, looking into her eyes. 'I wanted us to get a house.'

Catherine knew this, how he had longed to provide for her. She nuzzled into his embrace now and let him put his arms around her. And strangely, instead of feeling pity, as she thought she would, or a sense of obligation, she felt pride. A fierce, loving pride. 'Percy,' she said, pulling away and looking at him.

'Yes?' he said.

'I love you.'

Outside a woman holding some boots for repair

peered through the glass door, smiled and walked away.

# Chapter Twenty-Nine

**Lucy**

Lucy shook her head for the umpteenth time and said a vehement 'No!'

'But it will do you the power of good,' Susan was saying, looking at Angelo.

Lucy stared at this dark, foreign man in her front room. He was nodding too and smiling. 'Your little one will enjoy it,' he said, allowing Florence to grab his finger from her spot on the floor.

'What would I do at a fairground?' Lucy asked, wiping her wet hands on her apron.

'Smile a little?' Susan said. She walked over to where Lucy stood. Lucy instinctively put her a hand on her now bulging stomach. 'I know how you are feeling. I lost a brother and father too. But Joseph would want you to smile again,' Susan was saying.

Lucy looked at her baby. She'd gone nowhere for weeks, save for queueing to get some cheaper cuts of meat at the very end of the day, or passing the Salvation Army in the hope of any spare blankets or clothes going.

The only other outing Lucy had taken her daughter on was to Royce's Pawn Shop. There, in the window, she had now worked out which shoes had belonged to Joseph. They were still there. No one had bought them. Perhaps men felt it was unlucky to buy the shoes of a dead man, particularly in a seafaring town where all men went to sea. Lucy longed to buy them back herself, to take them home where they belonged. But some weeks she didn't even have enough money for stale bread. Buying back the shoes would be impossible. She looked at her daughter, starting to stand now and toddle, before crashing to the ground again.

'Eh, eh, eh!' laughed Angelo, scooping her up, and letting the child grab onto his fingers and try to walk again.

'Doesn't Florence deserve a day out at least?' Susan said quietly.

Lucy nodded. The child did deserve some joy. 'All right,' she said, reluctantly.

Next day, Lucy pushed the pram out of her front door and Susan and Angelo were waiting. The walk to the Common took half an hour on a good day but today the streets were teeming with people. Teeming with people who had had enough of death, drawn curtains, black clothes and misery. Mourning, Lucy thought, could only last so long. Life had to go on. It always did. When they finally reached the Common, the colours were what struck Lucy first. Gaudy reds and garish yellows, all the primary colours tossed together on merry-go-rounds and rides, stalls and games. Lucy watched as a man around Joseph's height and build punched the air as his ball hit a coconut in the coconut shy. The stallholder handed him his prize, and the man handed the coconut to his sweetheart, putting an arm around her. Lucy felt a stab of jealousy, gripped the pram and walked on.

By now Florence was sitting up in the pram, struggling to get out. 'Here, let me,' Susan said, lifting the baby out and setting her down on the grass. 'Want to walk, Florence?' she asked.

The child stood, fell, stood, tried to walk and fell again. 'Allow me,' Angelo said, and he heaved Florence up onto his shoulders where she began slapping his cap gently and giggling at his reactions.

Lucy smiled. Her cheeks hurt a little as she did so, so strange was the action to her. But she couldn't help it. If Joseph had been here, he'd be carrying their girl that way on his shoulders. If Joseph was here, he'd have won them a coconut on the shy. *If Joseph was here ...* It was a refrain that went around and around in her head day and night.

They walked on, past the strong man who Angelo stood watching, transfixed. Susan wrinkled her nose at the creature in his tight shorts and stiff, waxed moustache lifting a pair of huge weights into the air. As he lifted them, groaned, grimaced and dropped the weights to the floor, Angelo cheered. Florence laughed now too, clapping her hands again on Angelo's cap.

'I think she likes him,' Lucy said.

Susan smiled.

'And you've taken a shine to him, too,' Lucy added.

Susan blushed and kicked a clump of grass with her boot. 'What of it??' she shrugged.

'You, who wanted to fight government and the King for women's votes,' Lucy said. 'What happened?'

'*Titanic* happened,' Susan said simply.

Lucy nodded at that. She could not argue. *Titanic* had changed all their lives. It made them realise what was important.

'Don't look now,' Susan said, staring over Lucy's shoulder.

She turned and saw a couple walking arm in arm. The woman was licking at a cottony froth of candyfloss. The woman saw Lucy, tried to look away, but it was too late. Instead, she walked over, bringing her partner with her.

'Lucy,' Catherine said.

'Catherine,' Lucy replied. 'Percy.'

Percy doffed his cap and smiled. He seemed oblivious to the strange feeling between the women.

Susan broke the ice.

'Have you been on the merry-go-round yet?' she asked.

'Twice,' Catherine said. 'Percy said no more.'

Percy rolled his eyes. 'Too up and down-y for me,' he

said.

'I take it you're not going on,' Catherine said, eyeing Lucy's bump.

'No,' she said, touching her swelling belly. 'I'm happy watching.'

Angelo came over now, with Florence still on his shoulders. 'This one seems to love the strong man,' he said. 'No matter what he does, how he groans, how he yells, she just laughs! Grown men ran away, but not her!'

Lucy smiled at her daughter, happy as anything to be out in the fresh air, away from their street, the mould, the damp, the memories. With a sudden pang of guilt, she realised she should have done this sooner. She should have brought her baby out before this. She'd kept her prisoner all this time while she sat staring at the walls, hoping Joseph might come home, that it had all been a mistake.

The rest of the day passed in a blur of fast-tempo piped organ music, garishly ornate facades and rides that went up and down, round and round. Lucy thankfully accepted a cloud of white candyfloss that Angelo bought her. The taste of sugary softness on her lips was the first time in weeks she'd tasted anything sweet.

The sun was shining down, couples were laughing and walking arm in arm, children ran between stalls, some holding coconuts aloft and being chased by their friends. It should have been such a happy day. And it was – for Percy and Catherine and for Angelo and Susan.

But not for her. Everywhere she went, even here, a place of such joy and colour, she felt an ache. It was as if half of her were missing, or a limb, or her heart. She felt as if she were viewing the world through a pane of thick glass. She was there, but she didn't *feel* she was there. Would it always be this way?

She was just watching a woman go around and around on her white horse on the merry-go-round when Catherine caught her arm.

'I wanted to say that I want us to be friends once again,' Catherine said, matter-of-factly.

Lucy swallowed. 'Of course we're friends,' she said.

'No, I mean like before,' Catherine said, turning to face her. 'Hating me won't bring Joseph back, you know,' she said.

Lucy averted her eyes. She saw a man on a stall hitting a machine with a hammer and a bell rang out loud. Everyone cheered. She knew Catherine was right.

'I know,' she said finally. 'I was wrong to call you names and to shout at you. I was angry and … I was jealous. Your Percy came back, and my Joe didn't. It was foolish but it didn't seem fair. Especially as you didn't even …' Her voice trailed off.

'I didn't even care for him,' Catherine said, wincing and looking over Lucy's shoulder.

Lucy nodded.

Catherine took a sharp breath then look at Lucy again. 'I didn't, truth be known,' Catherine said. 'Didn't care one jot. I just wanted what he could bring back. Tips you know. I've been dirt poor all my life. I wanted a taste of what it might be like not to be. But I've gone a bit daft since then …'

She smiled and Lucy smiled too. Lucy couldn't help but smile. Who'd have thought it? Stone cold Catherine feeling something akin to caring for someone … even love. She watched as Catherine gazed at Percy, larking about with Angelo and the baby. Lucy watched as something in Catherine's expression seemed to soften. All the hardness and coldness she'd always had seemed to warm up somehow.

Lucy suddenly reached for Catherine's hand. 'Then I'm happy for you. Truly I am,' she said.

Catherine squeezed back. 'And I'm truly sorry for you,' she replied. 'If one man deserved to come back it was Joseph. There's no fairness in life is there …?'

On their way home, the baby asleep, exhausted, and the rest of them wearily carrying coconuts and slabs of cake, they passed Royce's Pawn Shop. Darkness had fallen and a streetlamp cast its light onto the wares in the window. Lucy couldn't help but linger a little. The others walked ahead and only realised where she was a few seconds later.

'All right there Lucy?' Susan called back, stopping.

Lucy pulled her gaze away from the window and caught them up.

When they dropped her at her door and said goodbye, they watched her go inside.

'What was she doing looking through the pawn shop window?' Catherine asked. The smell of candyfloss, the joyful music from the organ pipes, the sound of cheers as someone hit a coconut from its shy, all seemed to vanish in an instant.

'Joe's shoes are still in there, in the window,' Susan replied. She walked off, arm in arm with Angelo, her head down.

Beneath the streetlamp, Percy and Catherine were left looking at each other.

# Chapter Thirty

**Susan**

The four of them stood together in Percy's family cobbler's. The sign in the door read 'closed' but already a queue was forming outside. Mothers had started receiving their compensation and *Titanic* Relief Fund money. At last, many could afford to get the boots repaired that they needed for their children to go to school. Susan was talking and Percy tried to keep his eyes from the queue outside as he, Catherine and Angelo listened.

'I heard he bought them for three shillings but would sell them back for four shillings,' Susan was saying.

Angelo nodded, stroking his chin. Catherine took a deep breath and said, 'All right, then I'm in.'

Percy looked around him. 'I've got ten dozen pairs of men's shoes here. Why not give one of them? Would she realise?' he said.

Catherine rolled her eyes. 'Yes, she would realise,' she said, sighing. 'She wants her husband's shoes back, not a new pair! You dafty!'

Percy blushed. He wandered off to rearrange the window display, avoiding eye contact of the mothers outside. He smiled and hummed to himself. He secretly loved Catherine chastising him. Even when she called him 'dafty' there was a tiny tinge of affection in it, he was sure.

'So, we need to get four shillings,' Angelo was saying.

'Yes. A shilling each. What do you say?' Susan asked.

Angelo nodded. 'Yes,' he said.

'I'm in,' Catherine said. 'Percy?'

He got up suddenly in the window and bumped his head. 'Er, yes my love?'

'Are you in for a shilling?'

He nodded, wide eyed. 'Well yes, of course,' he said, hurrying over to the till.

'Here,' he said, looking over his shoulder to ensure his mother wasn't there. The till made a loud ker-ching as it flew open. Percy took a shilling from inside and handed it to Susan.

Angelo felt in his pocket and got out a few coins. He counted them into Susan's hand. 'There, a shilling,' he said.

'Thank you,' Susan said. She looked at Catherine. She felt around in the small fabric purse she carried against her. Like Angelo, she had to pull a shilling together in coins. She counted them out.

Susan looked at Catherine's hands, so chapped from cleaning and scrubbing, from being plunged into hot water then cold. A shilling was a great deal to all of them but particularly to Catherine.

'Thank you,' she said.

Catherine shrugged.

'That's me. I have to be at the big house. I'll see you,' Catherine said. She wandered over to Percy behind the till, stood on tip toes and kissed his cheek. As she walked away, she reached the door and turned the sign to 'open'. As she stepped outside, three matrons pushed past her.

'At last,' one sighed, shoving her way in.

'It's ten past!' another hissed, a basket over her arm knocking into Catherine's hip.

Inside, Percy was still holding a hand to his kissed cheek and staring straight ahead, grinning inanely and feeling like the luckiest man in the world.

Susan and Angelo stepped outside. 'Come with me?' Susan asked.

'Of course,' he replied.

They walked across the street, down a lane, and into another road lined with shops. They reached Royce's Pawn shop. The door was wide open.

Angelo motioned for Susan to step inside first.

A large man with a red nose, a ruddy pair of cheeks and a pair of glasses walked forward from the back of the shop and stood behind the counter. He lay his hands down flat and Susan noted with disgust they looked like ten fat sausages splayed out. 'Can I help you?' he said, smiling the most unfriendly smile she had ever seen.

She had never been in a pawn shop. She knew her father had many times, and her brothers. But the smell, the dust, the mustiness, and this man's unpleasant demeanour made her feel sure she would never enter such an establishment again.

Angelo sensed her unease. 'We have come to buy back a pair of boots,' he said.

The man's face morphed into a sneer. 'Ah, Italian, are you?' he said. 'We get a lot of you in here lately. Coming up like mushrooms my wife says.'

Angelo ignored the remark and walked to the window. 'Which pair, Susan?' he asked.

She went over and pointed to the pair Lucy had shown her days earlier on a walk past. 'This pair,' she said.

The fat man waddled over. As he did, Susan cast a glance around the shop. There were men's best shoes everywhere. But there were sights that were worse, that made tears well in Susan's eyes.

One on shelf sat a row of children's school boots, pawned by their families to afford food. On another there was a rail with children's school coats and pinafores. Again, pawned by families so desperate they had to decide between their child's clothing for education or bread.

As he came nearer, a stench of stale underarm sweat washed over Susan and she grimaced.

The man picked the pair up, looked underneath, noted a number, replaced the boots and then walked back to his desk where a fat ledger sat. He opened it up, turned the pages, lubricating them with spit as he went until he came to a date in April. 'Ah, Joseph Williams, *Titanic* stoker,' he read, looking at Susan over his glasses. 'Didn't make it back, I take it?'

Susan looked at the floor.

The man continued. 'Of course, some would say if these stokers weren't forever drinking their pay away, they wouldn't need to pawn something as essential as a pair of boots, don't you think?'

Susan met his gaze. Her heart quickened. 'We want to buy them back,' she said.

The man smiled. 'Of course,' he replied. He slapped the ledger shut and a plume of dust erupted from it. 'Four shillings,' he said, waddling over to the window and collecting the shoes.

Angelo suddenly stepped in his way. 'You don't feel, as a neighbour of these men who lost their lives, that you might give some small discount to these wives who have nothing now?' he said.

Susan looked at Angelo. His face was full of fury.

The fat man was dwarfed by Angelo's tall frame.

'I am a businessman,' he replied, calmly. Then he pushed past and went back behind his counter. Susan watched as the fat man wrapped the shoes in paper. He pushed them across the counter and held out his sweaty red palm. 'Four shillings,' he repeated.

Susan counted out the money from her purse and placed it on the counter, rather than his hand.

The man noted the slight and smirked. He held one hand against the counter and with the other hand he swept the coins greedily towards him. 'Four shillings exactly,' he said. 'My, my, my …' He opened his till with and placed the coins inside. He handed Susan a receipt. 'Pleasure,' he said.

Susan couldn't help but register disgust.

'Tell her not to spend it on mother's ruin!' the man called out after them.

Angelo's hand formed a fist and he made to turn back but Susan grabbed him around his waist and pushed him out of the door.

When they stepped into the street, both took huge

gulps of fresh air. It wasn't just the stale, musty air in the pawn shop, it was the sense of desperation and despair that lingered there; the desperation of working people handing over boots, school uniforms, pipes, picture frames, jewellery – if they had it.

'Thank goodness,' Susan said, holding the shoes to her breast.

'I'd like to see that man face down in the Solent,' Angelo said, lighting up a cigarette and wincing as he took a drag. '*Che cazzo* ...'

Susan gripped the boots tighter and with her other hand, gripped Angelo's arm. 'We have them back, that's all that matters,' she said.

They walked away.

# Chapter Thirty-One

**Catherine**

Catherine stood on a wooden chair in her mother's kitchen eyeing up a cob loaf that was on the side.

'Can I have some with a bit of marge?' she asked.

Her mother slapped her legs. 'Later, keep still, seven bellies!' she snapped, a pin in her mouth.

Catherine felt she had been standing there forever, her mother murmuring inaudibly through the various sewing pins in her mouth and being tugged this way and that.

'Surely it's all right now?' Catherine said.

Her mother stepped back and admired her work. Catherine stood on the chair in a long yoked dress that was at least fifteen years old. Far from the fashions of the day, it was out of date, nothing like the brides Catherine had seen in the better part of town where she worked. Brides there wore empire line dresses with lacy bodice tops and a mob cap style headdress. This, with its sagging tiered skirts and plain upper bodice looked like something her grandmother would wear.

'Take that look off your face, missy, because this is the best we can do,' Catherine's mother said, standing back again. A few more nips, tucks and curses from her mother, and it was done. When she was finished, Catherine hopped down, pulled the dress down, stepped out of it, to the cries of 'careful!' and 'hey!' and then pulled her day dress back on again.

She hurried over to the kitchen, grabbed the breadknife and sawed her way through the bread. She grabbed a doorstep of the cob loaf, slathered it with margarine and bit into it.

'You won't fit in it if you eat that,' her mother said, folding the dress up.

'Wha' duzzi' ma'er,' Catherine gasped between mouthfuls of bread. 'I loo' li' a sack anyway.'

She and her mother laughed but Catherine's face fell a little. She wandered nearer the door, swallowed the last of her hunk of bread and saw her reflection. She'd always been told she was pretty. For some reason, she'd inherited thick, dark hair, dark eyes and rich thick lashes. She imagined herself on her wedding day in the most modern frock of the time, holding a huge cascading bouquet of roses and greenery, marrying the richest man in town.

How different life was.

Instead, she was dressing in an ancient, yellowing sack frock, marrying a shoe-maker's son who was a trembling mess after surviving *Titanic*. But as she moved a tendril of hair from her face, she thought of Percy and saw herself grinning. True, she'd wanted a strong, rich man. A man who could provide for her. But since meeting Percy, and since he'd come home, something had changed. She didn't know why but something about Percy's vulnerability appealed to her. He didn't shout or throw his weight around like other men. He was quiet, thoughtful. And the way he looked at her ... well, would any man ever look the same way at her? He made her feel ... loved. That was it. Loved and cosseted. It was a nice, warm feeling. She'd never felt it before.

'What'll happen once you're married?' her mother asked, hiding the bread away before it could be attacked further.

'Well, Kezia says I can move in with them and help in the shop,' she said. 'I can leave them pigs up at the big house to clean their own fireplaces. And, once we get some money, we can try and get a place. But at first, we'll have a room above the shop.'

Her mother nodded. 'Better than many girls get, my missy,' she said. 'You heard about Vi Brown's daughter?'

Catherine shook her head.

'Lost her husband on *Titanic*, four children, now in the workhouse,' her mother said. 'Took to drink, had her money stopped from the relief fund and now she's in there. They don't reckon she'll see the year out either and her poor mites … well …'

Catherine breathed in and nodded. She was lucky, she knew that now. So many wives, daughters, mothers and sisters of the *Titanic* men who'd died were now in dire straits. She knew of at least two women who had died in childbirth, no doubt from the shock of their husband drowning. Countless others had taken to drink and some had had their children taken away and put in orphanages.

No, she was one of the lucky ones. She had a fiancé, a future. Feeling buoyant at last she skipped over to her mother and planted a kiss on her cheek. 'And will father be sober enough to walk me into church?' she asked.

Catherine's mother shot her a serious look. 'Don't expect miracles, missy,' she said.

At work at the big house the following morning, Catherine scrubbed the front step and heard a noise. She stopped, then realised it was a tune. The tune was emanating from her lips. She was humming. She sat up and put her hands on her knees. She had never hummed before. Certainly not when cleaning a rich family's step.

She felt the folded up bit of paper in her pinafore pocket and knew the reason why. Her notice. Oh, she could not wait to see the look on her mistress's face when she handed that in. A few moments later, the woman returned. She and her three daughters stepped over Catherine as if she was not there as usual. Catherine moved her bucket aside for fear of being splashed again. As her mistress was about to shut the front door, Catherine stood up, wiped her wet hands on her pinafore and said, 'May I speak to you?'

The woman turned. 'To me?' she said, frowning.

Catherine nodded.

'Come around the back,' she replied, before slamming the door in her face.

Catherine stood there, wet through, tired, sweat coursing down her back under her corset. She picked up her bucket and rags and heaved it along the side of the house, around the back and to the tradesmen's entrance. She walked down some steps, into the kitchen scullery, left the bucket there, dropped the rags into the Belfast sink, and steadied herself.

She felt in her pocket and pulled out her handwritten letter. She re-read it once again. *'I am giving notice as of the end of this week on account of my marridge.'*

She knew she'd spelt things wrong. What did it matter? The woman could work it out. She tucked the letter back into her pinafore pocket and hurried up the servants' staircase, she opened a door and was suddenly in the house hallway. She wandered to the morning room, waited outside the door and stood there.

She could see her mistress through a crack in the door. She was rearranging some flowers. Catherine coughed. Nothing. She coughed again. The woman came to the door and opened it fully.

'Ah, yes, you, do come in,' she said. 'I had quite forgotten.' The woman went to her mahogany writing desk and sat down.

Catherine lingered by the door.

'Come on then, out with it,' she said.

Catherine walked nearer, her hand over the letter in her pocket. She pulled it out and carefully placed it on the writing desk.

The woman unfolded the letter. She read it, before placing it back on the desk.

'So, you are leaving,' she said.

Catherine nodded and cleared her throat. 'Yes, ma'am,' she replied.

'And who is your husband-to-be?'

Catherine wiped her hands on her skirts again. 'A shoemaker's son, Ma'am,' she replied.

The woman leaned back in her chair. 'A shoemaker's son,' she said, thoughtfully. 'And was this man not a survivor from the *Titanic*?'

Catherine nodded. 'He was, yes, Ma'am,' she replied.

The lady shook her head. 'Must be so very difficult …' she said.

'Difficult?' Catherine said.

'Yes, walking down the street, having everyone's eyes on you, everyone wondering why on earth a man survived and women and children perished …'

Catherine swallowed hard.

'It beggars belief how they took those places in lifeboats,' the woman continued, smiling, Catherine noted, enjoying this. 'Does he feel embarrassed?' the woman asked, staring at Catherine now.

Catherine felt rage rise within her. She was about to speak, to let it all tumble from her lips, but something stopped her. Instead, she closed her lips tightly, stepped away from the desk and walked to the door. 'Friday will be my last day,' she said curtly.

Then she closed the morning room door behind her.

# Chapter Thirty-Two

**Lucy**

Lucy had no idea why the four of them had chosen to visit her all on the same Sunday afternoon. They all looked stern, worried. For a moment her stomach lurched. After all, when people come to your door without announcement and wearing uneasy expressions, that could only ever mean bad news. But then she realised; there was no more bad news anyone could give her. The worst had happened. Joseph was gone. Half her heart had gone too. There was no more bad news anyone could possibly dish out.

'Come in, then,' she said, stepping aside as Susan, Angelo, Catherine and Percy filed past her into her small scullery.

The men let the women sit at the table. Percy and Angelo stood. Susan, Lucy noted, held a package wrapped in brown paper and tied with string. She placed it on the kitchen table.

'Where's Florence?' Susan asked.

'Asleep,' Lucy replied. She lingered in the kitchen and paused. She didn't have enough teacups. She began, 'I'd make tea, but …'

Susan saw her expression and saved her. 'We don't

want tea,' she replied. 'Do, come and sit here,' she said, patting an empty chair beside her.

Lucy went over. She was huge now, her stomach too large to be restrained by a traditional corset. She gratefully pulled the chair out and sat down.

'Go on,' Catherine said, nodding to Susan.

Susan looked at Angelo. He nodded.

Percy nodded too, gripping his cap in his hands.

Susan pushed the wrapped paper package across the table to Lucy.

'This is for you, from all of us,' she said.

Lucy frowned. What was this? A parcel? Bread and butter? Some groceries? Lucy felt embarrassed and began to flush. 'I have help now, from the Relief Fund,' she said. 'I don't need food.'

Susan shook her head. 'It's not a food parcel,' she said.

'Open it,' Catherine added.

Lucy reached out and felt the string between her fingers. She undid the knot and the string fell aside. She turned the package over and pulled the brown paper apart. She turned it back upright and unfolded the remaining paper.

And then she saw them. A pair of black shoes. At first, she recoiled. She leaned back in her chair, her hands falling into her lap. She stared at the shoes. It took her breath away.

Catherine and Susan exchanged glances, that said, *Have we done the wrong thing?*

The men looked worse. Angelo cleared his throat and walked towards the window, pretending to look outside.

Susan broke the silence.

'I'm sorry ...' she said. 'We thought ...'

Lucy spoke now. 'No, you thought right,' she whispered. She reached forward and picked the shoes up. They were so shiny, cleaned up for the pawn shop window. She remembered Joseph had bought them for their wedding day. He'd never worn them since, keeping them for best.

'I'll wear themm to walk Florence down the aisle,' he'd laughed. 'Not much need for them in a furnace.' She could hear his voice now, ringing out. His laugh, the lilt of his intonation when he became excited or hopeful. This pair of shoes had represented that.

'One last trip,' he'd said.

The shoes were more than a deposit at the pawn shop, more than a way of raising some coins for Lucy to live off while he was away. The shoes had been given as a guarantee of hope, a guarantee of the new life they would surely have when he came home.

One last trip.

Lucy held the shoes on her lap and felt tears fall down her face. Then she looked at her friends – at Susan, at Catherine, at the men who surely loved them.

'You did this for me?' Lucy asked Susan.

'We all did this for you,' she said. 'Angelo, Percy, Catherine and I, we all chipped in, didn't we?' she asked.

They nodded. Percy blushed. Angelo made a circle in the steamed up window with his thumb. Susan looked wide-eyed at Lucy. Catherine picked at a nail.

Suddenly Lucy reached her two hands across the wooden table to her friends. She reached for Susan's hand, then Catherine's. They sat there in a triangle, each squeezing the others' fingers, like a coven of witches.

'You did this for me,' Lucy said again. She leaned across to Catherine, lifted her hand to her lips and kissed it. Next, she did the same with Susan's.

She stood up, carrying the shoes , and took them over to the 'best' sideboard. She moved aside a candlestick and placed the brown paper down. Then she placed the pair of shoes on the top. 'I will keep them there,' she said, gazing at them.

Susan and Catherine nodded.

'You can tell Florence when she's older,' Catherine ventured.

Susan added, 'Something to remember him by.'

Lucy patted the shoes, so shiny and unused. She sat back down and touched her bump. She felt the child moving inside, turning to get comfortable, she thought. She looked at her friends and smiled. 'Do you know, when Joseph first died, I was angry at the whole world,' Lucy said.

Catherine looked at the floor. Susan nodded.

'I thought, why did my Joe die and some didn't?'

Percy blushed and wandered over to the window with Angelo.

'I hated you,' she said, looking at Catherine. 'And I hated you,' she called over to Percy. 'I hated men who didn't go on *Titanic*,' she said to Angelo. 'And I hated anyone who still had a future, the chance to get married, to have children, to have a life. But now I don't hate anyone. Because I know I was truly lucky.'

A tear coursed down her face and into her mouth. She swallowed its saltiness. 'I know I was lucky because I knew true love,' she said, shrugging and smiling. 'I found a man I loved straight away and we wed. We laughed, we had plans, we loved. We had Florence, and now another,' she said, patting her stomach. 'I knew what it was like to get up every single day and feel joy. I never felt alone because even when he was away at sea, I *felt* him thinking about me. And I knew he felt me thinking of him. We were connected here,' she said, touching her head, 'and here,' she said, touching her heart. So, how can I be angry when I have had all that? I have truly loved,' she smiled, tears running down her face.

'And now, you have shown me what wonderful friends I have too,' she said, reaching again for the women's hands. 'So I wish for you both this; a truest love that you can find, a deep love, and a wonderful long life together. I wish you both this – happiness.'

And later, after more tears had been shed and goodbyes had been said, the two couples wandered down the street, Lucy's words ringing in their ears.

As Percy and Catherine went back to his shop, she snaked an arm through his and rested her head on his shoulder.

Susan was planning to walk back to her parents' house, but Angelo stopped her and said, 'Can we walk by the water a while?'

# Chapter Thirty-Three

**Susan**

The moon was full, and it cast a yellow glow on the sea. Catherine could smell sea salt and seaweed on the wind. The breeze was mild now that it was late summer. Angelo held out his arm and she took it as they walked along.

On the horizon, at the docks, another big liner was in. Nothing ever changed. Ships came and went, life carried on. Sailing was in this city's veins.

Angelo kicked at a stone covered in seaweed. He turned to Susan now and his face was lit by moonlight. She longed to reach out and touch his lips, but he began speaking.

'What Lucy was saying back in her house,' he began. 'It was ...' His voice trailed off. He started saying words in Italian she didn't understand – *emotive ... triste ... stimolante ...*

He gazed back at her. 'Sorry, I find it easier in my language sometimes,' he said.

Susan smiled.

He frowned and looked out to sea. 'I had friends on *Titanic* too,' he said.

'You never said anything!' Susan said.

'Oh, I was not close but I had two friends who were

waiters. We knew their families. They drowned.'

Susan shook her head. 'So many died …'

Angelo nodded. 'All this death, all this mourning …'

Susan gripped his hand.

'It makes you want to …'

'Live!' they both said at once.

Susan laughed and Angelo smiled.

'Yes, live,' he said.

'Do you know, my mother said there's no such thing as love for people like us. She says life's too hard,' Susan whispered.

Angelo was silent. He understood. 'Back in Italy, my mother's family were so poor they ate leaves,' he said. 'That's why we came here. It's poverty but a different poverty,' he smiled.

'But I don't agree with my mother,' Susan said. 'I do think people like us can love. I do think people who are hungry, or desperate, or lost, or bereft … I think we can love as well as anyone.'

She turned to Angelo. His eyes shone in the moonlight. He wrapped an arm around her and they walked to a sea wall. It curved slightly round, and they crept around behind it, until they were out of sight of anybody. The night was silent. Some fishing boats bobbed on the water and some masts made a noise as the wind passed them, but nothing else. No voices, no carts, no horses' hooves.

Susan looked into Angelo's eyes. Her heart was racing so hard it made a *swoosh-swoosh*, *swoosh-swoosh* sound in her ears. She felt sure he could hear it too.

'Susan, since I met you I know that I can only love you,' Angelo said.

She nodded, feeling every word he was saying, mirroring them exactly.

'Oh, Angelo, I feel that way too,' she said.

He pulled her towards him, pushing her lovingly yet firmly against the sea wall. She placed her hands flat against it and felt soft wet moss underneath her fingertips. Then her lips found his in the darkness. They felt warm and soft. He kissed her with a hardness then and she had to pull away and gasp.

Her body ached with a strange sensation she had never experienced. It was a sweet ache. She arched her body to his and felt his hands snake lower, past her back, past her waist, touching her thighs now.

She gasped and he kissed her neck. Then suddenly it all stopped. He pulled away, trembling, running a hand roughly through his black hair.

'Angelo?' she said, her voice husky.

'Not here and not like this,' he said.

She stood up against the wall, pushed herself away from it and held herself straight again. 'Have you done this before?' she ventured.

He was silent. Then he saw her gaze and knew it was pointless lying. 'Once, yes,' he replied.

Jealous rage surged through her. It was a stupid emotion, but it gripped her like a vice. 'And yet you won't with me? What is wrong with me? Is it because I am a suffragette? Is it because I am strong? Tell me!' Angry tears filled her eyes. She grabbed her purse which had fallen to the floor. It was wet with mud and seaweed. She made to leave but he grabbed her elbow.

'Susan. You don't understand,' Angelo said.

Moving away from the wall as she had, a streetlamp from a road behind the sea wall caught her face in its light. Angelo could see her usually warm, calm eyes flash with an anger he had no idea she could express.

'Susan, don't you see it is because I respect you ...'

'Oh! Oh! That one, I see!' Susan cried out, her voice on the verge of tears.

She made to leave but he chased after her. He stood in front of her, blocking her way.

'Because I am a strong woman. Because I believe in the vote for women. Because I believe in equal pay. I'm not quite your type of woman, am I?' she spat, pushing past him.

She strode off into the night, through the wet marshy ground and to a tunnel under a bridge that went over the causeway. It was dark down there. A place no woman would dare venture. But she strode on and he chased after he. He pulled her back again and held her fast.

'It is precisely because you are a strong woman that I feel this way about you,' he said. 'Precisely because you do want votes for women and a better life that I respect you.'

Susan wanted to weep. 'I don't want respect!' she cried. 'I want your love, don't you see!'

'Then have both!' Angelo cried out. He grabbed her shoulders and looked into her furious eyes. 'Susan, you are like no woman I have ever met. You are brave. You are fierce. You are true. You are kind. I didn't want to possess your body that way, in the mud, by a wall, by the water. Trust me, it took a lot to fight it. But I want us to do this properly. The right way …'

Susan's head was spinning. She knew she was plain, knew she wasn't the type Angelo could have if he wanted. She had none of Catherine's glamour and none of Lucy's sweetness. Yet now, as Angelo gazed at her, she dared to hope.

'Don't you see, I did not want to do it like that because I want to marry you!' Angelo cried.

Susan stopped. She gasped. It was a sentence she never dreamed she would hear relating to her. 'Marry you?' she whispered.

He let her go now and staggered backwards, back into the wet, manure-strewn street. 'Yes,' he said. 'Susan, will you be my wife?'

She froze then, thinking of all the hurt, the death, the pain, the poverty, the loss, the bereavement. For months a whole city had ached collectively together through their hunger. So why was hope surging inside her whenever she looked at Angelo? She stepped nearer. 'You want me? As your wife?' she said.

He nodded.

'And you know I am not a "wife" type of woman?' she said.

He laughed. 'That's precisely why I am asking you,' he said.

She placed her hands flat against his chest. The feminist within her wanted to push him into the road, to shove him into next week and run home, proud that she'd turned down a patriarchal marriage proposal, a proposal of shackles and imprisonment. But it didn't feel like that. This proposal felt nothing like prison. In fact, it felt like someone was handing her a giant, gleaming key to get out of prison. She realised then she could still have her opinions, could still attend her meetings, could still fight for women's rights. But she had always thought she had to deny herself love. Now, as she looked at Angelo's face, she knew that was not the case.

'Yes,' she whispered, almost inaudibly.

'Yes?' he said,

'Yes, I will marry you!' she cried. She leapt into his arms then and he spun her around. In a house a few yards away, an old lady looked down into the street from her window. She saw a pair of young lovers spinning around and around beneath the streetlight.

Over the sea, the moon shone on regardless, as the boats swayed in the breeze.

# Chapter Thirty-Four

**Catherine**

'Wash-house keys,' the housekeeper barked, holding her veiny old hand out, palm up.

Catherine unhooked the wash-house key and keys to various cupboards for scrubbing brushes in the house from her key belt and handed them over. She held her hand out then for her wages and the housekeeper duly obliged. Catherine opened the package and counted it.

'It's all there,' the housekeeper said. 'Besides I hear you're going to be a great shopkeeper now.'

Catherine was counting under her breath. *It never hurts to count,* her father had always said about pay. Goodness knows he'd been done over enough times by the liners.

'It's all there,' Catherine said.

She unfolded her work pinafore and slapped it onto the servants' table. 'Won't be needing that no more.'

The housekeeper laughed heartily. 'Oh, yes? I think you'll be swapping one pinny for another!' she spat.

Catherine did not care an ounce. The words of this woman – and anyone – simply washed over her. She had never felt more free, never felt her shoulders more relaxed and her spine more straight. She walked to the back door and cast one final look back over the kitchen, the place she'd come to work every day for four years. It smelt of carbolic soap and aching limbs, of shame and starch.

'Cheerio, then,' Catherine said, and she slammed the door behind her.

Out on the street, the early autumn sun beat down. Catherine walked past fine ladies with their frilly parasols up. Where they ran from the sun, Catherine turned her face up towards it. She closed her eyes and walked, precariously, along the roadside, hoping people might move if they got in her way. She felt the sun warm her skin, skin that had been turned down to the floor, steps, the bottom of fires for too long. It was her time to look into the sun. At last.

Back at Percy's cobbler's, she saw him serving a particularly large lady with rotund legs. As she tried to shove her bloated foot into a shoe, Percy was breathing heavily trying to get it to fit.

When he could get away, he hurried over to Catherine.

'How was it?' he asked, searching her face.

'Oh, you know,' she smiled.

Percy's face fell. 'You didn't ... *do* anything did you?'

She knew what he meant. For days, Catherine had been threatening to leave a dead mouse in the mistress's teapot, or to put manure in her writing desk drawer.

'I resisted,' she said.

Percy looked visibly relieved. 'Thank goodness,' he said. He took her behind the counter and held her hand out of view of customers. 'Three days 'til our nuptials,' he said.

Catherine smiled. She stroked his earnest face. 'Three days,' she said.

'Are you ... you know, nervous?' Percy asked.

She looked into his eyes. She knew what he meant. With her beauty and knowing expression, many people surmised Catherine was not a virgin. People talked. She didn't care. But the truth was, she'd only ever kissed one man before Percy. A sailor. Who had turned out to be married. It had put her off.

'I'm not nervous, because it'll be new to both of us,' she whispered.

Percy blushed furiously. His hands still shook now and then. And he still avoided walking down the street on a busy day and sent his mother to serve the *Titanic* widows when they came in the shop. But gradually, bit by bit, the nightmares he had were fading. Sometimes they came back, so huge and with such a force of terror he feared going back to sleep again. But as the wedding day neared, and all the hope that came with that, he began to feel safer, stronger again. With Catherine, he felt he could achieve anything.

'They're unveiling a memorial garden,' Catherine said. 'Up at the common. It's in memory of those that died on *Titanic*. My family are going and Susan and Lucy. Will you come?'

Percy suddenly looked terrified. 'I, I don't think I can. The shop …' he stammered.

Catherine knew better than to try and persuade him. 'All right,' she said. She kissed his cheek and made off for home. 'Until our wedding day,' she said.

He nodded and waved. 'Until then,' he said.

Back at her house, her mother was bending over her father, who was collapsed at the table.

'He's back,' Catherine said. Her father had been away two weeks on *Olympic*.

'Yes, back via the King's Arms,' she said, rifling through his pockets for his wages.

Catherine sat at the table, opposite her comatose father.

'Why do you think they do it, Mother?' she asked.

'Do what, girl?' her mother said, finally adding, 'Aha!' as she pulled his wages packet from his pockets.

Catherine watched as her mother hurried to the kitchen and hid the wages under a pot.

'Drink until they can't think or feel,' Catherine said.

Her mother came back over, satisfied her drunken husband would not find his wages again and sat down. It made for a strange scene – two women talking over the huge, comatose form of a man snoring drunkenly and emitting the stench of a brewery at the kitchen table.

'To escape,' her mother said finally.

'Escape what?'

'Oh, the life, the worry, the doubt, the fear of no work, the fear of dying at work. The furnace. The fire. The coal. The shovels. The worry of eating up to get strong before you go on the ship and the worry of coming home two stones lighter and so parched you're like paper. The senseless fightin' at the docks for a half day's work. I begrudge him, you know I do,' she said, hitting him hard on the arm. 'But I do understand it.'

Catherine nodded, looking at her father. Like all the stokers, he was hard, burly, smelly, drunk and angry-looking. People joked locally you wouldn't want to pass an angry stoker on a dark night. Others talked of stokers who disappeared, long before *Titanic*.

*'Another stoker took umbrage on the ship in the boiler rooms ... A fight broke out ... they fed him into the furnace. He never came home.'*

This was the type of men stokers were. Catherine knew nothing of soft cuddles, of loving words or encouragement. All she knew of her father was his burly mass, his drinking, his fighting, his hardness.

Was that why she had chosen Percy? Had she subconsciously wanted to escape the pattern that life had handed down from generation to generation; of angry hard women, and even angrier husbands, of drinking and fighting, not living but surviving?

She remembered her childhood playing in the street with Susan as their fathers strode off together, kit bags over their shoulders off on another trip. She recalled their mothers standing together, trying to work out the best way to survive another few weeks, sharing what food they had, helping each other out with fabric for pinafores.

She remembered in a class of twenty, seven of her friends dying of diphtheria as children. She also remembered how, as tiny coffin after tiny coffin made its way down her street, half of those mothers didn't even weep. Most already had at least six children. Life was cheap.

'They're unveiling a memorial garden tomorrow,'

Catherine said to her mother. 'I'm going along with Susan and Lucy.'

'Susan lost her brother and father, didn't she?' her mother asked.

Catherine nodded sadly.

'I'll be there. And so will this great oaf if he knows what's good for him,' she added, smacking him again.

# Chapter Thirty-Five

**Lucy**

Lucy craned her neck and stood on tiptoe, but it was useless. She could barely see a thing.

'Here,' Angelo said, 'let's try this way. He led Lucy and Susan away from where they were standing and to a different part of the crowd. A few yards away, a man was selling drinks. Angelo ran over and when he returned he was carrying an upside-down bottle box.

'Here stand on this,' he said.

Lucy reached out for his hand and stepped up onto the box. Susan was holding Florence's hand. She was now walking and refused to sit in her pram.

'Thank you!' Lucy said. 'I can see!'

They were gathered on Southampton Common to see the grand unveiling of a memorial garden to those lost on the *Titanic*. Catherine was supposed to have joined them with her mother, but the crowds were so large they hadn't found her. Lucy felt wobbly on the box, her bump threatening to topple her over at any time. Susan held her up and smiled.

'Thank you,' Lucy mouthed.

Some way away, the mayor of Southampton, Henry Bowyer, was talking about the plants and flowers that had been put together in honour of those lives lost on the Titanic.

Lucy strained to hear what was said.

# The Titanic Girls

'This is the memorial garden to the crew of those stewards, sailors and firemen onboard RMS *Titanic*,' the mayor was saying.

Lucy cast her mind back to the young lad who had come to her door weeks earlier, his hand out, asking for donations to a memorial to the *Titanic* crew. He'd lost his father on board, he had told her. She had only managed to get together a few coins, butt he had taken them gratefully. At least she had contributed in some small way.

'This Memorial Garden was created in memory of the crew who lost their lives on the SS *Titanic* disaster,' the mayor said. 'April 15th 1912.'

A strange non-cheer erupted from the crowd. A cheer felt wrong. A cry felt too loud. Silence was not enough. A noise of acknowledgement instead went through the hundreds of people there. Lucy clambered down from the box and thanked Angelo. 'You're kind,' she said. 'I'd not have seen it if it weren't for you.'

Angelo smiled. 'Niente,' he said.

Florence, always graduating towards men since her father had disappeared, toddled to Angelo and reached up to be carried on his shoulders. He obliged and he carried her while Susan and Lucy walked ahead.

'Well I am glad I saw that,' Lucy said, trying to sound bright.

Susan looked at her. She noticed how large Lucy suddenly seemed.

'How are you?' Susan asked.

'Oh, I am well,' Lucy said, stroking her bump.

'And Ernest?' she asked.

Susan shrugged. 'Gone back to sea,' she replied. 'Mother still talks about Jack as if he might come home. She says there can be no way of really knowing who drowned and who didn't without bodies …' She suddenly saw Lucy's expression – a mix of hope and horror – and stopped. 'Don't pay me any mind,' Susan said. 'I'm sorry.'

Lucy walked on.

'How long left?' Susan asked.

'Mrs Stoat …'

'Stout!' Susan laughed.

'All right, Stout,' Lucy smiled. 'Well, she seems to think October.'

'And will you manage? When the baby comes, I mean?'

Lucy nodded. 'Well. I get my compensation each month, and with what I get from the relief fund and the Lady Visitor sometimes brings me a food parcel. I manage …'

Lucy looked at her feet as she walked. *Manage*. That was all a widowed, working class woman could hope to do. 'Speaking of which, I have the Lady Visitor coming later today so I need to be on my way,' Lucy said. She waited for Angelo to catch them up, helped the child down and thanked him.

Back at her house, Lucy set the child down to play and set about tidying up. She stuffed clothes in cupboards, lay a blanket flat on the arm chair, put her pots and pans away and opened a window to let the smell of mould escape. She sat down and surveyed her home. It wasn't pristine. The mould that was on the ceiling in just one corner a few weeks ago had now spread to half way across to the kitchen. She could never get high enough to reach it, not in her condition. It was something Joseph would have done in a heartbeat, if he'd been home.

She closed her eyes. She was tired. So tired. She was tired of smiling for others whose lives were moving on, as they should. She was tired of tidying her home once a month to ensure she put on her best 'widow' display to be bereft and yet respectable enough to receive her hand out from the charity. She was tired of feeling twenty years older than her years. This should have been a happy time. A new life was on its way. Instead, some days, she only wanted to sleep … and sleep … and not wake up.

Sleep came then. The noise of Florence with her doll evaporated and she was back in Eling, the village where she'd grown up, during haymaking. She was hot and lying on the ground. Joseph was beside her. She leaned in and laid on his chest. She felt his hand on her back.

'We can't stay here,' he was saying.
'I know,' she said.
'You can't stay here,' Joseph said.
'I can't stay?'
'You can't stay with me …'

Just then, there was a knock at the door. Lucy was ripped from her dream, Joseph's voice ringing in her ears. *You can't stay here with me …* What had her dream meant?

She pushed herself up from the armchair and heaved her pregnant body towards the door. She opened and it saw the smiling Lady Visitor there, her bicycle propped up next to the door.

'Mrs Williams,' came the sing-song matronly voice.

'Come in,' Lucy said, letting her pass.

The afternoon passed in the usual way; the Lady Visitor asking how she was, checking Florence over, casting an eye surreptitiously over the house that Lucy was sure could never be clean enough, no surface shiny enough.

'And how old is the girl now?' the Lady Visitor asked.

'A year and four months,' Lucy replied.

'Well it is a way off, but there are scholarships and grants for young pupils to attend schools thanks to the Titanic Relief Fund,' she said. 'I shall put Florence's name down now in good time. That way, she will be sure to get what's rightfully hers when the time comes. A great many of our orphaned students are doing very well,' she went on. 'We have apprenticeships some might never have taken had their fathers not … had their fathers not …'

Lucy stared at the Lady Visitor. 'They would not find themselves in so fortunate a position had their fathers not died,' Lucy clarified.

'Well, yes,' the Lady Visitor said. 'A great many are experiencing pathways to things they might never have dreamed of. Education. Apprenticeships. We even awarded a grant to a young lady who wants to be a seamstress to get her own sewing machine,' she smiled proudly.

Lucy was too exhausted to smile. She didn't want scholarships or apprenticeships or sewing machines. She wanted Joseph back.

The Lady Visitor stood up. 'Well, everything is in order and satisfactory,' she said. 'I will see you in one month's time. More parcels of food now that the baby is imminent?' she added.

Lucy nodded, a blush of shame making its way up her neck. This was the fine line she always trod. The anger at how the widows were treated like dependent babies, but always having to show gratitude and subservience in order to get what she and Florence needed.

'Then I shall arrange that for you today,' the Lady Visitor said. And with that, she let herself out, hopped back onto her bicycle and was gone.

# Chapter Thirty-Six

**Susan**

She'd taught mathematics, English and history so far but try as she might Susan could not concentrate. She cared deeply about the little children in her care. She was thrilled to see they all had boots now, thanks to the Salvation Army and, now, the *Titanic* Relief Fund. But there was still a lost look in most of the children's eyes. Many didn't speak of *Titanic* anymore. It was an unsaid loss they all shared. No one needed to voice it.

But that wasn't why she couldn't concentrate. She was thinking of all the things she had always sworn she was against – a white dress, flowers, saying vows, setting up a home together. How on earth had this happened?

After school, Susan went to Catherine's house. If she didn't know the address, she'd have found it simply by following the shouting and cursing from behind the closed wooden door.

'You'll be there and that's that!' Susan heard Catherine's mother shouting.

A muffled male reply came that was inaudible and Catherine's mother yelled again. 'You can damn well tell them you're not working that afternoon on account of your daughter getting wed!'

The door opened before Susan could knock and a hulk

of a man stumbled out past her. He didn't even recognise Susan or speak. He simply stumbled off across the road the few feet away to the King's Arms.

Susan tentatively stepped inside.

'I came to see the …' her voice trailed off as she saw Catherine wiping the bottom of a pan at the kitchen table with a hunk of bread. 'Er, blushing bride,' Susan said, taking in the dripping falling down Catherine's chin.

It had always amazed Susan how Catherine could get her hands on so much food when no one seemed to have enough. It also amazed her how Catherine looked like something out of a newspaper, a famous singer or dancer from London, and yet she ate more than her brothers put together.

'No nerves then?' Susan smiled, sitting at the table.

Catherine licked her fingers and shook her head. 'No. Why should I have?' she said.

Susan shrugged. 'I don't know. Marriage. A husband. It's a new beginning.'

Catherine's mother came over wiping her hands on her pinny.

'I don't think young Percy has any notion of what he's letting himself in for,' her mother said, ruffling Catherine's hair.

'Get off, Ma,' Catherine said, shoving her hand away.

'St Augustine's, isn't it?' Susan asked.

Catherine nodded. 'Yes. Then finger sandwiches at the back of Percy's shop.'

'Dress all right?' Susan asked.

Catherine shrugged. 'Like a sack from the last century,' she said.

'Shuddup girl!' her mother called from her place back in the kitchen.

Susan leaned back in her chair. 'Truth is, you'd look a beauty even if you were in a sack,' she said. She cleared her throat. 'I'll be … I'll be coming along with Angelo, if I may?' Susan said.

Catherine's dripping-covered face erupted into a mischievous grin.

'Part of being a suffragette is it? Getting wed?'

'I'm not getting wed!' Susan lied. 'I'm just bringing him to your wedding!'

Catherine laughed, spitting crumbs of bread everywhere as she did so, and picking up stray bits off the table and putting them back in her mouth. 'I believe you,' she said. 'Hundreds wouldn't.'

Susan stood up, blushing and far too in love to lie any further. Not to Catherine anyway. 'I'll see you at church tomorrow,' Susan said, before taking her leave.

She stepped through the front door and closed it behind her. Out on the street, the September mild sun sun was shining down. May was the best month for a wedding, didn't they say? Yet as she walked along the streets, that were now thankfully dry for once, she felt all the joys of spring in the air, despite it being the end of summer. A wedding, a new life coming for Lucy, and … and Angelo. Susan put her hand to her mouth to stop passers-by seeing her smiling. It was so involuntary. She couldn't stop it. She shook her head and turned the corner at the King's Arms.

That's when it hit. The sadness. An aching, tugging feeling in the pit of her stomach that told her, no, all was not right with the world. Somewhere, at the bottom of the Atlantic Ocean, her brother and father lay. Their bodies had still been unaccounted for. Her new love with Angelo had been a welcome, incredible distraction. But every few hours, the horror would hit her again as she remembered Ernest's words … *the cold … the horror … the noise … the screams … the dying …*

As she bit back tears, anger surged too. The White Star Line had added extra lifeboats to all their liners in view of what had happened on *Titanic*. There had even been a new international convention drawn up to ensure every boat would always have enough lifeboats, so this horror could never happen again. But the cost of this had been her brother and her father. And countless others.

Five hundred and forty-nine men from Southampton had died on *Titanic*. Many of them fathers, sons, brothers. All breadwinners for their families. And as she walked on, involuntarily towards the sea, Susan felt a familiar emotion that always vied inside her for ownership of her mind. Guilt. How could she enjoy her life when her father and brother were drowned just trying to provide for their family? How could she feel love and excitement and joy, when so many wives had lost their men too young?

She thought of all the children she knew who had lost fathers on *Titanic*. There was the lad whose father had died leaving his mother to raise six of them. There was the little girl whose father had died and her mother was pregnant. Then there were the family of four she'd seen playing in the street who had all been separated when their father had died. Some were in orphanages, some were God knows where.

She walked on, nodding occasionally at some woman she knew. But they all had the same vacant, lost expression. Every other woman she passed was a *Titanic* widow. They shared the same look, a look that said, I survive but no longer live. Gaunt faces, hollow cheekbones from giving what food they had to their children, hunched shoulders from the worry of suddenly being head of a family in a man's world.

A man's world …

Susan had been fighting that until she'd met one of the enemy – a man. She shook her head as she reached the sea and picked up a pebble. It was wet and slimy from seaweed. She threw her hand back and tossed the pebble into the water. She watched it fall with a splash. Regardless of her views on women's rights, on the vote, on the patriarchy she hated, was marriage really a safe haven?

And did she really dare give her heart to someone, completely, utterly, when she knew that person could be all too easily torn away from her?

# CHAPTER THIRTY-SEVEN

**Catherine**

He stumbled away from the sink and Catherine's mother began wiping his face down with a dishcloth. Her father looked at Catherine through soapy eyes and slurred, 'You wearing that get-up to work, missy?'

A slap to the side of his head made him look more awake. 'It's her wedding dress, you oaf! It's her wedding' day today!' her mother cried.

Catherine shook her head and wandered over to the mirror. She had left work days earlier but her father, either inebriated or coming round from another binge, was never truly aware of what was going on. She peered into her reflection. Her face was shiny, rosy, from the harsh scrub her mother had given it over the sink that morning. She'd twisted her long, dark hair into a 'do that she'd seen on the front of a magazine. She pinched her cheeks and smiled.

'I'll do,' she sighed.

She sat at the kitchen table and wondered what Percy was doing now. Her dress made her sit upright, the new corset she had on stiff as a board. She imagined him nervously fiddling with his cravat, shining his shoes until they shone, pacing the cobbler's. He was nothing like the man she believed she'd marry one day. But, truth was, he was everything she wanted. Kindness, honesty, sensitivity and trust, she realised, were worth more than any brash, loud, hard man any day of the week. And even though he had not brought home the tips he'd promised, and she had worried that would break it for her, she now realised that she was not as shallow as even she believed she was.

Percy was a grafter – even his nervous cough had vanished since the hardship of being at sea. He worked long hours, morning until night, in that cobbler's. He'd never go to sea again, never be a steward in first class. But she knew he'd provide for her in the shop, the best way he could. That was all she could ask for.

Her mother walked over to the table now and Catherine gasped, stifling a snigger.

'What?' her mother asked.

Catherine fought the urge to snort. Her mother, who always donned a uniform of misery which consisted of a long brown dress, a grey pinafore and a scowl, was wearing a green dress and a hat with fruit decorating it. It looked as if it had seen better days and was rather wonky on one side.

Her mother touched the hat and stuck her nose in the air.

'I won't have that Mrs Lynch down the road sayin' I didn't look my best today!' she said.

Catherine stood up and hugged her hard, bony mother. 'Oh, no one will miss you today, Ma,' she said, avoiding her eye being taken out by a sprig of something that looked like cherry blossom but wasn't.

The church was not full. Despite its size that could accommodate hundreds, a working class wedding was a quiet affair. Percy waited at the front, his mother fiddling with his collar. His father sat quietly nearby, smiling and shaking his head, still in shock their son had come home.

Susan and Angelo sat in a pew with Lucy and Florence.

'Here, let me,' Susan said, taking Florence. The child

was in her best frock and smiled at Susan, reaching for her hair.

Lucy, no longer having to hold her wriggling daughter, looked around. There had been a service here, a vigil, days after the *Titanic* disaster. She vaguely remembered standing at the back, for it was too busy to get a seat. She remembered the vicar's words, so patriotic and rousing.

'The widows will be able to teach their children that their fathers died as Christian Englishmen should die; that England would always remember them with thankful pride, and that England was the better for what they did …'

She closed her eyes, recalling another line he had said. 'The heroic steadfastness with which the crew remained at their posts in order that others might be saved teaches us that we share a common humanity …'

Lucy felt tears rising. But then a creaking of a wooden door opening made her turn.

Outside the church, Catherine stepped through into the church porch. Her father, she knew, was supposed to be leading her, but it was Catherine well and truly leading him.

Her mother spat on a hankie and wiped her father's face. 'Now, remember, walk her in, get her to the front, sit down, stay quiet,' she whispered.

Her father nodded, looking around him at a building he had not set foot in in over forty years.

Her mother slunk inside and Catherine heard her footsteps echoing on the tiles of the church floor. When her mother had taken her seat, Catherine said, 'Now, father.'

They entered into the aisle. Catherine gripped her father's arm and walked him along. As she neared the front, she saw a man waiting in a smart wool suit. When he heard the noise of her boots, he turned around.

His hair had been slicked to one side and he wore a stiff, starched collar and cravat. For the first time in her life, Catherine's stomach did a somersault. As Percy smiled at her, the kindness and love he felt for her was tangible. She could almost touch it. He took in her dress, so simple and old-fashioned, yet so lovely. She cast her eyes to the floor in the best coy expression she could muster, before looking up and meeting the vicar's gaze.

'Please, be seated,' he addressed the handful of people in the congregation.

The words that followed were a blur. It was obey this, and thou shalt not that, but Catherine smiled her way through it and nodded in all the right places. Then she heard the vicar say something and time seemed to stop. She paused, then registered what had been said.

'You may now kiss the bride.'

Percy gazed at her. He had never looked so ... was the word 'handsome'? Catherine looked at him. Yes, she thought. The word was indeed 'handsome'. He had changed since *Titanic*. The baby face had become that of a man. The soft, rounded jawline seemed to have hardened in his distress.

For a second Catherine wished there was no one else in the church. She closed her eyes and felt something connect with her lips; Percy's lips. He kissed her and she felt no fireworks, no jolt of electricity. But what she felt was something warmer, bigger, better. She felt in that kiss a promise of faithfulness, of protection and true love.

She opened her eyes, pulled away and smiled at him.

What followed was another blur. Catherine stepped out of the church porch, holding her new husband's arm. Angelo and Susan threw rice down on the new couple. Percy protested but Angelo said, 'It is what we do in Italy!'

Catherine laughed, shaking stray pieces of rice from her hair.

Back at the shop, the wedding party passed the pairs of shoes and boots and arrived at the back to a spread of finger sandwiches, cakes and pork pies. Kezia smiled proudly as she welcomed Catherine's parents.

Catherine tried not to giggle as she saw her father lean into Percy's father and say under his breath, 'Any ale?'

Susan had managed to get a gramophone from a colleague and music began to play. Elsie Baker's *I Love You Truly* rang out into the shop.

*'I love you truly ... My dear ... Life with its sorrow, life with*

*its tear … Fades into dreams when I feel you are near*
*For I love you truly dear.*
*Ah, love, tis something to feel your kind hand*
*Ah, yes, tis something by your side to stand*
*Gone is the sorrow, gone doubt and fear*
*For you love me truly*
*Truly dear …'*

Percy held out his arms and Catherine stepped forward. The pair danced in the back of the cobbler's, Catherine seeing boxes of boots and shoes all around as she slowly turned. The song was a slow, romantic tune. Elsie Baker sang with a heartfelt sound that was verging on melancholic. Yet, the words … Catherine felt the words with all her heart. 'Tis something to feel your kind hand …'

It was exactly how she felt with Percy.

And as the song ended, and her family and friends clapped and cheered, Catherine smiled, tipped her head back and felt like the happiest, luckiest girl in the world.

No one noticed, in the midst of joy, and happiness, as Lucy took Florence's hand, backed away, and silently stepped out through the shop door.

# Chapter Thirty-Eight

**Lucy**

She was thankful for the thick, not-at-all-delicate finger sandwich stuffed with corned beef. She watched as Florence greedily devoured one before holding out her sticky hand and asking for another. Lucy handed her the other sandwich from the wedding spread she'd stuffed into her pocket and on they walked. It was early afternoon. Bright sunlight beat down. Catherine and Percy would still be dancing to gramophone tunes and the others would be drinking and eating and laughing.

She just couldn't.

She couldn't face going home either.

So, she'd taken some wedding sandwiches and decided they would take a walk. Florence, now tired, held her hands up to be carried. Lucy touched her bulging stomach and then bent down to Florence's level.

'Mother can't, sorry, my love,' she said. 'But hold my hand and we'll walk to the sea.'

Florence held her mother's hand and on they walked. As they passed the bakery, Mrs Dean, the baker's wife, was cleaning the front window.

'Eh, Lucy, dear, how are you?' she asked, getting down

from a footstool.

Lucy tensed, dreading the questions.

'Oh, so so,' she replied, touching her stomach.

'Not long left now,' Mrs Dean said, nodding at Lucy's tummy.

'Around two months, so they say,' Lucy said.

Mrs Dean shook her head. 'Must be hard,' she said. 'Mrs Woodyard – you know her?'

Lucy nodded.

'She lost her husband, a second class steward on *Titanic*, and now her two children been taken off her!' she said. 'She couldn't cope with them no more!'

Lucy took a sharp breath. This was on everyone's lips, all the time. Who was suffering, who had lost this, who had lost that. She reached for Florence's hand. 'I have to go,' she said, quietly.

'Oh, all right, then. Cheerio-bye!' the baker's wife called out.

Lucy trudged on. She kept hearing tales of *Titanic* widows unable to cope, having to go into a workhouse, having their children taken away into orphanages. She held Florence's chubby hand tighter. That would not happen to her. She could manage with two children. She could. She would …

'Lucy!' came a voice, coming up behind her.

'Susan, go back, enjoy yourself,' Lucy said, walking on.

'I can't leave you,' she said. 'You should have stayed. There'll be cake in a minute. Fruit cake.'

Lucy smiled. 'Tempting,' she said, sadly. 'But no thank you.'

'Where you going?' Susan asked.

'Oh, nowhere,' Lucy said. 'To the sea, probably.'

'Can I come along?' Susan asked. 'I could do with it, the amount of corned beef I've eaten today.'

Susan smiled and Lucy nodded.

They reached the sea front. Susan blushed as she saw the sea wall where she and Angelo had kissed a few nights earlier.

The tide was out today and Florence was stepping over

the wet stones, slipping in her best shoes.

'Careful, Florence,' Lucy said, gripping her hand tighter. 'Stay near Mother.'

The child saw another corned beef finger sandwich in Lucy's pocket grabbed it, and sat on the stones to eat it. Finally, not having to watch her, Lucy stared out to sea.

'Ever wonder where they are now?' Lucy said, not taking her eyes from the horizon.

'Who?' Susan asked.

'Your father, your Jack, my Joseph,' Lucy replied.

Susan looked down at the stones covered with tendrils of seaweed. 'I try not to,' she said, quietly.

Lucy suddenly turned to her. 'You see. I can't stop thinking about it. I try not to. Truly I do. But I can't. I imagine him swimming, trying to survive, then sinking and sinking down, down, down and all the while me not knowing a thing here. They found bodies. That ship the *Mackay Bennett* brought some up. Why not Joseph? Why not your brother and your father?'

Susan looked at the skyline. She felt uncomfortable. She knew the answer, but would it help?

Lucy stared at her friend. 'I read in a paper some rich passengers were retrieved and given burials. Why not our men, Susan? Why?'

'Because they were poor!' Susan suddenly blurted out. Her voice echoed off the sea wall. A seagull, disturbed, flew away.

'Pardon?'

Susan stared at Lucy. She was so naïve, so sweet, never quite savvy enough for the city.

Lucy looked at her friend and sought answers in her eyes. 'Go on,' she said.

'I read about the *Mackay Bennett* as well,' Susan said. 'Yes, it found a lot of passengers and yes, some crew. But many poor ones ... the poorest of all ... well, they were thrown back in. They didn't see the point. Who could pay to get there? Who could go to a funeral? Who could pay to inter them?'

Lucy was silent as Susan stopped speaking. She

watched as Susan formed a tight ring with her lips and suck in sea air. She looked so much older all of a sudden. 'So, they might have been found and just … just thrown away?' Lucy asked, turning her face to Susan.

She nodded. 'That is what we think happened to Father and Jack. And so many more.'

Lucy was silent. She watched as Florence licked her stubby fingers and kicked at the stones. She couldn't find the words. A man who was the most precious thing in the world to her, more than a diamond or a ruby, the man who she got up for each day and the man she prayed for every night, was probably at the bottom of the sea bed now, rather than buried and given a proper religious service. Because he was poor?'

'If it's any consolation,' Susan said, wiping her eyes, 'Captain Smith's body was never found either.'

Lucy shrugged.

'No help to you, I know,' Susan added.

'Mrs Smith grieves too,' Lucy said.

'Yes, I suppose she does,' Susan said.

'Except she has money, a fine house, food,' Lucy said. 'Those things must help.'

Susan swallowed and nodded. 'Oh yes I think they really do,' she said.

The wind whipped up suddenly. A cloud covered the September sun and for a moment it felt chilly.

'Strange wind ,' Lucy said, shivering.

'Come on, I'll see you home and later on I'll bring you a slab of fruit cake each,' Susan said, helping Florence up.

Susan began to help the child away, to walk carefully over the wet stones and back to dry land.

Lucy let them walk ahead a little. 'I'll be there,' she called after them.

Susan smiled.

Lucy turned back to the sea. She gazed as far as her eyes would reach. Clouds had formed, causing a grey stripe to slash its way through the previously blue sea.

*The sea … the sea …*

They'd come to Southampton from the countryside for

the sea. The sea had promised regular wages, a house, food in their stomachs. That same sea had stolen the man she loved from her in a second. The same sea that had kept them alive so long had now killed her beloved Joseph. She had not been academic. She'd left school at fourteen. But she remembered a small book of poetry her mother had now. She recalled a poem by a lady poet, Emily Dickinson. Her mother had once attempted to embroider it onto a cushion.

> *'As if the Sea should part*
> *And show a further Sea—*
> *And that—a further—and the Three*
> *But a presumption be—*
> *Of Periods of Seas—*
> *Unvisited of Shores—*
> *Themselves the Verge of Seas to be—*
> *Eternity—is Those—'*

# Chapter Thirty-Nine

**Susan**

Ever since the conversation with Lucy down at the sea, Susan had felt it; a rage that would not sleep. She felt it at school when she was teaching. She felt it when she looked into the eyes of the pupils who struggled in despite poverty, despite the pain in their stomachs, despite their mothers' grief. She walked faster. Angelo noticed.

'Is something the matter?' he asked.

She shook her head. But there was something the matter. It was called life. What she had said to Lucy was hard-hitting and upsetting. She regretted causing her friend any pain. But it was the truth. Their men were gone because of their class. And now, because of the women's class, they too suffered, asking for handouts, being checked by the Lady Visitor to ensure they were behaving themselves and thus still eligible for their award from the Relief Fund. And hand in hand with this, was her desire for freedom for women. Surely women getting the vote was a step in the right direction for every poor person – man or woman? She might have been in love, but her principles were still alive and well.

Days later Susan came to Angelo holding a leaflet. She

slapped it on his ice cream counter and he read it.

'You're going to this?' he asked, eyebrows raised.

'Yes,' she nodded. 'Seven women are in jail in London on hunger strike. I'm going to stand outside with other women and protest. They're force-feeding them!'

Angelo flung a tea towel over his shoulder. 'And how will you help?' he asked.

Susan felt the same anger snake up her neck in the form of a red rash.

'By showing I care!' she said. 'I may have *softened*, no thanks to you. But I still have my beliefs, you know that.'

He nodded.

'And, when I think of the women here, suffering, waiting to be checked to ensure they're behaving just to get their few shillings a week. Do you know, Mrs Beton had her award suspended because she had a few drinks. They said she was an inebriate and threatened to take her children away. Instead of helping or asking why she drinks, they've taken her award away. She'll starve!'

Angelo rolled his eyes. 'Maybe taking those children is for the best,' he said.

'But don't you see, this would never happen to a rich woman! Or the wife of an officer! These women are treated like infantile children, women who can't even organise their own money. Lucy is given her award at 12 shillings a week! They can't even trust them to have it in a lump sum. They want to keep them down, that's why!'

Susan was trembling now, pacing the floor. For weeks, the way the *Titanic* Relief Fund was giving out money had angered her, but now suddenly she was furious. Why did it feel that working class women could not handle their own money? After all, they had been experts at it when their husbands had been at sea. Why did the powers that be think women were unable to handle money now their husbands were gone?

And what about the checks and the way women were discussed? Susan had heard countless stories of women struck off the relief fund because they'd been found drinking, or even if they had begun a relationship with another man.

Children had been taken away, women had been reduced to begging and 'behaving' to get what was owed to them.

She saw the good it did, she knew that. She'd seen children leave her school to go to apprenticeships they would never have had access to without the relief fund. She was grateful for how the food parcels had kept her mother going in the early days after the sinking. But surely, there had to be a better way? A way to give these women a hope of forging their own lives? Not being reliant on hand outs forever?

'The people in charge want these women reliant on them,' Susan said. 'It's not about helping, it's about keeping them poor.'

Angelo folded his arms on the counter. 'I agree with you completely,' he said.

Susan stopped. 'You do?'

He nodded.

'But I thought … I thought you'd tell me women should be grateful for the help.'

He shook his head.

'Not at all. These women deserve all the money that is theirs, not to have it dripped down to them in tiny pieces. But this is how it is. Susan, how do you think supporting the starving suffragettes in London will change this?'

Susan sighed. 'Because it's a start,' she said. 'We can't talk about *Titanic* without talking about suffrage. The very reason these women are so poor and held down is because they are women. If we had the vote, and respect, and freedom, this would not happen. These wives are being tested each month by a woman visiting their homes to report back to a load of men. They're judged if they drink. Judged if they meet someone else. Judged if their children are untidy. This is about women and suffrage! The whole *Titanic* disaster is!'

Angelo nodded.

Susan sat there, seething.

He turned his back, rummaged around in a cupboard, bashed some spoons and metal and then turned around.

'Here,' he said, pushing a bowl towards her. He handed her a scoop of ice cream covered in cream and a toffee sauce.

'What's this?' she said, exasperated. 'I'm talking about suffrage, you're giving me an ice cream!'

He laughed. 'Try it,' he said. 'Go on.'

Angrily, she stabbed the spoon into the ice cream, took a scoop and slipped it onto her tongue. The vanilla was sweet and warming and the toffee sauce was sticky and homely. 'Is this supposed to calm me down?' Susan asked, licking her spoon.

'No,' he laughed. 'But I am softening you up so that you make me a promise.'

'Oh,' she said, trying desperately to resist having another spoonful.

'That you let me come with you, to London I mean,' he said.

She scowled at him. 'This is for women,' she began.

He held his hands up. 'I won't attend the rally. I will stand to one side and have a cigarette. But let me come with you?' he said.

She dug her spoon in and took another delicious taste of the vanilla ice cream and toffee sauce. He was right. The sweetness did soften her up. 'Oh, all right,' she said.

He turned around to tidy up. Then he turned back, smiled and said, 'Aren't you going to ask what this creation is called? My new ice cream?'

Susan shrugged. 'What's it called?

Angelo laughed. 'Sweet Susan,' he replied.

She giggled and threw her spoon at him and he ducked behind the counter.

# Chapter Forty

**Catherine**

She was stacking a particularly smart-looking pair of ladies' brown boots when it popped into her head again. A thought. One of many. She – Catherine – felt herself do something that she had never done in her entire life.

Blush.

She placed the boots in the shop window and grabbed a dustpan and brush. As she brushed around the new shoes on display, it happened again. A thought popped into her head from the night before. From their bedroom. With Percy. A furious pink rash snaked up from her neck and made her cheeks flush crimson.

'You all right there, dear?' Kezia asked, coming over with more boots. 'You look flushed. Don't tell me you're coming down with something.;

Catherine bit her lip and smiled. She wafted her face. 'Just this heat, especially in the window,' she said. 'Baking, it is.'

But it wasn't that. The truth was, since their wedding night, Percy had shown Catherine a side of him she had no idea existed. He seemed to know exactly how to touch her. How to kiss her. He had a sixth sense about what she needed and how she wanted to be caressed. The first night, she'd had to bite into a pillow and goose feather had erupted everywhere. Next morning, Kezia had come in to open a window and asked if a cat had got in with a bird. Since then, night after night, Catherine and Percy had consummated their marriage again ... and again ... and again. Some mornings she could barely function, remembering what they'd done in the tiny bedroom above the shop. She walked around in a strange, pink, fuzzy haze. Catherine blushed again as she helped stock the shelves with the new boot arrivals.

Just then Percy came in, pulled his apron over his neck and smiled at his wife. He blushed too now, looking at the floor.

Kezia looked at her son, touched his forehead and shook her head. 'I reckon you're both coming down wi' something,' she said, before going off out back.

Catherine and Percy erupted into giggles.

He rushed over to her, grabbed her around the waist and kissed her neck. A thousand volts shot through her and she arched her back.

'Oh, Percy,' she sighed.

There was a noise. They darted apart like guilty children.

It was only as the door opened and the shop bell rang that the mood changed. A woman they both knew walked in. She had a pair of boots for mending. She saw Percy, he smiled, but her expression changed and she stopped dead. Then she began to walk out.

'Excuse me, are you all right? Can I help you?' Catherine asked.

The woman stood still for a moment, her back displaying a stiffness and anger that was visible through her dress. Then she turned.

'I'd forgotten,' she said.

'Forgotten what?' Catherine asked.

'Forgotten that a coward worked here,' she said, so quietly and yet so full of anger.

'I beg your pardon?' Catherine said, stepping nearer.

'Him, a coward, that's what,' the woman said, pointing

at Percy.

Catherine stepped nearer. 'Care to explain?' she said, putting a hand on her hip.

The woman took a breath. She said, 'Getting a place in a lifeboat while women and children drowned. Walking around here while real men lay dead and drowned. I'd forgot he worked here. That's all. I'll take my custom elsewhere.'

Percy opened his mouth to speak. Catherine interrupted. 'I'll have you know Percy waited and waited to get into a lifeboat and didn't want to get in one,' Catherine said, squaring up to the woman.

Silence. The woman made to leave. Then she stopped again. 'Then why,' she cried out now, 'why is he here and my two sons are not?'

The woman dropped her shoes that needed mending and looked about to faint.

'Er, Missus,' Catherine stammered.

The woman's eyes rolled back.

Catherine helped her to a stool and sat her down.

'Oh, dear Lord,' the woman sighed, her legs barely able to hold her up.

'Loosen her collar,' Percy said, coming nearer.

Catherine did so. The woman fanned her face with her hand.

'I don't need your help,' she said, slapping their hands away. 'I'll be right, got to be, haven't I?'

Catherine gave the woman space. She was torn between feeling sorry for her and wanting to slap her judgemental face.

Percy broke the silence. 'Your sons,' he said. 'What did they do on *Titanic*?'

The woman looked up at him, hatred visible in her eyes.

'Both greasers,' she said. 'Youngest 23, eldest 25. Both drowned. It was my youngest's first time at sea.'

Percy nodded and looked at the floor. 'Greasers were hard workers all right,' he said. Then he sighed. 'You're right. I shouldn't be here,' he mumbled.

Catherine let go of the woman and said, 'You have

every right to be here. Tell her about that night Percy. Tell her.'

Percy looked at the mother. All her hurt, pain and anguish of a thousand mothers like her seemed to be painted on her face. It was as if this one mother was the embodiment of every other mother in their streets who'd lost a son.

'You don't want to know my story,' Percy said, beginning to walk away.

'No,' she said suddenly. She paused. She said, 'I do.'

Catherine raised an eyebrow and nodded. She made space for Percy next to the woman. He sat down, let his hands rest on his knees and he began sharing his story. He told her of how it had been such a quiet night. He told her about how the stars had been out and how the sea had been so calm it had seemed like a still pond, not an ocean.

He told her how even when the horrific noise of the ship hitting the iceberg erupted from the silence, no one believed they would drown. He told her how the rich refused to stop drinking in the cocktail lounges, and how those in bed were reluctant to come onto the freezing cold of the top deck.

He told her how, in the chaos, that he lost his friends and the family he was caring for, the man who had been tipping him each day.

He told her how he had experienced a cold he had never felt or even imagined could exist. And then he told her how only when he'd seen the women in his rich family to safety and when he'd waited and waited, only then when someone told him to get into a lifeboat did he do so.

'I've seen that moment again and again in my head,' he said, tapping the side of his head sharply with his finger. 'I see it every single night. I wished for a long time I'd never got in that lifeboat.'

Silence fell.

The woman seemed to be taking it all in. Catherine felt furious. All her hard work, all her encouragement to make Percy live again and try to forget, and now this woman had made him fall back into despair and guilt.

But then Percy's expression changed. He suddenly held his head up. 'Except now,' he added, reaching for

Catherine's hand, 'except now I no longer wish I was gone.'

The woman stared at him.

'Yes, yes, I was a coward. Perhaps. But I want to live. I can't help it. I'm young. I found a girl who loves me. I want to live my life. I will always be a coward and I will always hate myself. But I want to live now …'

He began to wipe tears away from his eyes. He stood up. 'That's all I wanted to say,' he said.

Then he let go of Catherine's hand and walked out to the back of the shop.

Catherine stood in the silence of the shop, looking at the floor. Finally, after what seemed an age, the woman stood up. She took her package of shoes that needed mending, walked to the counter and placed them there.

'I'll come back Monday week, then,' the woman said, wiping her eyes as if nothing had happened.

'Yes,' Catherine said, taking the pair of shoes and giving her a ticket.

'Goodbye, then,' the woman said, walking out.

'Goodbye,' Catherine replied.

# Chapter Forty-One

**Susan**

Hyde Park was so busy that Susan could barely move from left to right. It was ironic that her first time in London was a time she could not see a thing – not a building, not a road, not a monument. Instead, jostled from side to side by women all around her, she strained her ears to hear the speaker better.

'It is known that working class women prisoners are more likely to be force-fed in prison than upper class women,' the speaker shouted. 'These sisters suffer pain, suffering, emotional distress, humiliation, anguish and rage!'

The crowd erupted into angry cheers.

'Our sister Violet Bland was force-fed in prison,' the speaker continued over the din. 'They twisted her neck, jerked her head back, closed her throat off and held her all that time as if in a vice.'

The crowd booed and shoved forwards.

'The victim could not protest. She could not speak. When they finished and she could not get up quick enough because of her helpless and breathless condition, the brutes snatched her chair from under her, throwing her to the floor!' the speaker cried out.

More jeers and angry cheers. Susan cried out in rage and punched a fist in the air.

'We want an end to force-feeding! And end to force-feeding! End to force-feeding!' cried the speaker.

The chant reverberated around the crowd. Susan cried out the refrain, one hand in the air. She felt women all around her, pushing her, jostling her, but still she cried out the same phrase, her hand punching the air, the invisible patriarch, the oppressor.

Across the way, Angelo stood against a wall, smoking his eighth roll up of the day. He'd lost sight of Susan. All he knew was that somewhere her summer bonnet was among all the other hundreds of summer bonnets. He promised he'd wait at this location and wait he would. Susan, meanwhile, was listening to more speakers. Women told of how they were beaten and brutalised in police custody. Some spoke of how their families were threatened. Others spoke of more force-feeding until they passed out. The rally was peaceful. All the women around her seemed decent, listening carefully to the speakers, raging only when asked to reply. But then Susan noticed a small splinter group of women to her right. She saw one woman's two hands clenched around a brick.

What followed happened so fast, Susan barely saw it. A brick was thrown at a window, then another, then another.

'Votes for women!' came the screams.

Some women ducked. Others ran away. Some, who wanted action, ran towards the splinter group, reaching into their sacks for bricks, to join the battalion. Susan stood there, like a trapped animal too afraid to move. The more docile members of the crowd had dispersed. The angrier ones were throwing more bricks now, some were pulling bicycles away from railings and tossing them into the road.

A loud whistle followed by male voices made Susan's stomach lurch. This wasn't just the locl coppers. This was the London Metropolitan Police.

She looked left and right. She didn't know where to run. She felt a hand tug her and turned. A male hand.

'Thank God,' she said.

Angelo pulled her from the crowd and they ran down an alley. They passed a restaurant, passed a bar which had its front windows all open and was full of drinkers taking in the London air. He led her down a tiny alley that was wet on the ground with urine and mess. He threw them both against a wall. Flat against it, panting, he said, 'Never again, Susan.' He had his eyes closed.

She peered past him. She saw boots and uniforms running past in a blur. He pushed her back.

'That could have been you. Do you want to go to prison?' he asked, fury in his eyes.

'I did nothing wrong!' she cried out.

'They don't think like that. Guilt by association,' he said. 'It's the same with being foreign. One does something wrong, we're all bad. It's the same for you as women. Right or wrong. That's how it is.'

When the noise died down, he inhaled deeply. He rolled a cigarette and lit it, then he passed it to her.

'Thanks,' she said, hands trembling. She took a drag. The nicotine hit her brain immediately and she felt alert, fit to run, fit to fight again. Angelo saw this look and shook his head.

'The fight is over now,' he said. 'We need to get home.'

When the crowds had completely dispersed, Angelo and Susan made their way through London's streets.

'Shall we get the tram?' he asked.

She shook her head. She had never been to London before. 'I'd like to walk,' she replied. 'I've never been here before. Probably never will again.'

They walked down streets and lanes. Susan stared up with awe at beautiful, imposing buildings. The streets were so much wider here. There were cars too. Many more than she'd seen in her life. They walked on until they reached the Thames. The river glistened as the evening light faded. Lamps were lit and Susan gasped as Waterloo Bridge became lit up as well.

'What a beautiful place,' she sighed.

'It is, if you have money,' he said.

'You know London?' she asked.

'It's where we first came when we arrived here,' he

replied. 'I was fourteen. We found a whole community of Italians like us. It was wonderful.'

Susan frowned. 'So why on earth did you move to Southampton?'

He shrugged. 'Old family history came over from Italy and found us here,' he replied.

Susan opened her mouth but he put a finger to his lips.

'One day I will explain,' he said.

They walked arm in arm across the bridge. The Thames swelled and glistened beneath them. 'They say London smells, but it smells fresh as a daisy compared to home,' Susan said.

'Trust me, there are parts that don't smell so good,' Angelo smiled.

At the railway station, a plume of smoke told them their steam train had arrived. They boarded third class and sat together. As it chugged out of London, Susan turned to catch a last glimpse. 'I came to London and barely saw any of it,' she said, as the train gathered pace.

'One day, after we are married, I will bring you back here,' Angelo said. 'I'll take you to the finest Italian restaurants, buy you the finest cakes, I'll take you dress shopping …'

She turned to him. 'After we're married? And when will that be?' she asked.

'Well, you're the lady. You tell me,' he smiled, watching as great London buildings flew past through the window. It was September, almost October. She thought of the lights flickering over the Thames and suddenly said, 'Christmas. Let's marry at Christmastime.'

Angelo held her hand in his.

'Then we shall,' he said, lifting her hand to kiss it.

She leaned her head on his shoulder and felt it judder as the train chugged along the tracks. She felt exhausted, sleepy, so tired. As she closed her eyes, images of the day flashed before her. Women chanting, women shouting in solidarity, women throwing bricks, angry faces, women damaging property, the police …

She felt Angelo's arm tighten around her. She smiled

to herself, feeling safe, warm and oh, such a hypocrite.

'Susan, Susan …' she told herself inwardly. 'Call yourself a Suffragette?'

# Chapter Forty-Two

**Lucy**

In the last few days so much had changed that Lucy felt she was living another woman's life. The Lady Visitor had given Lucy a way into earning some extra money. She'd started just two days earlier and at last would have some money coming in.

The job was as a shirt finisher. The shirts were made in a nearby factory, then were given to women in their homes to 'finish' with hand stitching on the collars and cuffs. Lucy had done a night's trial with ten shirts and the foreman at the factory had been pleased. Now, between the hours Florence went to bed, and the hours she woke, Lucy worked at home, at her kitchen table, finishing men's shirts in the comfort of her own kitchen.

It wouldn't be a lot of money. Around three shillings a week to be precise. But it would help. And even better, Lucy thought, finishing off a stitch on a stiff collar, it meant she no longer laid in bed staring at the ceiling thinking of Joseph. This was what she needed. A job to occupy her fingers and her mind.

'Do they not care that you're about to pop?' Susan said when she visited Lucy one teatime.

'They don't have to know,' Lucy said. 'Besides, if I pop here, it's my business, not theirs. I'll make sure I don't dirty the shirts.'

Susan laughed. Lucy laughed too. She felt strange doing it. But somehow getting this bit of work made all the difference to her. It was as if the simple act of doing something with her fingers, and being paid for it, meant she was no longer foundering. One afternoon, before Florence's tea and bedtime and before Lucy's night shift began, Catherine and Susan visited together.

Lucy eyed Catherine. There was something different about her. – she'd noticed it gradually over the weeks that had passed since their wedding. Her angular cheekbones that had jutted from her beautiful face seemed softer, somehow. And her eyes, which had previously always darted around sensing danger – or food – were more docile, watery, full.

'You're pregnant,' Lucy announced, reaching across and taking Catherine's hand.

Catherine held her other hand up.

'Guilty as charged, your honour,' she smiled.

'That's wonderful news!' Lucy cried.

Susan choked on her tea. 'You're going to be a mother?' she said, feigning wide-eyed horror.

'Hey, give over,' Catherine said, smacking Susan's forearm. 'I'll have you know I have every intention of being everything my parents were not!'

Lucy smiled. 'You seem happy, that's what counts,' she said, shaking her head in awe at how joyful and peaceful Catherine seemed at long last.

Catherine took a sip of tea and a slice of bread and butter from the plate on the table. 'I am,' she said, pushing the bread into her mouth. 'In fact-'

'Still talks with her mouthful though, doesn't she?' Susan laughed, leaning into her and nudging her.

'Shu' yer mou',' Catherine said between chews.

Lucy laughed. She saw Florence sitting in an armchair and making her dolly dance. She felt her baby kick inside her and smiled once again. She couldn't help it. Maybe life was looking up? She had a small income now, a bit of extra money. She had a new baby on the way, something to occupy herself with for years and years.

Now one of her closest friends was to be a mother too.

'We can help each other,' Lucy ventured, sipping her tea.

'Too right you'll be helping me,' Catherine said. 'I can't be doing it all on my own!'

'And what about you?' Susan asked. 'How long left now?'

Lucy felt her stomach. It touched the table she was so huge.

'I don't know. Days? Close, that's all I know,' she said.

'And Mrs Stoat – Stout! – will be doing the job?' Catherine asked.

Lucy nodded.

'Old Mrs Knittin' Needles,' Catherine laughed.

'Hey! She helps deliver babies as well as kill them!' Lucy giggled.

'Well, if you want us here too, just shout,' Susan said.

When the tea was drunk and the bread and butter had vanished, the women stood up.

'Right, off to mark the children's mathematics book,' Susan said.

'Off to stock the front window,' Catherine smiled.

Lucy stood up slowly, a hand in the small of her back. Everything ached. Her legs, her arms, her back. Her ankles were swollen and she couldn't even do her hobnail boots up anymore.

'I'll see you then,' Catherine said, walking through the doorway.

'Bye for now,' Lucy said and the girls set off down the street.

The rest of the day passed happily for Lucy. She gave Florence her tea then set her down to bed. The nights were dark now in now. It was almost November. At last she could get the child to sleep without blazing sunlight creeping through the curtain.

When she could no longer hear Florence gurgling and chattering to herself, Lucy got out her batch of finishing to do.

She got out her sewing box, laid the shirts out on the kitchen table and brought the oil lamp over. She got out the first shirt and smoothed it flat. She threaded her needle and made a stitch. She pushed the needle through, pulled the thread and pinched it tight. She started the process again. And again. As she did so, the rhythmic movement of her fingers soothed her. Push in, pull through, tighten. Push in, pull through, tighten. It was repetitive. Predictable. Gloriously unemotional.

*Knock-knock.*

The sound made her jump. She held her needle and thread aloft in the half light. It was after nine o'clock at night. No one knocked at this hour. She put her shirt down, laid the thread and needle on top and heaved herself off her chair.

Ankles aching with the swelling, she made for the front window and peered through. Useless. She couldn't see her front door from there because it was set in an alcove. Besides, the glass was thick with soot and smoke stains from the wretched margarine factory. She thought of ignoring it. Maybe it was some drunk stoker, staggering back to the wrong house.

*Knock-knock.*

She jumped out of her skin again. Maybe it was the police? Maybe a robber had passed by? She smoothed her dress down and went to the front door. Her pulse quickened as she unlocked it, turned the latch and pulled the door open. She gazed out into the night. She stared at the man standing on her doorstep.

She made to speak, held a hand to her stomach, retched, and felt nausea come over her. Then she fell, hit her head and everything went black.

She felt a wet rag on her forehead. Then she felt the rag move and take residence on the nape of her neck. She was lying on one side. She opened her eyes and could see every speck of dust on the wooden floor. She could see a wooden toy of Florence's under the armchair from here, one she thought she'd lost.

'Don't try to get up,' came the voice. 'Just rest.'

She closed her eyes again. She smiled sweetly. She was

dreaming, that was it. The voice was one she knew, one she loved and trusted. She felt his hands on her, soothing her, pressing that cooling rag cloth to her face and neck.

'Joseph …' she sighed, not caring anymore for the wood that pressed hard into her cheek from the floor. 'Oh, I have missed you.' She knew if she opened her eyes the dream would fade, would vanish. She kept her eyes tightly shut. If she could just stay here, he'd stay too.

'Lucy, Lucy,' his voice was pressing, urgent. 'Come on, love.'

She opened her eyes. She managed to prop herself up on one elbow. The male voice was coming from behind her. She shook her head. Was she still dreaming? She felt a strong hand lift her and the other carefully support her back. She was turned and sat on the armchair.

Then she saw him.

He was standing in front of her. He was wearing clothes that were too big. He had a hat on that looked ridiculous. Foreign. His shoes looked brand new but too small. He came nearer, bent down and reached out to touch her knee.

She shook her head. The room was still spinning. Desperately she tried to focus.

'Lucy, my love,' the voice kept saying. 'Please don't fall again. Breathe. Breathe.'

She focused now. She took in his face. The same brown eyes. The same face. Except it was thinner than before, so much thinner. She reached out and pulled off the daft hat and looked at his hair. It was the same.

She tried to form a word, but it wouldn't come out. Finally, she managed, 'Joseph?'

He smiled and tears welled in his eyes, threatening to overflow. 'It is me, my love,' he said.

She closed her eyes. 'I'm dreaming,' she said. 'I'm surely dreaming.' She opened them again. But there he was. He was alive. He was here in her front room. She had imagined this moment thousands of times. She'd clung to the insane hope that, because there had never been a body or a funeral, he might one day walk in, saying it had all been a mistake. But now that it was happening, she couldn't take it in. In the dreams when this had happened, she had run to him, hugged him, showered him with kisses. Now that this was really happening, truly happening, she could not speak, think, cry or touch him. She was in suspended animation, stock still; she even wondered if her heart was still beating.

'How?' was all she could finally say, her voice no more than a croak.

'At first I didn't know who I was,' he began. He sat on the floor now, in front of her. He seemed afraid to come too near in case he made her faint in shock again. 'I was in a hospital bed and the nurses, the medics, everyone they all spoke in an accent. It took a while. I had such a headache and I had lost the sight in this eye,' he said, pointing to his right eye. 'They said it might come back properly one day. Now this eye is blurry, the left can see.'

He cleared his throat. 'I realised I was America. I was in a hospital and they told me I had been there for weeks. They said I'd been in a comatose state, unable to talk or even see. I just took their word for it. I had no idea who I was, where I'd come from, nothing.'

Lucy sat there, looking at a spot of dust in one corner. She couldn't look at him. She couldn't do it in case he disappeared and she broke the spell.

'I laid there for weeks. They fed me, got me up and walking. My muscles had rotted something rotten. I tried to walk first time and fell flat on my face. The nurses were kind. They kept at it, making me walk. Then came this doctor. He kept asking who I was, what I remembered. I said I remembered nothing. They kept talking about *Titanic*, saying I must have been on that and did I remember? But I didn't even know my name. I had never heard of *Titanic*, I told them, and didn't know what my job was. They asked if I had a wife. I said no. They asked if I had children. I shook my head at them and I laughed. I had no memory, see? I had no recollection …' He cleared his throat again. Lucy slowly dared to shift her eyes from the floor, to the table, to his hands. She could not look at his face.

'Anyway, I had talking therapy. You know? I had to

talk and talk and try to remember things. They asked me what I remembered in my life, childhood, that sort of thing. I must have vexed them something proper because I remembered nothing. They said I had amnesia and it would come in time, but I wasn't safe to be let out. I could barely feed myself and one eye wasn't working. I was useless.'

He paused, reaching for her again. She tore her hand away. She couldn't meet his gaze. 'Anyway the weeks went on like this. I got better at walking. I could do it without sticks. Then I could eat all right. My sight started coming back, blurry-like, but getting better. Then one day, this new doctor walked in. From my viewpoint on my bed on my side one of the first things I saw about him was his shiny black shoes. 'I said as he came over, 'Nice shoes there doctor.' And he looked at me and he replied, 'They're my best ones.'

And when he said that, something in me snapped. A memory. Something. A phrase. A thought. I don't know … but the shoes made me think of a shop. I could see it but not name it. I kept closing my eyes and trying to see it. And then one day, yes! I remembered it was called Royce's Pawn Shop and I'd taken a pair of my best boots there.

'Well, I told my doctor and he set about asking everyone he knew to find out if there was a shop called Royce's in all of the world. I knew that would take forever, so I kept forcing myself to remember it. The walk there, the street, what it was like outside. I kept trying. I thought about it so much I dreamed it. Then one night, I was dozing off, when I remembered someone there giving me money in a paper envelope. In my memory, I walked down the street, along another alley and to a house. It was number 24. The door was green and wooden. I walked in through that door and I put the money on a table. And I …' His voice trailed off to a whisper. He sounded choked. She was able to look at him then and saw he was weeping.

'And I remembered passing this money in an envelope to a pretty girl. I gave it to her and I told her to take care of herself and our baby. I kissed her, hugged her and she hugged me back and she told me she loved me …'

He dared to touch her face then and turned it to him.

'And that's when I remembered you, Lucy. You and Florence.' Their eyes met properly for the first time. Her pulse was twitching in her neck. Her hands were sweaty but ice cold.

'All that time I'd been lying there, not knowing who I was and I realised somewhere you were, thinking I was drowned and dead and grieving. Well, I threw the hospital covers off me and I ran out. I thanked them all, I did, but I had to get home. I got a passage on a steamer ship, cleaning and mucking out toilets. I told them I'd been on *Titanic*, and they thought I was crazy. Still, they let me on. I got here just today …'

Lucy felt her hands shaking. She raised them and let them fall on his cheeks, to trace his face. She felt his cheekbones, prominent now, and ran her hands down to his chin, where a soft beard had grown. He placed his hands over the top of hers and blinked away tears. She gazed into his eyes and felt her own fill with tears so much that he vanished behind a wall of water.

'You're really home?' was all she could whisper.

He took her in his arms then. She felt herself enveloped in his embrace for the first time in five months. She felt him wrap his arms around her as he always had done, felt his heartbeat, smelt his scent. She closed her eyes then and let herself exhale and let her face fall against his neck. If this was a dream she did not ever want to wake up. But when she opened his eyes, she was still there, still being held, still being told she was loved and so missed.

It was only then that she felt the armchair beneath her grow so wet, drenched. She took her hands away from him and a searing pain slashed across her stomach and down into her most intimate parts.

'Joe,' she said.

He pulled away and for the first time registered how big she was. 'You're …?'

She nodded, wincing in pain then she cried out.

'It's due now?'

She shook her head. 'Days, I don't know. It's the shock …' she cried out again. 'Joe,' she cried. 'The baby's coming!'

# Chapter Forty-Three

**Catherine**

Mrs Stoat wiped her hands on her apron then stood with them on her hips. 'When was your last bleed?' she grunted.

'I've missed two,' Catherine replied, pulling her stockings back up and swinging her legs off the bed.

'May then,' Mrs Stoat said. 'May the littl'un will be here.'

Catherine nodded. A spring or summer baby.

'One thing to keep an eye on, though,' Mrs Stoat said.

'Oh yeah?' Catherine asked, getting up from the bed.

'Bit of blood there was when I had a check. Tiny, like. Only pink. But go easy.'

Catherine frowned and nodded. 'Is that usual?' she asked.

Mrs Stoat shrugged. 'Can be, can not be,' she said, 'I've seen girls bleed every day and have a healthy little 'un and I've seen girls never bleed a drop and give birth to a dead 'un. I'm not a fortune teller. Don't mean a thing other than to go easy.' She held out her hand.

'Oh,' Catherine said. 'Ask Percy downstairs. He's sweeping the shop. Ask him to open the till.'

Mrs Stoat nodded. 'Right you are, then,' she said. She leaned sideways to get her ruddy girth through the bedroom door then trudged down the stairs to accost Percy at the till for the payment.

Catherine touched her stomach. *Bit of blood* ... Did that matter? She felt fine. She shook her head and stood up. Mrs Stoat said girls bled all the time. It didn't have to mean anything. She wouldn't tell Percy. He was so happy, and he'd been through enough. No, all would be well. She was sure of it.

She went to the window and pulled back the curtain. It was dark outside. November night had fallen. Grey mist fell onto the roofs and chimneypots like a soft blanket. She heard the plaintive sound of the ships' horns at the docks. They'd be going all night with this weather. As she went to the top of the stairs, she heard Mrs Stoat asking Percy for her payment. He opened the till and she heard its bell ring and Mrs Stoat trudge off through the shop front door. She walked down the stairs to help Percy tidy up ready for the morning. She hovered before entering the shop front room. Did she tell him about the blood?

He heard her lingering and ushered her through. 'So, my love, what's it to be?'

Catherine forced the worry from her mind. 'A May baby,' she said.

Percy threw his arms around her. 'Magic, just magic!' he cried. She let herself be hugged tightly. But on one of her hands the forefinger and middle fingers were crossed for good luck.

# Chapter Forty-Four

**Lucy**

Joseph had banged on so many doors that everyone in the street was now peering through their curtains. He had no recollection of where a doctor lived or a midwife. He just banged on every door, asking the same question, 'Where can I find a medic?'

Everyone had said the same thing – Mrs Stoat.

But when he'd arrived at the door they all said was hers, there was no answer. 'Mrs Stoat?' he cried, cupping his hands around his mouth to shout louder.

'Who wants 'er?' came a voice behind him.

He turned and saw a fat woman standing in the street behind him. 'I need a midwife. My wife's having a baby,' he panted.

Mrs Stoat rolled her eyes. 'Always the way,' she said. 'Come on, son, show me where …'

He ran back in the direction of the house. He noted, in frustration, that Mrs Stoat did not mirror his speed or urgency. She simply waddled along as if she was walking to the bakery.

He reached his open front door and pointed inside. 'Here, here,' he said.

Mrs Stoat frowned. At first she refused to step inside. 'But this is Lucy Williams's place,' she said.

Joseph nodded. 'Yes, come in, come in now,' he urged.

'But you're ... you're dead,' she said, pointing to him and staggering back in horror.

'I'm not, I'm not dead, Mrs Stoat,' Joseph said. 'It was all a mistake. I just came back. Please, please come in. I can explain it all, I swear to you.'

Mrs Stoat reluctantly followed him inside. She shivered a little as she stepped through the front door. She was a superstitious woman and attended a spiritualist church. She was worried this man was a ghost. She saw Lucy on the edge of the armchair, her legs splayed and her stockings off.

'Please,' Joseph begged, his face strained with fear and worry.

Mrs Stoat pushed her fear of ghosts aside and rolled her sleeves up. 'How long you been hurtin'?' she asked.

'Not long,' Lucy replied.

Mrs Stoat saw that her waters had broken beneath her. 'This one's on its way, then,' she said in her usual matter-of-fact way.

'Shall we get her on the bed?' Joseph asked, hands on his head.

Mrs Stoat crouched nearer to Lucy and Joseph watched as she put her hands under Lucy's dress. 'No time,' she said, pulling her hands away. 'This one's comin' now. Here.' Mrs Stoat grabbed Lucy's knees. 'Bear down now,' she said.

Lucy groaned and her face went purple as she pushed.

'Don't just stand there,' Mrs Stoat said to Joseph. 'Get some towels or a blanket.'

'All right,' he said, 'all right.' He raced to the kitchen. He had no idea where anything was; he had no idea where to find anything. Instead, he grabbed a rag hanging before the hearth and brought it over.

Mrs Stoat grabbed it and rolled her eyes. 'Blimmin' useless,' she said. She turned her attentions back to Lucy. 'Right, wait now, wait,' she said.

Joseph watched as she rummaged beneath Lucy's skirts again. Lucy's face contorted in pain and he put a finger in his mouth and bit on it.

'Right, cord's round the neck, missy, so you gotta do this a minute,' she said, forming her mouth into a little O and panting.

Lucy nodded and desperately formed an O with her mouth too. 'Huh, huh, huh,' she began panting.

'That's it, you done this before,' Mrs Stoat said.

Lucy stared at Joseph. He was pacing the floor, biting down hard on his fist. Pain seared through her body, threatening to tear her in two. The urge to push was so big, so irresistible but she saw Mrs Stoat shake her head.

'Not yet, not yet,' she was saying, still doing something down below. Mrs Stoat suddenly looked triumphant and said, 'Right, maid, push now!'

Lucy let the urge to push come now and with relief and agony, she opened her pelvis up and pushed with all her might. Joseph's eyes widened as an animalic sound emerged from his wife's mouth, that seemed to come from deep inside her.

'Push, once more, just one more, that's it,' Mrs Stoat said.

Lucy gave her final push. It was less pain and more sweet relief. Then she felt a surge of freedom hit her as she felt the heaviness taken from her body.

'Knife,' Mrs Stoat said.

Joseph patted his pockets. Nothing. 'Er …' he stammered.

'Scullery!' Mrs Stoat cried.

He ran over, found a bread knife on the side and brought it over. Mrs Stoat looked at the serrated edge and rolled her eyes again. She sawed through the umbilical cord with ease, though, and then she grabbed the rag Joseph had brought her and deftly wrapped the baby in it. She wiped its face of white mucus and blood, to reveal a perfect button nose, round cheeks and blue eyes.

'You've got yourselves a boy,' Mrs Stoat said.

Lucy rested back into the armchair. She gaped as Mrs Stoat passed her a small bundle. He was small, so much smaller than Florence had been.

'He's a little early,' Mrs Stoat surmised.

'No matter,' Lucy said, not taking her eyes from the baby boy.

'He'll be all right,' Mrs Stoat said. 'Good colour he has. Sturdy legs.' She put her hands over her ears as the baby let out a piercing cry. 'Good pair o' lungs too,' she said. She stood up and wiped her hands on her skirts.

'Water to wash?' Joseph said, seeing Mrs Stoat's blood-covered forearms.

'No, don't mind me, I'll wash back home,' she said. She suddenly remembered she was talking to a ghost and peered at Joseph from the corner of her eye. 'So, you're not dead?' she said.

Joseph shook his head and smiled, staring over at his new son. From across the room, a small girl with bare feet toddled out into the kitchen. Joseph turned and saw his daughter. She was taller now, standing straight and toddling, hanging on to the door frame, then the chair to walk towards him.

'Florence?' Joseph whispered.

The child smiled sleepily and wiped her eyes. Joseph went over and scooped her up against him. Florence looked at him close up, touching her chubby little fingers to his beard.

'I'm your father,' he said.

Lucy felt tears welling as she placed her new son to her breast. Then Joseph walked over and stood there, Florence in his arms, gazing down at the new addition to their family.

Mrs Stoat cleared her throat. 'Right, I'll make my way, then,' she said.

Lucy knew Mrs Stoat usually lingered, holding her right hand out for payment. But on this occasion, she didn't.

'Wait, Joe, there's some money in the drawer, in the kitchen,' Lucy said, nodding in that direction.

Mrs Stoat held her ruddy hands up. 'No, not today,' she said.

Lucy's eyes widened. If there was one thing Mrs Stoat never did, it was give concessions.

'But Mrs Stoat,' Joseph said, thinking in horror of the cord around the neck, of the silence as she begged Lucy not to push. 'You saved our baby.'

She shook her head, eyes closed.

'I won't take money from a ghost,' she said. She performed what could only be described as a toothless smile. Then she left.

Joseph looked at Florence, then at his new son. 'What shall we name him?' he asked.

Lucy looked at their son and murmured, 'Luke. It means light.'

# CHAPTER FORTY-FIVE

**Susan**

The bang on the door was so loud and so fast it shook the house. Susan looked in horror towards the door and thought, *Oh God ... the police know about me ...* But how could they? Did anyone know she'd attended that rally? No one had seen her. Angelo had seen to that. Heart pounding, she went towards the door. Relief washed over her as she heard Catherine's voice outside.

'Open up!' she was calling. 'You will never believe this!'

Susan opened the door and was pushed flat against the wall as Catherine barged in.

'You might need to sit down,' Catherine said, breathlessly, her eyes as wide as dinner plates.

'What? Why?' Susan said.

Catherine took a deep breath. 'Joseph Williams is alive.'

Susan clapped a hand to her mouth. 'What? Lucy's Joseph?' she said.

Catherine nodded. 'And there's more. Kezia ran into Mrs Stoat, and she said she delivered their baby last night right there and then!'

Susan frowned. 'But Lucy wasn't due for a while, surely?'

Catherine shrugged.

Susan grabbed her hat and made for the door. 'Well, come on, then,' she said, grabbing Catherine's arm. 'Let's go!'

The pair hurried through the streets. Delivery boys came and went, the newspaper boy sold his papers, the bakery smells wafted past, stokers filed in and out of the King's Arms. Everything was as it was. And yet, if Catherine was right, Susan thought, everything had changed. They reached Lucy's door and knocked. A while later, the door opened and a man peered around.

'Oh, my good God,' Catherine gasped, crossing herself for good measure.

Susan didn't have time to ask why on earth Catherine was suddenly religious. She gaped, staring at Joseph. The man looked like him, but not like him. Joseph had been big built, heavy, strong. This man was slim, wiry, light. But the eyes – they were the same.

'Joseph? Is it really you?' Susan said.

He nodded. 'Come in,' he said. He let the women in. He recognised them at once. They stood nervously in the kitchen, fearing to sit down.

'Where's Lucy?' Susan asked.

'Up in bed, with the baby,' Joseph said.

'Can we see her?' Susan asked.

'Of course,' he replied.

As he made his way to the stairs, Susan touched his arm lightly. 'Do you remember us?' Susan asked.

Joseph looked at her sadly. 'Of course,' he replied.

They followed him up the stairs and into the bedroom. Lucy was in bed, propped up, feeding the baby. Florence sat at her side, holding her doll.

'Oh my, oh my,' Susan said, nearing the bed and perching gently on the mattress. 'Your little one came!'

Lucy smiled and nodded. 'A boy. We called him Luke,' she smiled.

Catherine stood up, refusing to sit. She couldn't take her eyes from the man standing in the doorway. 'I can't take it in, I just can't,' she said, peering at him from head to foot. 'It looks like Joseph, but not. I can't understand any of it.'

Joseph shrugged. 'I don't even know how I am supposed to look,' he said.

The women sat on the bed as Lucy and Joseph told the tale and explained it all. Susan and Catherine gaped and gasped, sighed and even cried as Joseph recounted his story.

Susan listened intently. She was trying to push down a sense of hope that was bubbling inside her, threatening to come out. If Joseph had survived and come home months later, well then maybe Jack and her father could? She didn't want to spoil this moment of happiness, but she longed to ask Joseph. She couldn't help it.

'Joseph, can I ask, do you remember my father and brother? Jack and Thomas Jarvis?'

He saw the hope on her face and felt suddenly very guilty. He looked at the floor and shook his head.

'I never saw them again. I don't remember anything. I hope it'll come to me in time, truly I do. I'm sorry …'

Susan nodded and forced a smile. 'No need to be sorry,' she said. She stood up and went nearer to him. She stepped forward to kiss his cheek. 'You're home safe, that's all that matters. And you have a son.' She saw Florence looking a little lost and left out and went to her. She picked her up and blew a raspberry on her neck. 'And you, little miss, you have a brother!' Susan cried.

Florence giggled.

Catherine was still staring around her, stunned. 'I can't believe any of it,' she was saying. 'I can't. One minute a person's dead, the next they're alive. I mean, how did they say you were dead if you weren't?'

'White Star Line sent letters and telegrams to anyone who wasn't found after a certain time, assuming they were drowned,' Lucy said. 'That's what happened with Joseph. Except all the time, he was in a hospital not knowing who he was.'

Catherine was shaking her head in disbelief. 'Percy doesn't know yet. He was at the market. I don't know what he'll say when he hears this!'

'Percy?' Joseph said.

'We're marrie,' Catherine said. 'He was on *Titanic* too, if you remember.'

At thee word *Titanic*, Joseph winced visibly. He did so, the women noted, whenever the ship's name was mentioned. 'Then I should meet with him and see if anything comes back,' Joseph said.

'All in good time,' Susan said, jigging around with Florence on her hip. 'All in good time. Now you have to get well, get fed, get some meat on you,' she said.

At the end of their visit, Susan and Catherine said their goodbyes and stepped out into the street. It was still foggy, and horns went off at intervals from the docks. They walked past the greengrocer's and Susan noticed turnips and parsnips and other root vegetables were beginning to appear. Autumn, then winter, then Christmas. Jack had always loved that time of year. When he was home, he would always dress up silly at Christmastime and play tricks on them all. Catherine saw Susan's expression and interrupted her thoughts.

'Penny for 'em?' she asked.

'Oh, just so happy for them,' Susan replied. 'And …'

Catherine linked her arm through Susan's. 'And, you're wondering if your pa and brother might come back just like Joseph?' she said.

Susan nodded, biting back the urge to cry. 'Daft, isn't it?' she said.

Catherine walked on at her side in silence for a while. When they reached the cobbler's, the pair stood together.

'Lucy was lucky,' Catherine told Susan. 'But good luck don't strike twice.'

Susan looked at Catherine and nodded. She could always count on her for some straight-talking and sense, however hard it was to hear. 'I know you're right,' she said. She watched as Catherine went in through the door to the cobbler's. She stood in the street, watching people come and go, thinking how every single one of them lived off the sea in some way – delivery boys, stokers, greasers, the grocers that supplied the ships, the coal merchants, the haberdasheries that supplied the uniforms. She walked on, making her way home, thinking that the sea can give on one hand but always be ready to take with the other.

# Chapter Forty-Six

**Catherine**

Percy was frowning and shaking his head and pacing all at once. 'You're telling me Joseph Williams is back? Back from the dead?' he said.

'That's the truth of it,' Catherine replied. 'I've just seen the body. He's alive and kickingall right.' Catherine sat on the seats in the shop where ladies sat to try the shoes. She was a woman who was always hungry yet always retained her figure. But pregnancy had made her even greedier than usual. She sat there, holding a paper bag of boiled sweets and was crunching them rather than sucking them.

'You're supposed to suck not crack them,' Percy said.

'I'm starving,' Catherine said. 'That or feeling sick. It's always one or the other.'

Percy hurried to her and sat beside her. 'Everything's so good,' he said. 'We'll have a family. Joseph is home. Funny how life can change, isn't it?'

Catherine smiled. She could see the joy in his eyes. This would be the one thing that would seal their happiness, the one thing that could chase the demons of that terrible night in the Atlantic away.

She'd been ignoring the regular pink spots in her underwear. She'd had more this morning. Mrs Stoat made it clear some girls had it, some didn't. She'd tried her best to take it easy but what working woman really could? She got Percy to haul around the heavier boxes but the rest of the time she carried on as usual. And besides, life at the cobbler's was a lot easier than life in domestic service. It still felt like a holiday to her. No, she would keep the pink blood a secret. No need to worry Percy.

'So how did he look?' Percy asked.

Catherine was brought back to the present. 'Oh, Joseph?' she said, crunching another boiled sweet. 'Thin. Ill looking. Tired. Nothing like him at all.'

Percy suddenly had a thought. 'You don't suppose it's an imposter?'

Catherine rolled her eyes and patted his hand. 'I think Lucy can be relied upon to know her own husband,' she said.

'Ah, yes,' Percy said.

The shop doorbell made a ting-a-ling and two matronly women came in.

'You heard about Joseph Williams?' one said, placing her shoes on the counter.

'He's back from the dead,' said the other, placing her bag of vegetables on the seating area. 'Mrs Tinks down my way said she saw him the night he came back – running around knockin' doors, shouting.'

The other woman nodded and added, 'It'll be the shock. He won't be right in the head now, will he? After all he saw.'

Percy turned and feigned tidying behind the counter.

'I've seen so many men gone in the head,' said the woman, tapping the side of her head. 'They can't get over *Titanic*. Can't get the screams out of their heads, they say.'

Catherine scowled at the two women. 'Can we help you?' she said, taking the shoes from the counter.

Percy gave her a thankful look and went out the back.

'All I'm sayin' is, that even when they go back to sea or look normal they're gone up here,' the woman carried on, still prodding the side of her head with her forefinger. 'Mrs Brown's son wakes in the night wetting the bed,' she said, with what Catherine noted was a gleeful sneer.

'And Eleanor Jones's husband smacked her so hard

one night she had to call the police,' the other woman said. 'A stoker. He blamed it on what he saw on *Titanic*.'

'Right, well thank you, ladies,' Catherine said, giving the lady her ticket and ushering them towards the door. Before they left, one of the women took Catherine's hand. 'I'm just saying,' she said, her voice a whisper, 'be careful with your one.'

'My one?' Catherine frowned.

'Yes, he came back, didn't he? Acting fine now, ain't he? I'm just saying, you can't let your guard down. You can't trust 'em. They're in a mess, up here,' she said, tapping her head for the umpteenth time with her finger. 'One moment they're nice as pie, they next slapping you into next week. You can't just come back from *Titanic* normal and as if nothin's happened. That's my tuppence-worth, that's all.'

Catherine smiled and let the ladies out. Then she closed the door. She put the boots away ready to be mended and dusted down the sides. Then she felt an overwhelming urge to go to the toilet.

'Percy,' she called. 'Can you mind the shop?'

He came back to the shop front and smiled. 'Of course,' he said. 'Sorry about that. I can't be doing with old women like that. The rubbish they spout …'

'I know, I know,' Catherine said.

She made off to the back yard and into the outside toilet. She felt her bottom connect with the freezing cold seat. She looked up and saw a new spider had taken up residence in the corner.

Then she looked down at her underwear. Her grey knickers were now crimson. Not just a drop of pink or a spot. Her heart thudded. She grabbed a square of newspaper that Kezia kept in a pile by the toilet for wiping. She felt its paper against her skin and looked at it. The grey words and letters were now scarlet red. A sudden urge to cry out came but she put her hand over her mouth. Should she call Mrs Stoat? She sat there, feeling more and more blood coming from her, hearing it fall into the toilet with a slop. She perched up a little and looked down, seeing big clots fall into the toilet pan. A pain seared across her stomach and she gripped it with both hands.

There was no use calling Mrs Stoat. She felt more clots fall from her. She had to push some out, biting her cuff as she did so. It was too late. Nothing Mrs Stoat could do. She sat there, feeling everything inside her emptying. She no longer felt the cold of the toilet seat, or feared the spider. She sat there, feeling the life of her baby fall from her.

'You all right?' came Percy's voice. 'Thought you'd fallen in!'

Catherine swallowed a sob. 'I'll be there,' she said. 'Got a bit of stomach ache.'

'That's too many boiled sweets for you!' Percy called out. Then she heard his footsteps make their way back to the shop.

When she was certain he was gone, she leaned over her legs and stared down at the cold cement floor. Only then did she see a single tear fall past her underwear and onto the damp, cold ground.

# Chapter Forty-Seven

**Lucy**

The Lady Visitor from the Titanic Relief Fund was staring so hard at Joseph Lucy worried her gaze might bore a hole into his already thin face.

'I'm terribly sorry, but I may need this repeated to me,' she said. 'This is most irregular.' She looked at the notebook she was carrying, opened it and found a page relating to Lucy. 'You were given a letter in May informing you that your husband was drowned,' the Lady Visitor said.

'Yes,' Lucy said, 'I have it here. Look.' She pushed a letter across the table to the Lady Visitor.

She examined it and nodded. 'Right, right, and then you were given your compensation from the White Star Line …'

'Yes, but at £4 a month,' Lucy said. 'Not in a lump sum.'

'Indeed, and you received your award from the *Titanic* Relief Fund at …' she ran her finger down a list of figures. 'Twelve shillings a week.'

'That's right,' Lucy said.

She closed her book with a snap. 'And yet here he is,' she said.

Joseph was holding the baby. He had no idea what this woman was talking about. But if Lucy had been given money due to his death, then he knew she deserved every penny.

'I'll report to the Fund of course. I'm sure it will need nothing more done. After all, you accepted that money in good faith, believing your husband to be dead. But now, obviously with your husband returned, the payments from the Fund will cease.'

Lucy nodded.

The Lady Visitor stood up. 'Well, I am thrilled for the two of you,' she said, smiling, Lucy believed, a genuine smile. 'This is the second "back from the dead" story I have seen occur, although the other one happened only days after the sinking. This truly is a "big story"!'

Lucy reached for Joseph's hand. 'Whatever money has to stop, I understand,' Lucy said. 'I'm just so glad he's home where he belongs.'

The Lady Visitor opened the front door and stepped through. 'This will be our last visit, then,' she said. 'Good luck to you both.' Then she was gone.

Lucy came back to the table and lifted Luke from Joseph's arms. Florence, who had been waiting, clambered onto her father's lap and took her brother's place.

'I'm sorry the money had to stop,' Joseph said.

'Don't be daft!' Lucy said. 'You're back! What else matters?'

Joseph saw the pile of shirts Lucy was finishing at night. He sighed and said, 'I'll have to go back to sea.'

Lucy's stomach lurched. She sat down.

'You will do no such thing,' she said.

Joseph crooked his neck back and stared at the ceiling. 'And how else are we to manage?' he said. 'I'm a stoker, so you tell me. I need to go back to where I can earn. We have two little mouths to feed now. I won't sit here doing nothing, Lucy.'

She reached for his hand. 'But don't you remember...'

'I remember nothing,' he said, tearing his hand away. 'That's the problem. Don't you see? I remember nothing!' He stared angrily straight ahead.

Lucy fell silent, then she said, '*Titanic* was to be your last trip.'

He looked at her and laughed. 'And what on earth was I going to pay the rent with after that?' he said. 'Dust?'

She went over to the sideboard and found the newspaper article. She unfolded it and placed it flat on the table before Joseph. 'There,' she said.

He stared at the newspaper. There was an advert for ladies' hand cream and a list of people who had been before the magistrate's court.

'No, there,' she said, seeing his gaze and pointing to a photograph. A photograph of a charabanc.

'A beautiful thing,' Joseph said. Then he shrugged. 'And?'

Lucy pulled her chair up next to him, her baby falling asleep in her arms. 'And, that was to be our plan,' she said. 'You were doing one last trip on *Titanic*, then you were going to purchase a charabanc, like this one,' she pointed to it.

He stared at it. 'Me? Get me one of those?' he laughed.

'Joseph, listen!' she cried, suddenly irritated. 'You had plans before you left. You weren't going to do this anymore. No more fighting at the docks for half a day's work, no more coming home with a black eye if you did get a day's work. No more heaving coal into the furnace and coming home so dehydrated you could barely stand. *Titanic* was your last trip, so we could buy a charabanc and start our business!' She was shaking now, trembling with anger that he had forgotten their plans, the life they wanted.

He looked at the image. He focused hard, desperate to remember something. 'I don't remember this at all,' he said, pushing the article away. He stood up, pushing his chair back behind him. 'I'm going down White Star to see if they have anything going,' he said, going to get his overcoat.

Lucy stood up, her legs weak and her head pulsing with her own heartbeat. She stood in front of him in the doorway. 'I won't let you, Joseph,' she said. 'I will not let you go back to sea.'

'Lucy I am a husband and a father. I need to earn.'

She stood her ground. 'But you've only just come

home!'

He shrugged. 'Money won't come in through that door,' he said.

'I've lost you once to sea. I can't go through that again,' she begged, standing in his way.

But Joseph merely moved her gently to one side and kissed her cheek. 'Florence and Luke need food and blankets,' he said. 'The Relief Fund money's stopped and soon we'll run out of bread. I'm going where I can find work.'

And with that, he stepped past her and out into the street.

# Chapter Forty-Eight

**Susan**

The fine young man standing before her wore a smart jacket, trousers tucked into knee-length socks and held a grey cap in his hand.

'Eustace, what are you doing back here?' Susan asked. She looked down at his shiny shoes and recalled how just months earlier, she had taken a pair of donated boots to his home from the Salvation Army. Weeks later, Eustace, like so many boys his age, had found out his father had died on the *Titanic*. He had finished school that summer and had left. Now, he was before her once again.

'Fancy coming back to school?' she joked. 'Missing the mathematics?'

Eustace smiled and gripped his cap. He cleared his throat. 'I wanted to come back to say thank you, Miss,' he said.

Susan stopped. It was the end of the day, and she was tidying the classroom. The children had long gone, and she was due to go home herself. 'You wanted to thank me?' she repeated.

He looked at his shiny shoes then met her gaze. 'Truth is, Miss, when I had no boots, my ma told me not to bother comin' to school no more,' he said. 'I wasn't going to but I …' he blushed.

'Yes?' Susan said.

'Well, I liked it. It was better than bein' at home. And I learnt things here.'

Susan smiled. 'I should hope so,' she said.

'And then,' the boy went on, 'when Father drowned, Ma told me again not to bother comin' in. But I had my boots then, didn't I? So I kept coming. I don't think I would'a done if you hadn't given me those boots.'

Susan put her books down and looked at him. 'Well, that makes me very happy,' she said.

'And now, the *Titanic* Relief Fund got me an apprenticeship to a chauffeur,' he said, proudly standing a little straighter and fingering his cap. 'I'm still learnin'. I don't drive yet or nothin'. But I'm learnin' my way around an engine and I'm polishin' and I'm earnin'.'

Susan's face broke into a smile. 'Well, I'm over the moon for you,' she said. 'This is the best news I have heard in a long while.'

Eustace smiled again too. 'It's thanks to you, Miss. I'd never have bothered comin' back to school after my father died if you hadn't given me them boots. Thank you.'

Susan fought the urge to hug the boy. But he was standing so tall, she didn't want to baby him. She watched as he walked away, putting his cap on and adjusting it as he walked proudly out of the school gates and down the street. Standing in the school yard, she remembered the sea of faces in her class when she'd asked, 'Who here has lost a father on *Titanic*?' Most of the hands had risen into the air.

*Titanic* had devasted their school, their streets, their whole community. Worse, it had fuelled a mistrust even greater between rich and poor, servants and their betters. Susan kept a stack of newspaper articles on the *Titanic* under her bed. She knew every fact, every statistic about the tragedy. When only thirty-nine percent of first class passengers but seventy-six percent of third class passengers perished, it was clear there was a huge road ahead before working class people would be anywhere near close to being recognised as worthy or important. Susan recalled another article which had stated that only one child from First Class had perished, whereas fifty-two children from steerage had died. Then there was the crew. The devoted, exhausted, work-weary crew. Seventy-six percent of them had died on *Titanic*. Five hundred and forty-nine from Southampton alone.

But now, as she watched Eustace disappear, a whole new future ahead of him, she felt confident that they would rise out of this horror like phoenixes from the ashes. And as she went back to collect her bag and coat, and shut her classroom, she realised there were ways she could make a difference every single day.

She didn't have to go to rallies, risking arrest or breaking windows. True, she'd always believe in the cause and back the Suffragettes in all they were doing. But she knew she didn't have the fight in her that way since *Titanic*. She longed for a time when women would get the voteand be treated as equals. But in the meantime, she had a life to live and could make a difference in other, smaller ways. Just seeing Eustace's proud face and his smart uniform made her sure of that now.

Leaving the school, she walked her usual way home, passing people she knew and recognised. She passed a newspaper stand and saw the headline 'Cat and Mouse Act will be passed'. She bought a paper and started reading. The headline 'Cat and Mouse Act' referred to a new proposed act in Parliament called the Temporary Discharge for Ill Health Act. It gave police the powers to let Suffragettes on hunger strike go free from prison and then re-arrest them once they were stronger. Susan took the paper home under her arm. She didn't know if this was good or bad. She turned back on herself and decided to pay a visit to Angelo to ask his thoughts. She pushed open the ice cream parlour door and saw him and his mother behind the counter. His mother was holding up an ancient-looking gown in a style she had never seen before. She saw Susan and thrust it immediately behind her back.

'What's happening here?' Susan asked, as Angelo's

mother blushed.

'Mamma?' Angelo said.

The woman brought the dress back from behind her back and laid it carefully on a clean unused table in the shop.

'Dillo a lei,' his mother was saying.

'What is she saying?' Susan asked.

'She's saying "tell her",' Angelo said. 'Va bene, Mamma, va bene,' he said to his mother. He took the dress from his mother and held it up. 'This is your wedding dress,' he said.

Susan's face fell.

# Chapter Forty-Nine

**Catherine**

For days Catherine had been making her excuses whenever he came near her. He didn't push for any intimacy anymore. But when he tried to caress her tummy or whisper happy, sweet things about their impending arrival, Catherine would bat Percy's hand away and say, 'Give it up, Percy.'

He had no idea what was the matter with her. It was the pregnancy, his mother had said.

Catherine plunged herself into working. She got up early and swept the shop, then she polished the shoes until they shone, then she arranged and rearranged the window display so many times that Percy had no idea where women's shoes ended and men's boots began.

'What's wrong with you?' he asked finally.

'Nothing,' she said, 'I'm tired, that's all.'

'Mother said you shouldn't be working so much,' Percy said. 'You can rest you know. You have a home, a job, we're all right Catherine.'

She felt herself blush and tears rise up in her throat. 'I'm going out,' she said.
She grabbed her overcoat and pulled it on.

'But it's raining,' Percy called out.

She ignored him and slammed the shop door behind

her. She walked. And walked. She trod through puddles, through the wet streets, not caring if carts splashed her or children doused her with muddy water as they ran past. Her stockings were wet. It didn't matter. She walked on, and on until she reached the King's Arms. She stood outside, the rain dripping off her hair and down her neck. Women never went in the King's Arms. Well, she thought, some did. But they were the type of woman you didn't talk about.

Now, raging and on the verge of screaming, she pushed the double doors open and walked inside. A group of stokers was on one side of the room. A group of foremen were on the other side. She walked up to the bar and said, 'Gin and water please.'

The barman looked at her. 'You old Gregory's daughter?' he said.

'So what if I am?' she said.

He shrugged, poured her a gin and water and shoved the glass towards her. She handed over her coins, lifted the glass and downed it. She felt the gin coat her throat. Then a warm feeling cascaded through her, down her neck, across her tense shoulders and down her back. The barman had come back with her change when she said, 'Get me another. The same.'

He looked over her shoulder. The group of stokers were watching her now. Many of them she knew. There was no threat or menace. They knew she was her father's daughter. She took her second glass of gin and walked to a seat at the back of the bar. She sat down and sipped this time, feeling the numbing sensation as it coated her tongue. Her blood felt warmer now. The cold from the rain was easing off. Her stockings were still wringing wet, but she could feel her blood pumping again.

She held her glass, swishing the transparent liquid around and around. She thought of her underwear and stockings, stuffed into a bag of rubbish at the back of the shop. She'd hidden it well. No one would ever find it or know what had happened. Because she'd hidden it so well, Percy still believed she was carrying their baby. Kezia still talked about a day far off when 'little feet' would be trying the shoes on. Try as she might, Catherine had been unable to find the right time to tell Percy. He had bloomed so much since their marriage. He still suffered nightmares and still had that lost look and shook sometimes. But love was healing him, she knew that now. The notion of being a father soon was the one thing keeping him going, stopping him from sinking under as so many other survivors had done.

She cast her mind back to those two women who had come into the shop. They'd had nothing good to say about surviving crew. Men who hit their wives, men who screamed out, men who could no longer work. Percy walked that line every single day. She knew that. And she knew her pregnancy had been the antidote to fear and suffering. The antidote, she thought, to death itself.

She downed her glass and winked at the barman. 'One more,' she said.

He obliged and brought a glass over. 'You know,' he said, eyeing the stokers who were laughing and slapping the table, 'you should be careful in here. A woman alone.'

Catherine, now feeling wonderfully tipsy, threw her head back. 'I'd like to see 'em try,' she said. 'I'm my father's daughter.'

She was also her mother's daughter. She'd grown up seeing her mother whack, slap and hit her way through marriage. She'd also seen her father fight outside the pub, fight for work, fight over pay, fight over an insult. Fighting was in her blood. She feared no one.

Two more gins later, Catherine's world began to spin. She stood up, woozily, and fell back down again.

'Waaa-haaaay!' yelled the stokers, seeing her slump down into her chair.

She steadied herself and got up. She paid her final bill and staggered out through the double doors and into the early evening darkness. The nights were cold now. She walked in the direction of the shop. Then she turned and walked back the way she'd come. She thought of going back to her home. She saw the light in the front room across from the King's Arms. Tears began to well in her eyes. What would she tell them? That she'd failed where every other woman seemed to succeed? There was no end of pregnancy around her way. Every day another baby seemed to be born and another woman sprouted a new bump. Not her. She shook her head. Maybe she was too poisonous, too hard to be a mother. She walked to the left and down towards the docks. The ships' horns called out over the misty streets. The rain had stopped.

She walked on. The streets were quiet now. She left the bustle of the high street behind and could only hear the clip of her own boots on the cobbles. Just then a figure stepped out from the shadows. She turned and saw someone she vaguely recognised. It was one of the young stokers from the King's Arms.

How had he got here?

He stepped forwards. 'Had a few, have you?' he slurred, coming nearer.

She turned away and began to walk on but he grabbed her wrist. 'Hey! Get off!' she yelled.

'Come on, girl like you drinkin' alone gotta be askin' for it,' he said, pulling her into an alley. 'I'll give yer a few pennies.'

The light from the street disappeared as he dragged her further into the darkness of the alley. He had one hand around her neck, the other snaking its way downwards, pulling her skirts up. Sickened, she felt the clammy skin of his hand on her thigh. His breath, close to her mouth, stank of stale ale and whisky. She kicked. She pulled away, she tried to cry out. He covered her mouth with his hand that had been on her neck.

'Shut it, right?' he said, shoving her head back against a brick wall so hard she felt dizzy.

She closed her eyes. She stopped fighting. What did it matter anyway? Her body was ruined, rubbish, a purposeless vessel that would never carry a child.

But then she thought of Percy's face. Dear Percy, who loved her more than anyone had ever done. She thought of the cobblers and suddenly remembered she always kept a pocketknife in her pinafore, for undoing the string on the shoe parcels in the shop. Heart racing, she made her body go limp, letting him carry out his disgusting desires. Fumbling, her fingers plunged into her pocket. They found the hard leather of the knife's sheath. She grabbed it, pulled it out and then, with a sudden jab, she thrust it into the stoker's side.

He staggered backwards. He didn't cry out. He didn't say anything.

She pulled her skirts down and ran. She ran and ran, through puddles, up and over kerbs. She ran until she couldn't hear her own pulse in her ears anymore.

# Chapter Fifty

**Catherine**

Lucy bashed the tea cup down so hard that hot liquid fell onto Joseph's hand. 'Is this the breakfast service I was always accustomed to?' he asked, smiling.

She didn't answer. She hadn't answered him in days. Not since he had signed on to sail on *Olympic* in just five days' time.

'Look, I have to go,' he said. 'I don't know what else to do. The Fund money's stopped. The compensation will next month. We can't live off air, Lucy.'

She walked over, ignoring Luke crying in the pram. 'But you had plans, Joe. You were going to buy the charabanc and we'd have a business! Why can't you just try and remember that?'

'I can't believe I'd say that. It would be a massive risk, don't you see?' he said. 'Besides, I've only ever driven a tractor!'

'What difference does it make?' she spat. 'You didn't care before you went on *Titanic*.'

He closed his eyes and sighed deeply. 'Don't you see, I don't remember a thing before *Titanic*. I don't remember who I was or what our life was like, let alone whether or not I fancied getting us a charabanc.'

'We were going to get out of this,' she said, gesturing to

the mould on the ceiling, the damp in one corner of the room, the windows that were never transparent no matter how much you cleaned them. 'You were going to stop risking your life at that furnace, dying young and leaving me. You see the state of them when they get off the killer ships. Skeletons, they call the stokers. I don't want you to go that way, Joe.'

He stared at the image of the charabanc. He felt nothing. No memory. No excitement. No memory of a plan.

Lucy groaned and pulled her winter coat on and pushed the pram into the street. It was a damp October day; the kind of damp that got into your bones. She tightened the blanket around Luke's neck and walked along the pavements, avoiding last night's puddles that seeped in through a hole in her left boot. She was walking with such anger and rage that she barely felt her pram bash into Susan's legs.

'Oh, steady there!' Susan said.

Lucy gasped. 'Oh, so sorry. I didn't see you.'

Susan took in Lucy's red eyes and frowned. 'What's wrong? Been crying?' she said.

Lucy shrugged. 'He's going back to sea,' she said.

'When?' Susan said.

'*Olympic*. Five days' time.'

Susan shook her head. 'So many men do, though,' she said. 'Half the stokers that came back signed back on again to different ships. It's all they know.'

They walked on.

'But this was Joseph's last trip,' Lucy said. 'This was the last one and then we were buying a charabanc. We had plans …'

'A charabanc?' Susan said, eyes wide. 'I'm all ears.'

They walked on and slowly Lucy was able to calm down enough to explain.

'Joe planned to buy a charabanc and run outings?' Susan asked.

'Yes, excursions and trips, you know,' Lucy said. 'We were saving for it. Now when I show him the article he kept, with a picture, he just frowns. He says he doesn't know anything about cars and can't remember even planning this.

He says the only thing he's ever driven is a tractor.'

Susan's face lit up.

'What if he actually saw a charabanc, up close?' she said.

'How?' Lucy said. 'Know anyone round here with one?'

Susan laughed. 'No. But I know an ex-pupil who does. Let me have a word with someone I know. I reckon I can set up a time Joseph can see a charabanc up close. Touch it, smell it. If that doesn't jog his memory, then nothing ever will.'

Lucy's face erupted into a smile. 'That would be marvellous,' she said.

Just then, Susan and Lucy felt a hand touch each of their arms. They both spun around and saw Catherine standing there. She had dark circles around her eyes and her hands shook.

'What on earth …?' Susan said.

'Catherine, what's wrong?' Lucy said.

'I need to talk to you,' Catherine said.

Susan ushered Lucy and Catherine into her parents' scullery.. 'Ma's at the market,' she said.

Lucy pushed the pram into a corner. Luke was asleep. Susan pulled three chairs out at the kitchen table and the three of them sat down.

'Tea?' Susan asked.

Lucy was about to say yes when Catherine shook her head and shivered. 'No,' she said.

They sat down. Catherine was silent. Finally, she said, 'I think I killed someone.'

The silence rang out in the kitchen. Susan finally said, 'What?'

'I think I killed someone,' Catherine repeated. 'Last night.'

Lucy stared in horror at Catherine. She knew she was a live wire and always had been. She had her father's attitude towards authority and her mother's temper. She was a born survivor, a city street woman if ever Lucy saw one. But kill someone?

Susan was shaking her head. 'What are you on about?' she said.

'Stabbed him, I did.' Catherine made an action of jabbing and twisting an invisible knife. 'He was all over me, pawing at me. I had to do something.' She shivered again and pulled her shawl around her.

'Who? Where? When?' Susan was asking.

'I was drinking,' Catherine began. 'I went in the King's Arms and had some gin and water.'

Lucy looked confused. 'What were you doing in there?' she asked. Even Joseph didn't frequent that rough place.

'Never you mind,' Catherine replied, shooting Lucy a scowl that said, *what would you ever understand?*

'Go on,' Susan said, leaning forward.
'I had a bit o' gin. Probably too much. I went for a walk to clear my head, like. I ended up walking by the docks. It was dark but the lampswere lit. I just wanted to walk a bit …' Her voice trailed off and she picked her nails, her hands in her lap.

Susan looked very grave. 'What happened, Catherine?' she said.

'I was walking. All I wanted was some air before going back to the shop. I swear it. But then he came along.'

'Who came along?' Susan said.

'I don't know. Never seen him before. A stoker. He was in the King's Arms. He came at me and told me I was askin' for it. He pulled me into an alleyway and started grabbin' at me all over.'

Susan closed her eyes. Lucy looked terrified.

'I tried to kick and fight, I swear it,' Catherine said, now staring at them with wide, imploring eyes. 'I fought and I smacked him but he was stronger. He had a hand round my neck. Then when I screamed, he put it over my mouth.' She sighed.

'What happened?' Susan asked.

Catherine paused. This was the moment. If she told them this part, there was no going back. Lucy was holding her now-flat stomach, sickened and disgusted that a man could attack a pregnant woman.

'I felt in my pocket. I remembered my pocket knife from the shop,' Catherine said. 'I didn't want to kill him, I just wanted him off me. I ...' Her voice trailed off and she put her head in her hands and slumped onto the kitchen table. 'I killed him,' Catherine said, her voice a muffle through her fingers.

Lucy had her hands over her mouth. Susan looked like a statue. No emotion crossed her face.

'Do you know? Did you see him die?' Susan said.

Catherine shook her head. 'I ran. I ran all the way back. I didn't see.'

Susan thought quickly. 'And did anyone see you, running away I mean?'

Catherine replied, 'No.'

'What happened next?' Susan asked.

Lucy was too stunned to speak. She just listened, a passive voyeur in the most bizarre conversation she'd ever overheard in her life.

'I went home and the shop was closed up. I let myself in the back of the shop and I took my pinafore off. It had blood on, you see. I threw that away in the rubbish and I washed my hands. Then I went up to bed.'

'And you told Percy?' Susan said.

Catherine looked up at her.

'You didn't tell him?' Susan said.

'No,' Catherine said, her voice no more than a squeak.

Susan kicked her chair from under her and began to pace the floor. Lucy noticed the floorboards creaked as she walked across them.

'So, no one saw you, no one knows and we don't know he's dead,' she said.

Catherine stared at her hands.

'Don't you see, then you're probably all right?' Susan said, hurrying over and crouching at Catherine's side.

'But what if they find him? What if he's still there by the docks?' Catherine said, tears finally welling in her hard-as-steel eyes.

'Then it was a scuffle between two stokers,' Susan said. 'Wouldn't be the first time.'

Lucy finally found her voice. 'Joe said a stoker vanished on a trip once. They reckon he ended up in a furnace because he never came off the other end. No one questioned anything.' With disgust she added, 'It's what stokers do.'

Susan nodded. 'Exactly. It's what they do. A stoker was drunk, he had a fight and he got cut up. It happens all the time. No one saw you and no one can connect you to it. It's our secret – mine, yours and Lucy's. All right?'

Susan looked at Lucy. She nodded, numb. Catherine stared at Susan. She knew she could rely on her. But Lucy? A sweet, soft-headed girl from the sticks?

'How do I know you won't tell?' she said.

Lucy swallowed hard.

'Because I'm a mother,' she said. 'That filth attacked a pregnant woman. He deserved it.'

Shocked at her reply, Susan said, 'See. She won't tell. No one has to know.'

Catherine looked at her hands again. They were trembling. 'That's the other thing,' she said, her voice no more than a whisper.

'Oh?' Susan said. 'What other thing?'

Catherine sighed and put her hands to her head. 'I'm not pregnant. Not any more.'

Lucy gasped. 'That brute did that? Made you lose the baby?' she cried.

Catherine shook her head. 'No. I'd lost it a few days earlier, in the lav,' she said. 'Why do you think I went drinking? I hated myself.'

Lucy nodded sadly. Catherine looked at her expression. She didn't think she'd seen a sadder expression in her life. She saw Lucy casting a glance over to the pram where Luke lay sleeping. Lucy turned back to Catherine and said, 'I'm so sorry. And I still don't blame you.'

Susan squeezed Catherine's hand. It was ice cold. Her fingers had turned blue. 'Have you eaten anything?' she said.

Catherine didn't answer.

'Look,' Susan said. 'What was said here stays between these walls. Agreed?'

Catherine nodded. They both looked at Lucy. She nodded too, her eyes full of tears.

'Our secret. Forever,' Susan said.

Catherine finally leaned over and wept.

# CHAPTER FIFTY-ONE

**Susan**

A day had passed since Catherine's revelations at her mother's kitchen table and in that time, Susan had imagined a hundred different scenarios. The stoker, dead, found by police. The stoker, injured, staggering off to die somewhere else.

Straight after leaving Catherine, Susan had walked down to the docks, to the place where Catherine said she was attacked. There was nothing there. No body. No trace or remnant of an attack. She got down on her knees and blindly felt the wet, marshy ground with her fingers. No weapon. Nothing. She tried to put this horror to one side. She had other things to do today – an important outing for Joseph. She waited at the roadside and then saw them approaching – Joseph holding Florence's hand and Lucy pushing the pram.

'Don't see the point of this, really I don't,' Joseph said.

Susan noticed his beard had been trimmed and he'd gained a bit of weight. He was starting to look more like the Joseph she recognised.

'It's just a quick day out to have a look at a car,' Susan said. 'See if we can't jog your memory a bit, all right?'

They walked on and met Eustace, dutifully waiting on the corner by the butcher's in his smart chauffeur's uniform.

'We all set, Eustace?' Susan asked.

'We are, Miss,' he said. He nodded at Joseph and then said, 'Follow me, it's not far.'

They walked along a road, a road that left shops behind and gave way to houses. Then, at a right turn, Susan saw Eustace leading them to a garage up ahead.

A sign outside said 'Harris's Transport'. Two men were smoking outside. One was wearing filthy overalls and was covered in oil, the other was wearing a smart uniform like Eustace.

'Eustace,' the man in uniform said.

'This is that gentleman I was tellin' you of,' Eustace said.

The man stepped forward and held out his hand. 'Jerry,' he said.

'Joseph.'

Jerry put a finger to his temple then said, 'You was on *Titanic?*'

Joseph nodded.

Jerry shook his head. 'And you came back.'

Joseph shrugged. 'I don't remember a thing, truth be known,' he said.

'And they tell me you wanted to get yourself a charabanc when you got back?' Jerry asked.

Joseph shot Lucy a look. 'Apparently,' he said, through gritted teeth.

'Come on in,' Jerry said.

He threw the remnants of his cigarette on the floor. Susan noticed that Eustace looked longingly after the still-smoking stub. She ruffled his hair and they followed inside. Two cars were in sight. Both with shiny chrome headlights. Both black.

'What's that?' Joseph said.

'That's an Anderson Electric,' Jerry replied. 'Beauty, in't she?'

Joseph reached out a hand to touch the shiny paintwork.

'But what you're here to see is out back,' Jerry said.

They all traipsed through. The smell of oil and fumes was overwhelming. Jerry led them to a huge vehicle with three sets of benches, a bench at the front for a driver and even space at the back for luggage. It was enormous.

'This,' Jerry said, feigning a magician wafting his hands as if explaining a trick, 'is a charabanc.'

Joseph hovered. 'Go on,' Susan said, pushing him slightly. He stepped forward. He walked around it, his hands behind his back. He was amazed at its length, its width. The seats were brown leather. The paintwork was spotless.

'And you take folks on outings in this?' Joseph said.

Jerry nodded. 'Worthing, Eastbourne, even as far as Kent,' he said. 'People willing to pay good money to get away from here and get some decent air.'

Joseph was still pacing around the charabanc, eyeing it, touching it, trying desperately to remember. As he peered into the backseat Susan noticed that he flinched slightly. He closed his eyes, frowning as if remembering something, something so small and intangible it might have been mist.

He opened his eyes. 'Do you know, I do recall this,' he muttered . He walked on, looking into the front seat, at the driver's seat, the steering wheel. 'May I?' he asked, looking hopefully at Jerry.

The man nodded. Susan felt her pulse quicken as Joseph opened the driver's door. He sat in the front seat and let his hands fall onto the steering wheel. Susan looked at Lucy as they both watched Joseph's fingers curl around the steering wheel.

And something happened.

He smiled.

Susan saw Lucy's face light up. It was a smile, she knew, that Lucy had not seen in all the weeks since his return.

Joseph nodded to himself, a flush of pink brightening his face. 'I was going to get a charabanc, just like this,' he said, his voice a tremor. 'I was going to come back off *Titanic*, and buy one like this and do outings,' he said. 'Lucy, you were right.' He gripped the steering wheel tighter. He felt around the side and grabbed the soft plumpness of the horn and gave it a squeeze.

Susan and Eustace jumped.

'Steady on,' Jerry said.

Susan and Lucy laughed.

Joseph climbed out of the charabanc and closed the door. He ran his hands one last time over its paintwork. He went to Jerry and held out his hand once more. 'Thank you,' he said.

Jerry looked puzzled. He looked at Eustace. He shrugged too. 'Anytime,' he said.

Susan went to Eustace and shook his hand. 'Now it's my turn to thank you,' she said.

Eustace blushed. 'T's nothin', Miss,' he said.

Susan looked at Lucy and Joseph, now hugging in one corner, as Joseph then lifted his wife into the air and kissed her cheek over and over.

'It's so much more than nothing, Eustace,' Susan said. 'It's everything.'

# Chapter Fifty-Two

**Catherine**

She reached for Percy's hand and held it. But his fingers felt limp in hers. 'And you're only telling me now?' he said. 'Why didn't you tell me before?'

Catherine inhaled. 'I didn't know for sure at first,' she lied. 'Then, when it happened, it was such a shock. Then I didn't want to cause you any upset.'

Percy finally felt the life come back into his hands. He squeezed her hand back. 'But you should have told me, my love,' he said, his eyes red.

'I know that now,' Catherine said.

Percy came nearer and wrapped an arm around her. They were sitting in the front of the shop window, surrounded by shoes and boots. Customers passed by outside, some stopping to peer in at the strange display of human emotion taking place in the window.

'So, are you, you know, are you all right?' Percy asked.

Catherine felt her throat ache with emotion. How did she tell him that this secret she was finally telling him, that she had miscarried, was only the half of it. Her biggest secret remained just that. She could never tell him that.

She'd lied, she'd kept secrets, she'd probably killed a man. But here was her man, ever loving, ever faithful, ever believing in her. She suddenly felt an urge come over her and kissed his cheek. 'I'm all right, Percy,' she said.

'Then we can try again, and it will happen in time, God willing,' Percy said, letting Catherine's head fall against his shoulder. He then whispered, 'Goodness knows, we have fun trying …'

Catherine suddenly jumped up. She smoothed her dress down and made for the other side of the shop.

'Something the matter?' Percy asked, confused. Normally when he mentioned their nighttime antics, Catherine smiled and blushed.

'Nothing,' she said. 'Just there's customers that will want serving, that's all.'

Percy looked into the street. There were no customers at the shop door. He watched his wife busy herself, dusting down the shop counter and moving a pile of boots to mend pointlessly from one area to another. He knew women could be funny, though. He knew they changed when they had babies. Maybe she was still grieving and didn't want to try yet. He decided to leave it for now. They'd talk another day.

When it was time for lunch, Catherine said she had errands to run. She met Susan at the end of the road.

'Ready?' Susan said.

Catherine nodded.

They set off along the route Catherine had taken that night. They reached the docks where she had wandered.

'Here,' Catherine said. 'This is where he grabbed me.'

Susan followed Catherine as they walked down an alleyway. Susan noted that no one could be seen from this viewpoint. It was completely deserted.

'Here?' Susan said.

Catherine nodded, nausea rising in her throat. She looked at the wall where he had pushed her. It looked so plain, with red brick and moss growing on it. Completely harmless. Yet that night …

Susan was scouring the ground for a knife, for clothing, for anything. 'There's nothing here,' she said.

Catherine held her hand to her head.

Susan spun around. 'Don't you see? This is good news. It means you didn't kill him. He got away and probably wandered off, got it bandaged and woke up the next day none the wiser.'

Catherine wasn't so sure. She closed her eyes and remembered the sickening sound as her knife tore into his flesh, his gasp as he staggered backwards.

'Did the knife have anything on it, any writing that anyone could trace back to the shop?' Susan asked.

'No, nothing. It was plain,' Catherine replied.

Susan came to her and said, 'Then, everything is all right.

She took Catherine by the shoulders. 'No body. No news. Don't you think we'd have heard if a stoker was found dead down here? Everyone would be talking about it.'

Catherine tried to smile.

'Here's what happened,' Susan said, 'he was drunk, he tried his luck, he got stabbed, he ran off home. God knows stokers do this all the time. He probably doesn't even remember what happened.'

Catherine was shaking. 'You're right. You're right,' she said.

'Would you remember what he looked like?' Susan asked.

Catherine bit her lip. 'I was tipsy. Well, I was drunk. And it was dark. I can't remember him at all.'

Susan smiled. 'Then he won't remember you,' she said. 'Do you think these men see a person when they look at a woman? He won't remember you at all. Probably not the first woman he's forced himself upon either …'

Catherine saw the rage that flew across Susan's face. They walked away, hurrying not to be seen and then stood outside a shop window. It was almost dark despite only being past one in the afternoon. The shop was a confectioner's, selling sweets and bon bons and chocolates.

'Remember all the times we stood here as children, our noses up against the window?' Catherine said.

Susan smiled. 'How could I forget?' she said. 'Old Mrs Wiggs back then used to move us on and I'd have saliva dripping down my collar from wanting a sweet so badly.'

'Never did get any did we?' Catherine said sadly.

Susan nodded. 'No, we never did.'

Catherine watched as a boy and girl ran past with their hoops, chasing them down the street. It was lunchtime and the children would be going back to school soon. Susan would soon have to go, too.

'I didn't see it before,' Catherine said.

'See what?' Susan asked.

'Oh, all your whinnying about women's rights and the vote and suffrage. I didn't see the point of it all,' she said.

Susan listened. Catherine watched the girl playing with her hoop in the street. 'I see it now. I see why you want it. There was never any hope for us, was there? Not just for a sweet in a shop like this, but for a future, or for not feeling hungry, or for not feeling to blame when someone grabs you and wants to do what they want with you.'

Susan reached for her hand.

'I can see now why you want that to change,' Catherine said, still watching the little girl. Susan said goodbye and set off back to school. Catherine stood there, watching the girl as long as she could, as she twirled and ran and chased her hoop down the street back to school.

She wondered what life that girl would have? Would she have to marry a local man? Would she feel a failure when she could not bear children? Would she have to run the risk of being grabbed and attacked when a man fancied it, just because she was a woman? Catherine watched the girl and her hoop disappear around a corner. She'd never thought about anyone's feelings in her life, except Percy and her friends. But now she made a wish for that little girl.

'Please make things get better for her,' Catherine whispered. 'Maybe one day even for all of us.'

# Chapter Fifty-Three

**Lucy**

Joseph walked in, slammed the door, hurried over and scooped Florence up in his arms. 'Fa-da, Fa-da,' the little girl sang out.

Then he set her down and went to Lucy feeding Luke in the armchair.

Joseph pulled a cap on, stood to attention and said, 'Well, what do you think?'

Lucy stopped feeding and put the sleepy Luke into the pram. 'You never …' she said.

'I did!' he said. He hurried to the table and rummaged in his pocket. He pulled out a piece of paper that looked very official. 'Look,' he said. He pointed to the words. Lucy struggled to take it all in but in essence it said, *First deposit 12 shillings. Balance due October November 1917*. 'It's the agreement, for the charabanc?' Lucy ventured.

'It is, my love,' Joseph said, grabbing her and spinning her around. 'I get it tomorrow. Beautiful black, she is. Shiny. One seat is a bit scuffed but no one will mind that.'

Lucy wriggled to be put down and laughed. 'This is incredible, wonderful!' she cried.

'And I signed off from *Olympic*,' he said. 'Give some other fella a chance.'

Lucy rolled her eyes upwards and silently thanked

God.

The charabanc was on order. He'd pulled out from the next trip. He was no longer a stoker with the long hours, the hellish labour and all the ill health and risk of death that came with it. They were going up in the world. Now they would own a business.

'I can't believe it,' Lucy said.

'Me neither,' Joseph replied, biting his lip and shaking his head. 'Me a chauffeur. Jerry, at the garage, he's been a good 'un. Says he'll give me a few lessons on driving. Says anyone who came back off *Titanic* is a hero in his book. He'll do it for free.'

'Wonderful!' Lucy said.

She went to the stove to check on the meat pudding she'd made earlier that day. She'd made a suet dough and piled meat inside and topped it with a thick, crusty 'hat' before tying a thin white sheet of muslin around it and plunging it into a pan of boiling water. It had been cooking three hours and Lucy checked it now. She reckoned it needed another hour. She was just about to tell Joseph this when he said, 'Said goodbye to some of the lads earlier.'

'Oh?' Lucy said, drying her hands on her apron.

'Yeah, they dragged me into the Grapes. I only stopped a while. I said my goodbyes. They can't believe I'm leaving the boiler rooms. Some said I was going soft.'

'Nonsense!' Lucy said. 'You have ideas, that's all. They can't understand that.'

Joseph smiled. He got out the charabanc picture on the article he carried everywhere with him. He gazed at it.

'Anyway, one of the fellas was in a bad way,' Joseph said.

'Oh?'

'Yeah, he got stabbed by a working girl down at the docks!'

Lucy froze. Her hands gripped the sideboard. She felt suddenly very strange and dizzy. She turned around. She tried to make her voice very calm, very matter-of-fact. 'Stabbed?' she said.

'Yeah, took a knife to his side, he did. He was walking

but had a limp. Doctor fixed him up. People were ribbin' him, sayin' even the whores won't take him no more!'

Lucy made a sharp intake of breath. 'Don't call them whores,' she said, quietly.

Joseph looked up from his newspaper picture. He frowned. 'Well, what are they, then? Selling themselves down at the docks. What's the word, my love?'

She fought the urge to cry, to tell him everything. Instead she turned back to her range and replaced the lid on the boiling pot. 'Maybe he deserved it,' she said.

'Too right,' Joseph said. 'I tell you, what people say about that one, he did deserve it.'

Lucy turned again. 'Oh, what about him?' she said.

Joseph leaned back in his chair. 'You, Mrs Williams, are very interested in this case,' he said, in a mock posh voice.

She felt a smile come and felt her shoulders drop. 'Sorry, ignore me. Just being silly,' she said.

He went back to staring at his charabanc picture. Lucy began to slice cabbage to boil and tried her best to contain her thudding heart.

# Chapter Fifty-Four

**Catherine**

Lucy and Susan piled into the back of the shop and Catherine closed the door between the shop front and behind the scenes. The shop was closed. Percy was at a market. Kezia was out at the shop and Percy's father could be heard snoring upstairs.

'What's all this about?' Catherine said, taking in the girls' nervous expressions.

'We have good news,' Susan said.

'Very good news,' Lucy added.

'Come on then, out with it,' Catherine said.

'That stoker's not dead,' Susan said.

'You never killed him,' Lucy added.

Catherine's eyes widened. She let out a huge sigh. 'Oh, thank God,' she breathed.

'Joseph saw him in the pub giving him a send off,' Lucy said. 'I managed to find out more that night – without him suspecting anything.'

'Go on,' Catherine said.

'Turns out, he's a stoker with a wife. And he's known to hit her. They had the police out twice last month. He broke her arm once.'

Susan shook her head, disgust registering on her face.

'Seems he does this a lot, following women, going

whoring at the docks. He told everyone …' Her voice trailed off. She was ashamed.

'Say it,' Catherine said, her voice like steel.

Lucy cleared her throat. 'He told everyone he picked up a working girl at the docks and she stabbed him. A doctor fixed him up. He says he can't remember the wh …'

'The whore?' Catherine said, her neck twitching.

'Yes. He says he can't remember but says it was a working girl. Anyway, that's not the best part,' Lucy said.

'Exactly,' Susan said. 'Turns out, according to Joseph, he's just signed on for six months on the Union Castle Line ships. He's already left. He won't be around here for a good while. You won't have to see him. Not ever.'

Catherine let out a long sigh. She closed her eyes. Then she opened them and said, 'Thank you.'

Lucy reached for her hand. Catherine held it. She'd always had a strange relationship with Lucy. She realised now, as she looked at her beautiful face, her wide eyes, her innocence, she envied her. She envied her softness, her hope, her lack of being tarnished. Now, as she felt more tarnished than ever, she realised she no longer had to feel that way. 'Thank you for telling me this,' Catherine said. 'And for keeping my secret.'

'You have nothing to hide or be ashamed of,' Susan said suddenly. 'It's him who should be … castrated! It's him who should be held to account.'

'But that won't get me anywhere now,' Catherine said.

'I know, I know,' Susan said. 'I hope he gets what's coming to him one day, that's all.'

Catherine smiled sadly. 'I hope that, too. But for now, it's my secret to keep.'

'Our secret,' corrected Susan, holding Catherine's other hand in hers. The three of them stood there, out the back of Percy's shop, in a triangle, like a coven of witches.

They heard the back door rattle open and Percy walked in carrying bags of new polishes and sprays for the shoes.

'What's going on here?' he said, smiling. 'You three doing spells?'

'Oh, you don't want to know!' Susan said, laughing.

'We wouldn't hex you, Percy,' Lucy giggled.

The women left, leaving Percy and Catherine together. He knew not to go to near to her, knew that she was unresponsive to him since their loss. She allowed a cuddle now and then, but he knew that was where it stopped. He was about to carry the bags through to the shop when Catherine reached for his hand.

'Percy,' she said.

'Yes, love?' he said, eyes wide.

She looked at his dear face, the face that she now loved with all her heart.

'Your mother's out,' she said.

'Yes,' Percy said.

'And your father … well, you can hear him snoring.'

Percy rolled his eyes and laughed.

'So …' she said.

'So?' he said, still oblivious.

'How about we go back upstairs and start doing what we are meant to do?' Catherine said.

'And what's that?' Percy said.

'Making a baby.'

# Chapter Fifty-Five

**Susan**

Susan stared at Angelo's mother and didn't know whether to laugh or cry. The woman had a pout and a scowl that could rival any little girl in her class. Her dark eyebrows, now specked with grey, were knitted together. Her lips were pursed. Angelo stood between the two women, trying to placate them.

'Look, Susan, she just wanted you to have her mamma's wedding dress,' Angelo said.

'And I am grateful, but I want to make my own dress,' Susan said.

Angelo sighed. 'Where we come from, the dress is handed down,' he said, gritting his teeth.

'And I come from here, Southampton, and I am a modern woman and I want to make my own,' she said.

Angelo ran a hand shakily through his hair and walked back behind the counter. He began washing scoops and spoons. Mrs Rizzi stood up and walked away, banging into chairs as she left.

'I am sorry, Angelo,' Susan said, 'I love your mother and I don't want to hurt her feelings. But I want to at least choose my wedding frock.'

Angelo turned. He was wiping the inside of a bowl with a towel. 'I know. But she is trying to help, believe me;

anyway dresses are expensive.'

Susan shook her head. 'Lucy does finishing for the factory,' she said. 'She says she'll help me. My mother has some material and I have a design in my head. We can do it ourselves,' she said.

Angelo leaned over. 'And you will look a picture,' he said, kissing her.

Susan felt content for the first time in a long while. It had been four weeks since she had introduced Joseph to the charabanc via Eustace. She'd seen the car arrive and all the street had come out and looked. Boys from all the nearby lanes and alleys came every day to look at it and touch it. Joseph had taken to draping a large bit of rubber over it that he'd got from Jerry at the garage. Lucy seemed so much happier. The *Titanic* Relief Fund was slowly filtering down to the children at school and many of them not only had boots now but new clothes, fuller tummies and apprenticeships on the horizon.

It was two weeks until Christmas. Which meant two weeks until their wedding day. 'I've got an idea,' Susan said.

She went out the back and found Signora Rizzi, sniffling into a handkerchief. She knelt down beside her and reached for her hand. Her fingers felt gnarly with work. Angelo stepped in behind her.

'Can you translate?' Susan asked, looking up at him.

'Si,' he smiled.

'Mrs Rizzi, I love your son,' she said.

'Signora Rizzi, amo il tuo figlio,' Angelo said.

'But I am my own woman and I want my dress to be about who I am,' she said.

Angelo rolled his eyes. Instead he translated simply and said, 'Io voglio un'abito che scelgio io.'

Mrs Rizzi dabbed at her eyes.

'But,' Susan said.

Angelo said, 'Ma …'

'I would be honoured if you could provide me your veil,' Susan said.

'Vorrei il tuo velo da sposa,' Angelo said.

Mrs Rizzi stopped sniffling and looked at Susan

through red eyes.

Susan squeezed her hand 'It would be a true honour,' she said.

Angelo was about to translate, but Mrs Rizzi stopped him and held her hand up.

'You may have my veil, my dear,' she said, kissing Susan.

Angelo rolled his eyes and escaped back to the ice cream shop. 'Grazie Dio,' he muttered.

# Chapter Fifty-Six

**Lucy**

She stood on her front doorstep as she watched people clamber into the back of the charabanc, or Bessie, as Joseph affectionately now called the car. 'This way, that's it, up we go,' Joseph was saying, as he helped ladies into the car and assisted gentlemen. This was his fourth trip and he was taking paying customers on a trip to the old capital of England, Winchester. It would be a long day but would involve trips along country roads, a lunch stop in the city, before a Christmas carol service at the Cathedral and a trip home again. As he packed the final passenger into the Bessie, he hopped in the front, doffed his cap to Lucy and grinned.

'See you after our trip,' he called.

She grinned so broadly she thought her face might pop. She waved him off, Luke in her arms, Florence at her side. They watched as their father drove Bessie away and turned the corner.

Lucy went back inside, still grinning. She set the children down safely, Florence to play and Luke in the pram, before there was a knock at the door. She knew who it was and beamed immediately.

'Enter the bride,' she said.

Susan stepped inside, holding reams of fabric. 'And you are certain about this?' Susan said.

'Certain,' Lucy said. 'I've had enough practice,' she added, motioning to a pile of shirts she'd finished. She still worked some nights, finishing shirts. Joseph hadn't liked the idea at first but, as Lucy explained, they needed some capital to start the business – some money for the car and advertisements. He'd accepted on the condition that once the business was running well, she would give up the night work. She promised she would but on one condition; they'd be partners in the business, running it together. Joseph had agreed.

Now, Lucy watched as Susan laid out reams of ivory fabric. Lucy fingered it. 'Ooh lovely,' she said. 'Taffeta.'

Susan nodded. 'God knows where she got it. I don't ask questions of my mother – she knows some rather unsavoury people But needless to say, I am accepting it because, well, it's beautiful!'

Lucy smiled. It really was. As well as taffeta, Susan had brought some chenille and soft cotton. Together, Lucy knew, they could combine to make a beautiful dress.

'And have you a pattern?' Lucy asked.
'No, but I have this picture,' Susan said, taking a ladies' newspaper article from her purse. Lucy gaped. The picture was of a woman with a dress above the ankle. It was like nothing she had ever seen before.

'You know that this is above the shoe line?' Lucy said.

Susan nodded. 'Yes. It represents my freedom as a woman,' she said. 'I might be a bride, but I don't have to conform to everyone's notion of what a bride ought to be wearing.'

Lucy rolled her eyes. 'Can one thing ever not be political?' she giggled.

'No,' Susan replied.

They set to work. Lucy sketched a pattern based on what she saw in the picture. The frock was modern and fresh. Instead of the tight, stern corseted bodice, this dress had loose fitting sides that came to a sash waist. The skirts instead of falling stiffly down, cascaded down in a mist of chiffon. It was everything that was beautiful about a wedding dress with none of the restraint or overt modesty.

'I think it's wonderful,' Lucy said.

When she'd finished her sketch, Susan surveyed the work. 'Perfect!' she said.

For the next few nights, when the children were in bed, Lucy worked on the dress. She stitched and unpicked, cursed and sweated. But a week later, it was done. For the grand unveiling, Lucy invited Susan and Catherine around one afternoon. The dress hung in Lucy and Joseph's bedroom. She made the women tea, then went upstairs to get it. She came down holding it aloft and then held it up for Susan to see.

Susan put her teacup down and ran over. 'Oh, Lucy,' she gasped. 'Oh, oh!'

Catherine came over now too. She put her hands on her hips. 'Certainly better than the godforsaken sack I was dragged down the aisle in,' she said.

Susan elbowed her. 'You look good in a sack, that's your trouble,' she said.

Susan dared to reach out and touch it. It didn't feel like fabric. It was so soft, so light, it felt like clouds.

'Can I try it?'

'I should hope so!' Lucy laughed.

Lucy and Catherine waited at the kitchen table while Susan went upstairs. They heard the floorboards creak above them as she took off her dress, corset and stockings and pulled the dress on. Then they heard the creak of the stairs as Susan made her way down.

The woman who entered the kitchen looked ethereal, like a fairy or a Roman goddess. The fit was perfect, Lucy thought. The fall of the fabric over her hips and legs accentuated her slim figure without being provocative. And the bodice, a far cry from the staid, tight, unbreathable fashions of the day, was soft, gentle and easy. It was a dress for a new era, thought Lucy.

Susan read her mind. 'I feel like this dress says everything I want to say,' Susan said. 'I know it sounds daft. But I feel like, in this dress, I am marrying someone but not giving anything up. Does that sound daft?'

'Yes,' chorused Lucy and Catherine, before collapsing

in giggles.

The truth was, Susan would have to stop her work as a teacher once married. But Angelo had promised to support her in her quest to help women get the vote. She'd work in the shop and they'd run the ice cream business as equals. That, for Susan, was enough for now – enough until she had changed the world.

Susan stepped forward and hugged Lucy. 'Thank you, thank you, thank you,' she said.

'It was a pleasure,' Lucy said.

Susan then hugged Catherine too. 'What's this for?' she said.

'And thank you too, for always being a friend,' she said.

Catherine wafted her hand away. 'Oh, give over.'

Susan went back upstairs and climbed carefully out of the dress. Lucy helped her wrap it up in pieces of fabric to be taken to her mother's house.

'I would like to pay you something,' Susan said.

Lucy stared at the picture of the charabanc in that article still over the fireplace, the article that had started everything. She looked at Susan, the woman who had gone to all lengths to get Joseph to see and touch a car, to bring his memory back.

'You already have,' she said.

# Chapter Fifty-Seven

**Catherine**

Catherine cast her mind back over the last few days. She counted once, then twice, then again and again. There was no avoiding it. She was late. She looked in the mirror. She still had her good looks, her dark eyes, her mass of black hair. But something had changed in her reflection now. The hardness, the steeliness from before was gone. She wanted nothing more now than to be a mother, and to give Percy a child. Being eight days late might mean nothing. Or it might mean everything. She made her way into the shop. Kezia was in the window, hanging thin garlands of tinsel and paper decorations.

'I know it's daft,' she said, turning around. 'But Percy felt it might draw more customers in.'

Catherine went closer and looked at the tinsel. It was three in the afternoon and the December day was already fading. Soon it would be pitch dark. She still hated the dark, ever since that night by the water. But she shook her head as if to shake the memory off. There was hope now. The man was gone. She watched as a fine piece of red tinsel moved in the breeze. Christmas was coming – her first as Percy's wife. That was something to celebrate. She didn't have the space to think about that man by the docks. She would not let him ruin another minute of her life.

Just then Percy came in holding a tiny tree. It had clearly been bashed so many times through the doorways half its branches were already bare.

'What's this?' Kezia said.

'A Christmas tree. I got it for you Catherine,' he smiled.

He set it down next to the counter. It was only three feet high. 'I thought we can have it upstairs and decorate it,' he said.

Catherine looked at the branches. Her parents had never brought a tree in at Christmas. They'd never had the money or the inclination. She felt a little girl deep inside her excited and joyful at the prospect of a tree, perhaps with baubles or even candles. 'You're too good to me, Percy,' she said, throwing her arms around him.

In the shop window, Kezia smiled.

Later that night, Percy and Catherine knelt together in their small upstairs room. Kezia had given Catherine some left over Christmas window decorations and now they decorated their own small tree together.

When they'd finished, Catherine stood up and admired it. 'It looks good,' she said.

'It looks lovely,' Percy said.

They sat on their bed together, admiring the tiny tree, so bare in parts. It didn't matter. Nothing mattered. Catherine thought of telling Percy she was late, telling him that she had hope and a sense of something changing inside her. But she thought better of it. She couldn't let him down again. She felt him reach for her hand. In the half light of their room, she turned to face him.

'I've not talked much about *Titanic* since it happened,' he began, looking at her slim wedding ring.

'You don't have to,' she said.

'Oh, but I want to now,' he said, meeting her gaze again.

'Go on,' she said.

He coughed a little. She noticed he'd stopped coughing, that little tic he'd had before he'd set sail. She'd longed to hear that nervous cough again. Now here it was. 'When I was standing on the deck in that cold, a hundred things rushed through my head. I looked at the stars. They were so beautiful. They sparkled. It didn't feel right, seeing them sparkle and gleam like diamonds while all around me women were screaming and crying and men begging them to get in lifeboats …'

Catherine nodded.

'Well, I thought of lots of things. I kept saying I would not get in a lifeboat. All the men were saying that. I thought of my mother and how she'd raised me, and how I loved her. I thought of my father and how I realised I barely knew him, you know, he's always so silent.'

'Apart from when he snores,' Catherine added.

Percy laughed.

'And I made peace with that,' Percy said. 'I knew I would never see them again and it pained me, but I made my peace.' He paused. 'But then I thought of you, Catherine,' he said. 'I thought of your face, of your beautiful smile, your hair, your laugh and how you made me feel. But most of all I thought of how I loved you and how dear you were to me. And that's when I made a decision.'

Catherine listened.

'I knew I could either drown there and be a man and go down like a true hero. Or I could get in a boat and be called a coward all my life. But it was an easy choice, when I thought of you. I had never wanted to live so much in all my life. I thought of us getting wed, having a family, the life we'd have. And I knew I could not die then. I didn't care if I was called a coward every day of my life. I had to live and be with you.'

Catherine was looking at her lap, too afraid to show the tears that were falling down her cheeks.

Percy gently lifted her chin and looked into her watery eyes. 'I don't regret it, not even when I hear the names behind me, or the women won't come in the shop,' he said. 'Not for a moment.'

She held her head to his neck then and let herself sob. 'Oh Percy, nor do I,' she said. 'Nor do I.'

# Chapter Fifty-Eight

**Catherine, Lucy and Susan**

The mirror in Susan's childhood bedroom reflected three excited faces. 'Let me,' Catherine said. 'You did the dress, let me do the hair at least.'

Lucy felt Catherine tug the hair pins from her grasp and gave in, laughing. She sat on the bed and watched as Catherine deftly twisted Susan's brown hair into a modern style that showed the nape of her neck.

'Very daring, Susan,' Lucy laughed.

Susan shrugged and smiled.

With the hair set, Lucy and Catherine set about helping Susan into her dress. Lucy steadied her arms, while Catherine shimmied the dress over her feet, ankles and calves and up to her waist. Susan then slipped her arms in and turned and Lucy did the satin buttons up that snaked up the back.

Susan turned. 'Will I do?' she asked.

Catherine suddenly recalled the muddy-faced girl Susan had been as a child. She remembered how they'd played together in these very streets, stomachs aching with hunger as the Muffin Man had passed, playing on regardless, jumping and running after hoops.

Now, Catherine thought, how did that child become this woman? This woman who fought for good and what was right? But Catherine didn't have the vocabulary to express this. Instead she said, 'You'll do.'

Lucy watched as Susan spun in her dress. All the nights of sewing and unpicking, of her eyes watering in the lamplight, had been worth it. She looked a picture. A noise interrupted their thoughts.

*Beep-beep!*

Catherine and Susan ran to the window and peered down.

'Joseph's here in Bessie!' Lucy cried.

Susan gave one last look to her reflection and picked up her small bouquet off her bed. 'Then we must go,' she said.

Three girls hurried down the stairs. The mother of the bride was nipping from a gin bottle next to the hearth. She hastily put it down and wiped her mouth. 'Ready?' she asked.

'Ready, Ma,' Susan said.

They stepped out into the December day. There was a sea mist and it felt cold to the very bone. Joseph smiled, doffed his cap and opened the door to Bessie.

'Bride first,' he announced. He held out his hand and aided Susan into the back. Her mother followed, then Catherine, then Lucy. As Lucy stepped in, Joseph gave her a playful pat on the behind.

'The children?' Lucy asked Joseph.

'Happily playing with Mrs Stoat,' he replied.

'Well, she certainly knows all there is to know about children,' Catherine said.

Joseph got into the driver's seat and started the engine. And suddenly they were off, the cold wind whipping their hair and faces.

'Couldn't you get one with a roof?' Catherine said.

'Next time!' Joseph shouted over the din of the engine.

As they drove through the streets of Northam, people stopped and gaped. Everyone knew about Bessie, but they also knew she was for the middle class outings only. To see local people in such a fine charabanc was something altogether new. Matrons gaped as the bride drove past. Little girls shouted and waved. Susan waved back.

'I feel like royalty,' she said.

They arrived at St Edmund's Catholic Church. Joseph parked outside and got out of the car. He walked around to Susan's side and helped her out.

'It's a shame Ernest couldn't be here,' Joseph said, proffering his arm.

'You'll do,' Susan smiled.

The women filed into the church. Susan's mother swayed a little as she walked down the aisle to her place. Mrs Rizzi saw her and feigned a smile. She would have to have words about this woman's drinking, she noted.

At the front, Angelo stood facing the altar. Percy stood nearby, nervously holding the wedding ring for Susan.

The wooden door to the church creaked open and an organ began to play. Angelo's cousin was a piano player in a bar. He'd persuaded the vicar to let him play. Susan walked down the aisle to a strange Italian love song she had never heard before. Mrs Rizzi stared at her new daughter and her ancient family veil that framed her face and dabbed at her eyes.

Susan reached the altar and Angelo turned. He took a sharp intake of breath. She had never looked more radiant.

'Hello,' he whispered.

'Hello,' Susan whispered back.

The congregation watched as they said their vows. Susan's side of the church was almost empty. Angelo's was packed to the back with cousins, brothers, sisters, uncles and aunts. As Susan promised to love and obey, Angelo gave her a wink. She smiled back. She knew he would be a partner, not a master.

As they sang a hymn, Susan thought of her father who should have walked her in. And her brother Jack who no doubt would have played pranks by now. She fought the tears that were trying to bubble up and pushed them down again. *Titanic* had taken enough from their lives. It would not take today from her.

As the vows ended Angelo leaned in and kissed his bride.

The Italians cheered and the English side frowned and

blushed. Then the Italian organ music started again and Angelo held out his arm. Susan linked her arm through his and they walked down the aisle again. This time, as man and wife.

As they stepped out into the freezing December air, rice rained down on them. Susan squealed as she felt rice fall down her bodice, down her back, all over her hair.

Joseph found his wife and wrapped his arm around her. 'I never thought I'd see her marry,' he said.

'Me neither,' Lucy said, shaking her head.

'Mrs Pankhurst will not be pleased,' Joseph grinned.

'Oh, I don't know,' Lucy said. 'The best way to change things is from within. I reckon Susan has a lot more to say and do yet.'

A few steps away, Percy held Catherine's hand as she threw more rice over the new couple.

'Remember our day?' Percy whispered.

Catherine nodded and kissed his cheek. 'That's when my life changed for the better,' she replied.

As the December mist knitted into a thick blanket and the plaintive ships horns sank out from the sea, the bridal party made its way back to the Rizzi's shop for a wedding breakfast.

As Catherine walked behind the others, holding Percy's hand, she smiled. Outwardly, she felt nothing but deep inside her, a tiny bundle of cells fizzed and fused and buried themselves deep into the rich, nourishing scarlet of her body. A countdown to life and hope began.

*Other titles by BLKDOG Publishing for your consideration:*

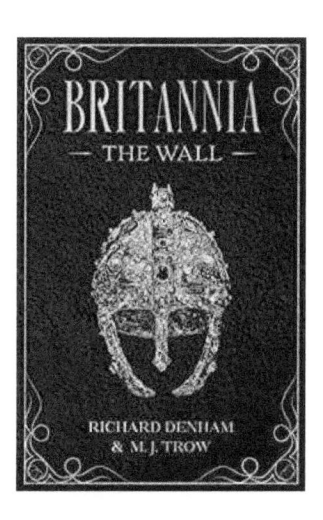

**Britannia: The Wall
By Richard Denham & M. J. Trow**

THE END OF ROMAN BRITAIN BEGINS.

The story opens in 367 AD. Four soldiers - Justinus, Paternus, Leocadius and Vitalis - are out hunting for food supplies at an outpost of Hadrian's Wall, when the Wall comes under attack.

The four find their fort destroyed, their comrades killed, and Paternus is unable to find his wife and son. As they run south to Eboracum, they realize that this is no ordinary border raid. Ranged against the Romans at the edge of the world are four different peoples, and they have banded together under a mysterious leader who wears a silver mask and uses the name Valentinus - man of Valentia, the turbulent area north of the Wall.

Faced with questions they are hard-pressed to answer, Leocadius blurts out a story that makes the men Heroes of the Wall. Their lives change not only when Valentinus begins his lethal sweep across Britannia but as soon as Leo's lie is out in the world, growing and changing as it goes.

**Maxwell's Zoom
By M. J. Trow**

When asked about when it all began, Peter Maxwell would always say that it was at breakfast one day, when his son said, 'It says in the news that bats are giving people colds.' At that point, that was all anyone thought, if they thought anything at all. Nolan was worried about the Count and Bismarck but of course, as everyone would soon know, it was more than that – much more.

What was perhaps not quite so obvious as the world started to pull together to halt the spread of the pandemic, was that it would also restart a killing spree, one that had been halted for decades. Old memories rising to the surface, old enmities and slights recalled and suddenly, in masked and socially distanced Leighford someone is prowling with a hammer raised to create mayhem.

As an historian, Maxwell is keeping his head while most people are running round like chickens minus theirs – loss and tragedy stalk the land, closer to home than anyone thought possible. In a world where death is striking everywhere, how can anyone hope to bring a murderer to book?

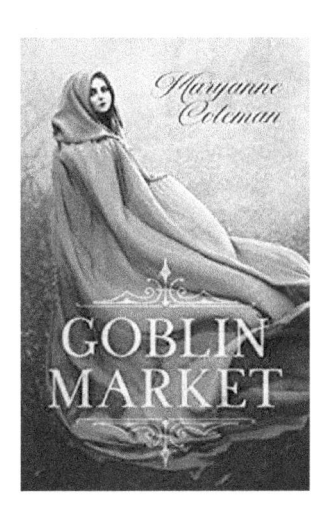

## Goblin Market
### By Maryanne Coleman

Have you ever wondered what happened to the faeries you used to believe in? They lived at the bottom of the garden and left rings in the grass and sparkling glamour in the air to remind you where they were. But that was then – now you might find them in places you might not think to look. They might be stacking shelves, delivering milk or weighing babies at the clinic. Open your eyes and keep your wits about you and you might see them.

But no one is looking any more and that is hard for a Faerie Queen to bear and Titania has had enough. When Titania stamps her foot, everyone in Faerieland jumps; publicity is what they need. Television, magazines. But that sort of thing is much more the remit of the bad boys of the Unseelie Court, the ones who weave a new kind of magic; the World Wide Web. Here is Puck re-learning how to fly; Leanne the agent who really is a vampire; Oberon's Boys playing cards behind the wainscoting; Black Annis, the bag-lady from Hainault, all gathered in a Restoration comedy that is strictly twenty-first century.

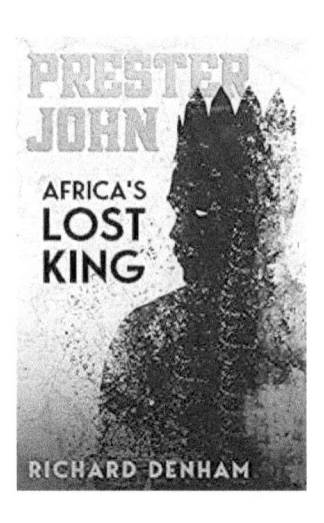

**Prester John: Africa's Lost King**
**By Richard Denham**

He sits on his jewelled throne on the Horn of Africa in the maps of the sixteenth century. He can see his whole empire reflected in a mirror outside his palace. He carries three crosses into battle and each cross is guarded by one hundred thousand men. He was with St Thomas in the third century when he set up a Christian church in India. He came like a thunderbolt out of the far East eight centuries later, to rescue the crusaders clinging on to Jerusalem. And he was still there when Portuguese explorers went looking for him in the fifteenth century.

Was he real? Did he ever exist? This book will take you on a journey of a lifetime, to worlds that might have been, but never were. It will take you, if you are brave enough, into the world of Prester John.

## Fade
## By Bethan White

There is nothing extraordinary about Chris Rowan. Each day he wakes to the same faces, has the same breakfast, the same commute, the same sort of homes he tries to rent out to unsuspecting tenants.

There is nothing extraordinary about Chris Rowan. That is apart from the black dog that haunts his nightmares and an unexpected encounter with a long forgotten demon from his past. A nudge that will send Chris on his own downward spiral, from which there may be no escape.

There is nothing extraordinary about Chris Rowan...

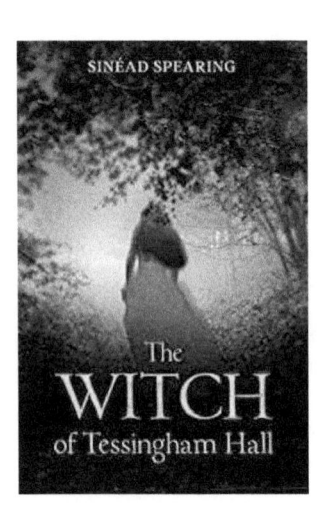

**The Witch of Tessingham Hall
By Sinéad Spearing.**

**England 1657.**

Alison, a folk- healer, stands falsely accused of murder by witchcraft, an allegation that sets in motion a powerful curse — "May your women forever wane!" — the spell haunting generations of her accuser's family, sending their women early to their graves.

**London 2022.**

Eden Flynn – an anxiety-ridden academic of Old English magic is invited for a job interview in the crypt of Southwark Cathedral, where her interviewer, the dashingly handsome geneticist Lord James Fabian, pulls her into the midst of his family secret: his sister is sick, and his daughter is showing signs of the same mental affliction.

Can Eden fulfil her part in the web which has been woven stronger and stronger over hundreds of years? Can she find the strength to break the bonds that bind her and Lord Fabian to the past? And can she live with the changes she will unleash?

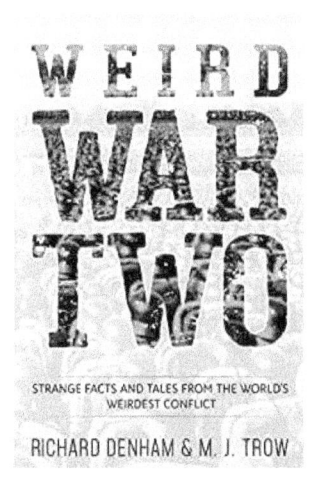

## Weird War Two
## By Richard Denham & M. J. Trow

Welcome to the wonderfully weird World War Two…

The Second World War was the bloodiest on record. It was the first total war in history when civilians - men, women and children - were on the front line as never before. With so many millions involved, the rumour machine went into overdrive, tall stories built on fear of the unknown. With so much at stake, boffins battled with each other to build ever more bizarre weapons to outgun the enemy. Nazi Germany alone had so many government-orchestrated foibles that they would be funny if they were not so tragic.

Parachuting sheep? Pilot pigeons? Rifles that fire round corners? Men who never were? You will find them all in these pages, the weird, wonderful and barely believable tales from World War Two.

www.blkdogpublishing.com

Lightning Source UK Ltd.
Milton Keynes UK
UKHW040631281022
411251UK00001B/212